ALSO BY ZOË S. ROY

Butterfly Tears

THE LONG MARCH HOME

A NOVEL

ZOË S. ROY

inanna poetry & fiction series

INANNA PUBLICATIONS AND EDUCATION INC.
TORONTO, CANADA

We gratefully acknowledge the support of the Canada Council
for the Arts and the Ontario Arts Council for our publishing program.

We are also grateful for the support received
from an Anonymous Fund at The Calgary Foundation.

Cover design: Val Fullard
Interior design: Luciana Ricciutelli

Library and Archives Canada Cataloguing in Publication

Roy, Zoë S., 1953-
    The long march home : a novel / Zoë S. Roy.

(Inanna poetry & fiction series)
isbn 978-1-926708-27-0

    I. Title. II. Series: Inanna poetry and fiction series

PS8635.O94L66 2011   C813'.6   C2011-905664-X

Printed and bound in Canada

Inanna Publications and Education Inc.
210 Founders College, York University
4700 Keele Street, Toronto, Ontario, Canada M3J 1P3
Telephone: (416) 736-5356 Fax: (416) 736-5765
Email: inanna@yorku.ca Website: www.yorku.ca/inanna

*To all those who suffered
during the Cultural Revolution.*

1.
NATURE'S COURSE

I'M HAVING A BABY! Meihua Wei was hoping for a girl; she already had two sons. She was washing her feet in the basin and couldn't wait to share this news with her husband, Lon, who had just come home for his monthly visit from the mine where he worked. After dinner, he had listened to the radio for a while and then climbed into bed. Now he was waiting for her to join him.

She dried her feet and stood up, catching her reflection in the small mirror above the wash basin. Her hair was just starting to gray, but she was still in good shape she thought as she patted her face dry, letting her thick hair tumble down her back. She turned the light off and opened the mosquito net covering the bed. Climbing in, she curled up beside her husband. Her long brown hair fanned out as her head sank into the pillow. Lon's hand lightly touched her face. In the dim light from the window, he noticed her wide open eyes as they swept over his face. Meihua reached for Lon's hand and covered it with her own. "Feel here, Lon," she said, guiding his hand onto her abdomen.

His fingers gingerly touched and circled her navel. Then his palm rested there, the warmth from his hand spreading throughout her body. Hesitating, Lon asked, "A baby?"

"Yes, a baby," Meihua murmured. Then, haltingly, "Do you think we should keep it?"

"I have always wanted a daughter," sighed Lon. "Maybe

this time we will have a girl." He turned to his wife, tenderly stroking her cheeks. "I won't be able to help you very much. I'm rarely home. I worry so much about you here alone." He had been living in the Red Flag Gulag, a mining camp, for the past seven years.

"Don't worry. Yao can help me."

"Yes, she can, but—" Lon flapped his hand in the air and clenched it into a fist, trapping the mosquito buzzing annoyingly around them. Turning back to her, a hot breath rushed from his nose and he blurted out, "I'm an ex-convict. This stigma will ruin our children's future. In fact, it already has."

Meihua knew her husband was referring to their eldest son, Dahai. He had recently been assigned to what could only be described as a mediocre high school rather than the much more prestigious Red Flag High School, a key school in the city. "His grades weren't great," Meihua said, her voice soft and soothing. Her fingers gently unclenched Lon's fist and lightly caressed his thick-callused palm.

"Liu, from work, told me his daughter couldn't get permission to marry her boyfriend at the military research complex where he was assigned over a year ago," Lon said. "You know why they mistrust her? Because of her father's background. Liu's an ex-prisoner like me."

A shiver ran through Lon's body. Liu had disagreed with the Party's Secretary and because of his outspoken complaints about the unfair treatment he had endured, he was labelled a political criminal and expelled from the Communist Party.

Only once had Lon dared to voice a different opinion, but the consequences were the same: first, time in prison and then probation and rehabilitation at the mining camp. During the Anti-Rightist Campaign launched in 1958 by Chairman Mao to persecute intellectuals who dared to question the government's actions or policies, each work unit was compelled to hunt and denounce at least one rightist who favoured freedom of speech and outspokenly disagreed with the ideology of the

Chinese Communist Party. Lon was the one at his high school who had dared to suggest the Party Secretary should have a university degree.

"Keep your hopes up, Lon," Meihua said, feeling her husband's fear. "Chairman Mao tells us not to judge a person by his family background." She tried to make him feel better, but she couldn't help but reflect on her own situation. She was an art instructor at Spring University in Kunming City, but was born and raised in America. Chairman Mao had been friendly to Edgar Snow, an American journalist, though he had called all American imperialists "Paper Tigers," meaning they looked terrifying but were actually fragile, as if they were made of paper. But, Mao had also written an article praising the Canadian medical doctor, Norman Bethune. It gave her a measure of hope.

Yet, like her husband, Meihua couldn't help but worry about the future of her children. *I'm not an American imperialist,* she assured herself. *Surely, no one would think so. My father was Chinese. And my children were born here. They are also Chinese.*

Lon exhaled in resignation. "I'm worried about Dahai's future. I don't want our children to go through what I have. And if we had a daughter, I would be even more worried. Maybe we shouldn't keep it."

"I understand," Meihua answered, hiding her disappointment, and rolling to face him. Lon was tall and lanky, his fine hair streaked with gray, his brow permanently furrowed with worry. Meihua was tiny and could curl her entire body into the crook of his arm. She snuggled into him and laid her head on his chest "Let's talk about it tomorrow, okay?" she said, her hand running over the hardness of his abdomen. "Rest now."

Lon said nothing. He was lost in thought.

Mosquitoes zizzed outside the net. Eventually Meihua fell asleep. In her dream, she watched a little girl in a bright red blouse and matching skirt, twirling on the green lawn. When Meihua embraced her, myriad pastel-coloured flower petals floated in the air around her.

The following morning, Meihua woke at around 9:00 a.m. Lon was already up. She put on a blouse and a loose, lemon yellow skirt, even though in 1965 most Chinese women wore only dark shapeless pants with tunics made of the same coarse fabric. Wearing a skirt or a dress was the only habit she had not relinquished since coming to China in 1948, so some of her colleagues had nicknamed her Skirt Wei. As Meihua thought about the funny nickname, Jar Qian came to mind. She was not the only one with a nickname at the university. Professor Qian at the Department of Mathematics had obtained his degree from Université de Picardie Jules Verne in France. It was said he stashed his money in jars and never invited any of his colleagues to his apartment, fearing his jars would be discovered, and his money stolen. So people called him "Jar Qian." Knowing this made her feel better about her own nickname, and her reluctance to restrict her wardrobe to shapeless gray pants and dark tunics.

She slipped into her shoes, and smoothed her hair down as best she could. In the heat, it tended to curl, so she often rolled it into a tight bun on the back of her head, her attempt to hide stray curls from curious eyes. Lon was home though, so today, she wore it long and loose around her shoulders, its waves hugging her cheeks. She opened the bedroom door and stepped in the living room. "I'm up," she announced to no one in particular, scanning the apartment for Lon, but he was nowhere to be found.

A familiar voice startled her. "He's gone back to Huize County," said Yao, who had just come out of the boys' bedroom, a cotton bed pad bundled in her arms. Yao, a woman in her late forties, worked for Meihua and Lon, helping with the kids and the household chores. She was a round woman, of stocky build, with long gray hair that she wore in a loose braid down her back. Her eyes were dark brown, always guarded, but warm and inviting around those she loved. She had been with the family for fifteen years.

"Why?" Meihua exclaimed. "What happened?"

"A telephone message came from the switchboard. The leaders at the mine wanted him to go back right away," said Yao, pointing with her chin at the small table by the door. "He left a note for you over there."

Pulling a slip of paper from underneath a glass paperweight, Meihua deciphered the scrawl: "Meihua, there was a mining accident yesterday. I must return for the rescue effort. Many people are still buried underground ... keep the baby if you wish. We must let nature take its course and accept its gifts. Lon"

Although overjoyed at Lon's sudden change of heart, Meihua was worried about his rescue mission. She envisioned the search team in the rubble, hour after hour, choking and coughing; their breathing passages filling with dark dust and pungent odours. Images of the mine caving or poisoning methane gas creeping into their nostrils, or another explosion filled her with fear.

Yao's voice interrupted her thoughts. "There's hot soymilk in the thermos," she said, having returned from laying the cotton pad out on a chair in the sun—her monthly chore to drive the dampness away. "I'll fry a steamed bun for your breakfast. Okay?"

"No need," Meihua said, heading for the wooden stand near the wall. The two-tier stand had a rack on the top for hanging face towels, an lower shelf to hold an enamel face basin and and another shelf below that one for a foot pan. She poured hot water from a thermos into the basin to wash herself from the neck up. Then she brushed her teeth. She liked to have some privacy, unlike other residents who brushed their teeth at the communal sinks.

"Can you boil some water for Teacher Yu? She's been sick these past few days," Meihua asked Yao, washing down some crackers with her morning cup of soymilk.

"I'll get some drinking water for her from the boiler at the canteen. Our ration of coal has almost run out."

"Thank you," Meihua said and then retreated to her room. She planned to work on her teaching materials before heading out to attend that Saturday afternoon's routine session of political studies. She pushed open the double-paned window and hooked the ring screws, so the wind could not blow the window shut. But she kept the light curtains drawn to maintain a bit of privacy from the windows on the adjacent building that faced hers. Sunlight, together with the scent of soymilk and fried buns, filtered through the gap between the curtain and window frame.

After opening the files on her desk and selecting a number of books from the shelf next to her, Meihua began to prepare her courses: "World History of Painting" and "Creative Paintings." Sometimes it was difficult to prepare for her classes because the lesson plans had to include artists and historical events based on the curriculum demanded by Marxism-Leninism. For example, artwork about the "Paris Commune" represented revolution and Picasso's "Guernica" condemned wars. The "Mona Lisa" had to be criticized as it was said her smile would corrupt revolutionaries. Everything that Meihua had learned seventeen years earlier at the Pennsylvania Academy of the Fine Arts in Philadelphia was not deemed appropriate in China now, and Meihua had trouble locating recent publications in English that would fit the necessary curriculum. Instead, Meihua opted for Chinese versions of the Russian communist textbooks used at other universities.

Teaching art was easier. She taught painting techniques that had no political implications. She even used live models in her third-year art class, without caring whether or not others would gossip about it. Critics were more interested in comparing themes of artwork or artists' ideology. Paintings about the revolution and the working class like Nikolai Niko-laevich Baskakov's "Lenin in Kremlin," and Boris Grigoriev's "The People's Land" and "Village," were greatly admired. Meanwhile paintings that had been labelled "bourgeois," like Claude Monet's "Women in the Garden," Dante Gabriel Rossetti's "Lady Lilith," and Eleuterio Pagliani's "A Reclin-ing Lady with a Fan," were simply ignored. Meihua liked to emphasize attention to detail and colour in her art classes, and avoided encouraging her students to create artwork dealing with revolutionary themes, like the paintings "On the Banks of the Yan River," and "Liu Hulan." Instead, she focused on guiding her students to practice mixing colours and brushwork techniques.

As she mulled over the teaching materials, a print that had been distributed among all the teachers caught her eye. The Party's Secretary wanted them to follow Mao and the Commu-nist Party's political viewpoints against the U.S. On the print, painted in bright red, were the words: "American Imperialists Should Get Out of South Korea!" Her heart sank. Meihua was born in America.

At noon, a pot of boiled rice, two dishes of pork and cabbage, and three bowls sat ready on the table. The door popped open, and Sang, Meihua's seven-year-old son, bounced into the room. He was lanky like his father, his hair also fine and dark. "Mama, please help me take off my book bag." His hand gripped the straps, as he struggled to pull them over his head.

"Okay, hold on a moment, Sang," Meihua said, helping to slip the pack from her son's shoulders.

At the same time, Yao pushed the door open with her ample hips, and placed two thermoses on the table, next to the bowls. She told Meihua the blue thermos was for Teacher Yu.

Sang's eyes were shining and darting around the room. "Where's Baba?"

"He had to go back to work because there was an accident at the mine."

"No!" Sang whined. "He promised to take me to the Golden Palace tomorrow."

"Baba will take you to the palace another time," Meihua said gently. "Why don't you play with the toy bus he made for you." She filled one of the bowls with the rice, topped it with some pork and cabbage, and placed it in front of him. "Eat your lunch, please, little boy. Then tell me what your plans are for this afternoon."

"All students are supposed to do good deeds at home," Sang recited, his legs dangling from the chair beneath the table. He told his mother that his teacher had asked the students to learn from the People's Liberation Army martyr, Lei Feng, and find ways to help others. "What things should I do to help?" he asked.

"You can help Yao," answered Meihua just as Yao returned. Meihua gestured for Yao to sit down. "Time for lunch, Yao. We're waiting for you."

"I'm coming," replied Yao, drying her hands on her apron, then pulling a stool up to the table. She sat down and picked up her bowl, and filled it with some rice. "At the boiler, I met Sang's teacher. She said there would be no extra activities this afternoon."

"I told Mommy first. I win!" Sang clapped his hands and the chopsticks he'd been holding dropped to the floor.

"My dear Sang, don't move." Yao bent over to pick up the chopsticks and tossed them into an empty pot. Then she handed Sang another pair. "Little one, be still. You are moving around too much."

"I'm not little." Sang took the chopsticks, wagging his head left and right. "I'm an elementary student."

"Okay, student Sang. Please discipline yourself and eat properly," said Meihua, her voice playfully stern.

"Yes, sir!" Sang straightened his back, casting Yao a sly

glance. "Mommy's really like a teacher," he whispered.

The adults both laughed.

"Your mama *is* a teacher," Yao chuckled. "She teaches big students," she added, and then slid a fried egg from a plate into his bowl. "Eat well," she said, pushing Sang's stool closer to the edge of the table.

After lunch, Yao cleared the table and stacked all the bowls and plates into the pot that also served as a wash pan.

Meihua helped her son rinse his face and hands. "Student Sang, can you wash your book bag this afternoon? That would be a very good deed."

"Can't do a good deed for myself. I must help someone else."

Meihua suggested that he help himself before helping others.

"But later can I help Popo Yao do laundry?" Sang asked.

"Sounds good. You help me wash quilts. I'll help you with your bag," Yao said, her hand dipping into the pot full of unwashed plates and bowls. "That way, after your nap, we will both do good deeds."

As Meihua hung the washcloth back on the rack, she spoke to Sang. "Did you hear what Yao said?"

"Okay," said Sang, as he sprinted to his room and clambered onto bed.

Yao trudged out to the communal sinks, the pot tucked under one arm and balanced against her waist. Meihua carried a basin of pots out with her, too. The communal sinks were centered in a spacious, square courtyard surrounded by four one-storey buildings made of uniform gray bricks with soft black roofs that matched the appearance of most of the people milling about with their sleek black hair and faded gray clothing. The court yard was called "Arts Paradise" because many of the residents in the complex were instructors and professors from the university's Arts Department, and their students often rehearsed their plays or displayed their artwork there.

Like some of the other staff dormitories built in the1950s on the university campus, the courtyard apartments were modelled on the Soviet Union's collective communes and thus did not include kitchens. All the residents in the complex shared six large concrete sinks, and a ramshackle building at the outskirts of the complex housed the kitchens where residents cooked their meals.

Yao placed her pot in one sink and turned on the tap. Meihua poured the used water from the other basin into the open drain underneath sink and then refilled the basin with fresh water to bring home. After replacing the basin full of fresh water on the wooden stand in their apartment, Meihua tiptoed into Sang's room to make sure he was asleep.

Back in her room, just the thought of that afternoon's session of political studies made her tired. She yawned and stretched out flat on the bed. A little rest would relax her, mentally and physically. She would put her hair up into its usual severe bun when she awoke.

By 2:00 p.m. Meihua was walking briskly along the road toward the Arts Department, a three-storey gray brick building located in the eastern area of the campus, about an eight-minute walk from her apartment. Rows of cedars stood solemnly in front of the building. A couple of students sat on low folding stools drawing pictures in the quiet garden. Red and yellow roses bloomed in the bushes along the walkway to the front door. The sight lightened Meihua's heart.

She climbed to the second floor where the room for the meeting was located. The double door was open; a large, framed portrait of Mao Zedong hung in the middle of the wall facing the door. Clad in a military uniform, a red star on each collar, Mao's eyes seemed to watch everyone who walked in the room. Several tables and chairs were scattered around. Entering the room, Meihua politely greeted a few of the teachers that were already seated, and then found a chair near one of the bookshelves lining the walls.

The Party's Secretary of the University's Arts Department began reading an announcement from the State Department. He talked about Premier Zhou Enlai's new policy on family planning that demanded each family have no more than two children. As Meihua listened, her abdomen contracted, as if the baby within her had responded in an unidentified voice, "I'm a life. I want to live!" She was puzzled by this new government policy on family planning. China had been following the Soviet Union's policy of providing childbirth incentives. Mao had said that the larger the population, the more powerful the country would be. She wondered if China's population policy was being changed because of the recent Sino-Soviet split.

After reading the document, the Party's Secretary raised his voice, "Comrades! At present, the Soviet revisionists are rampant. The international communist community faces crises. We should be alert to class enemies inside our country. They want to bring back the old days. Chairman Mao teaches us, 'After the enemies with guns have been wiped out, there will still be enemies without guns....'"

Many heads lowered as the secretary's tone rose. Miehua's eyes roved about and the room became a blur. Finally, her eyes rested on the cover of a journal set on the bookshelf near her. In the photograph, many arms raised portraits of Chairman Mao and Castro. A huge sign was stretched over the crowds and read, "Get out of here, Yankees!" Meanwhile a Chinese song taught at a previous political studies session resounded in her head: "We want Cuba, not Yankees!" Meihua was deeply disturbed by the photograph. She couldn't stand the sight of those raised arms. She turned her face away.

This is not meant for me, Meihua told herself. Her fingers pinched a corner of her blouse, twisting into a tiny knot. *I haven't done anything wrong. I'm serving China. I have nothing to do with American imperialists. My father was Chinese. My children were born here; they will also serve China.* These thoughts comforted her.

After the meeting, many of the teachers left without talking to one another; so did Meihua. But once outside the imposing building, Meihua's close friend, Ling Wang, caught up to her. She shook her head as if to rid herself of what she had heard. Her dark hair, usually tucked behind her ears, became loose and fell over her clouded face. Ling patted Meihua's arm and said under her breath, "You'd better be cautious. Take care."

The words touched Meihua, as the thought of her husband in the daring rescue operation also brought a lump to her throat. It was a time of uncertainty; a time of fear. Too many people knew her mother was American. Meihua hurried home, draping a light scarf over her head, not daring to lift her eyes or look at anyone.

2.
DRIED DATE SOUP AND LONGAN NUTS

A S MEIHUA APPROACHED HER ONE-storey building, she heard a voice from inside the apartment, half singing and half humming. "*The moon is high in the dark sky / casting its brightness over the world / In this deep and quite night, / I miss my hometown.*" It was Dahai, the oldest of her two sons. He was newly enrolled at the agriculture school some twenty kilometres away. Instead of a daily commute, he'd opted for weekly visits home. This way he'd save both money and time. Pushing the door open, Meihua was greeted by Sang standing on a chair, waving his arms up and down, as if he were a concert conductor. Dahai was singing while setting the table. Startled by his mother's entrance, Dahai abruptly stopped singing, chopsticks slipping from his hand and scattering across the table.

"What's that song?" Meihua asked, raising her eyebrows.

"It's called 'Nostalgia' by Ma Sicong. I learned it from my roommates," Dahai responded, quickly gathering up the chopsticks he had dropped. "I sing it because it helps me feel better when I feel homesick." He ran his fingers through his hair. It was as thick and wavy as Meihua's, but a lighter brown than his father's and brother's. He also shared his mother's smaller stature and graceful limbs. He hid the delicate shape of his body behind the baggy pants and tunics commonly worn in the schools of the time.

"How can you be homesick, Dahai? I know the school isn't

the one you dreamed of, but—" Meihua reached out to take Sang's hand and help him down from the chair. "You'll have useful skills after you graduate."

Dahai said, "Don't you ever miss your home? The home you grew up in? Even the country you grew up in ?"

His words startled Meihua. It was as if a bee had suddenly stung her in the face. She felt the heat rush to her temples, the apprehension tightening the muscles in her abdomen. She didn't like the thought that some people might misconstrue Dahai's homesickness as influenced by his mother's previous life in America. That was why Meihua hardly ever spoke of her time in the United States to her children.

She raised her voice. "I might have been born in the States, but China is my country. You were born here. Your home is here."

"I just feel so homesick sometimes," Dahai muttered.

"But you're home now," squealed Sang, wrapping his arms around his brother's waist.

"All right," she said, lowering her voice. Afraid that Dahai's feelings might be interpreted as the reflection of his parents' attitudes toward the Chinese government, Meihua wanted to prevent Dahai from being criticized in the future should he share these sentiments with the wrong people. It was so easy during this time to be misunderstood, and then accused. "Dahai, remember, this is your country, your home, and you do not want for anything. Now, go help Yao bring in our supper."

"Okay." Dahai shrugged and walked over to their kitchenette at the corner of the rectangular yard. The building that housed the kitchettes had been built several years after the complex had been finished, since most of the residents in the complex preferred to cook their own meals rather than eat in the university canteen.

Each family living in the apartment complex was allotted a kitchenette. Those who wanted to cook their own meals had to carry their food across the courtyard between their dwellings and kitchenettes, since the kitchenette was too small for a family to eat in. At mealtime, the residents crisscrossed one another's steps from apartment to kitchenette or to communal sink, carrying dishes of meats and vegetables, or empty pots and pans. Yao had almost finished cooking when Dahai stepped into the tiny room.

"Is your mama back?" she asked, passing him a pot of soup. "Take this with you. I'll be there in a minute."

"She's home," he answered, taking the steaming pot of soup from her hands and turning to walk back to the apartment.

Yezi was ready to follow him. In one hand, she held a large bowl of cabbage and pork, and in the other, a pot of rice. As she left the kitchen, she hooked her foot on the door to pull it shut behind her.

At dusk a child's voice burst in with the cool evening breeze. "Everybody, bring out your chairs. Performance tonight!"

Thrilled at the call, Sang asked Dahai, "Big brother, are you going?" He got no response, so he turned to pluck at a corner of Yao's blouse. "Shall we take our chairs out there?"

"Why not?" said Yao. Picking up a chair in each hand, she went outside with the excited boy.

"Mama," Dahai said, "I'm going to see a friend. I'll be back soon."

"Okay, don't stay out too late."

After Dahai left, a song and dance rehearsal began. A sprightly chorus rose after the announcer introduced the program. Back for a glass of water, Yao asked Meihua, "Are you going to join us?"

"No. I have a couple of odds and ends to take care of," Meihua said.

Yao hurried away. Going into her bedroom, Meihua rummaged through the dresser drawers and closet for used cotton blouses and bed sheets. With these soft materials, she could make baby clothing. Once she had drawn some lines and designed a pattern, she cut out the pattern on paper. Then she traced the pattern on the cloth with chalk. As she worked on the garment, she listened to the rehearsal outside in Arts Paradise.

The winter of 1965 had come and gone, but the temperature had never dropped below 12° Celsius in Kunming. There was no real winter in the city. Many trees remained green and leafy. That was why everyone called it Spring City. Instead of wearing a skirt, when it was chillier Meihua preferred a long, loose dress with warm woollen sweater over top of it. Spring was now just around the corner.

On her daily walks around the campus, she noticed the new buds on the trees and the signs of sprouting flowers in the gardens. Birds began building their nests, flitting overhead with bits of branches and dried leaves in their beaks, preparing for the birth of their chicks. Meihua felt her baby flutter and kick in her abdomen, a new life proclaiming its existence.

When Lon returned home for his monthly visit in March, he accompanied Meihua on a stroll in Broadview Park at Lake Dianchi. Delighted with the fresh air and swaying willow branches edging its shoreline, the couple ambled silently along the lake. Spring had painted all the branches a pale green. Jasmine added a hint of yellow. A pleasant fragrance filled the air.

"Lon," Meihua asked, "what should we name our baby?"

"How about Hope?"

"People might think we long to have the old days back," Meihua said, thinking about the Party Secretary's warning of the class enemy.

"What about Aihua?"

"Love China?" Meihua's name hinted at a link between America and China. She wrinkled her nose at her husband, and added, "Aihua is sure to be seen as too political."

"How about Yezi? It would be neutral," Lon said, "A leaf is green in colour. It is symbolic of new life. And it too is close to your American name, Mayflora, suggesting the delicate flowers that bloom in May."

"I like it," Meihua responded, nodding. "It's a pretty name for a girl, but what if we have another son?"

"Well, let's pick another name in case it's not a girl," he answered, Gazing at the mountains across the lake, he said, "What about Xiaopo?"

"That's nice too," Meihua said. "A hill, and a leaf. They are both names that are part of nature. I love them." As they walked, Meihua noticed the gentle babbling of the lake seemed to hum in harmony with the new life taking shape inside her.

In May 1966, like an unexpected squall on a vast ocean, a massive political tide denounced the "Three Family Village," the name given to three well-known writers in Beijing: Deng Tuo, Wu Han, and Liao Mosha. They had been accused of verbally attacking Mao and his political syste, because some of their plays and essays discussed and critiqued the current government's policies and programs. Similar to other cultural rectification campaigns launched by Mao Zedong, denouncing intellectuals was another of Mao's political weapons to implement the Cultural Revolution, whose dark waves crashed from Beijing and spread out to other places, including Kunming, this faraway city in the southwest corner of China. Mao's goals were to persecute anyone who questioned the authority of the current regime and its ideology, and to purge the country of his political rivals, Liu Shaoqi and Deng Xiaoping, in order to secure his dictatorship.

In addition to every Saturday afternoon's session of political studies, the department arranged extra sessions to denounce the "Three Family Village." Sometimes Meihua and her colleagues had to cancel their classes to attend these denunciations. Spring University was far from Beijing, but it reacted in unison, as the people had become accustomed to various class struggles since 1949, a year that witnessed the struggle against landlords with Land Reform, the Suppression of Counterrevolutionaries, and the Anti-Rightist campaigns.

Classes continued, but political meetings and denunciations of the "Three Family Village" increased. The meetings Meihua was told to attend occupied more of her time than her teaching. Enthusiastic students and staff members who had grown up under Mao's red flag were active in criticizing the works by the three writers. Many students started to denounce some of their professors and the heads of the departments at the university. Keming Dong, the head of the Arts Department, was branded as a capitalist lackey and accused of being an American spy. At the meeting denouncing Dong, Meihua could hardly breathe. *How did this respectable artist and leader become suspected of being an American spy? Is it because he was educated in the United States?* A shiver of fear coursed through her body.

Large-character posters, written with brush pens to protest and criticize, emerged everywhere on campus. Each time Meihua walked to the Arts Department, her steps became heavier. She looked at the large-character posters mounted on the walls of each building and listened to directives issued from the Central Party and Mao blasting from loudspeakers. She worried about her unborn baby and wondered what would become of all her children.

On May 31, an anxious Meihua received a brief letter from her husband, saying that all the ex-prisoners at the mine were forbidden to leave as authorities feared they might ferment dissent against the Cultural Revolution. He didn't know when he would be able to come home. He had to wait for further directives.

That night, Meihua tossed and turned in bed before falling asleep. She was awoken by a sharp pain in her abdomen. She checked her watch under the pillow. It was 5:50 a.m. She slowly rolled over to the edge of the bed, then she sat up and slipped her feet into her shoes. A slight noise from the living room told her that Yao was up and mopping the floor.

She dressed quickly and ambled over to the door. "Can you come to the hospital with me?" she asked.

"Of course," Yao said, straightening her back. She looked at Meihua with concern. "Let's get going." She leaned the mop against the wall and grabbed her house keys from the table. "Sang's still sleeping. I'll come back to check on him."

They trudged to the bus stop, Yao's arms holding Meihua around her waist.

Forty minutes later, they were in the emergency room. Meihua eased herself onto a bench against the wall and waited for her turn. Glad to be in the hospital, she urged Yao to go home.

"I'll bring your things here after Sang's gone to school." Yao called over her shoulder as she hurried away.

A nurse in a white gown appeared. "What's—" she covered her mouth with her hand, yawning. "What's wrong?"

"My water broke," answered Meihua.

"When is it due?"

"June 12."

"In eleven days," the woman frowned. "It's early."

"Yes, but the contractions are so strong."

Taking a sheet of paper and a pen from the table, the nurse said, "First, I need to fill out this form." She sat down and asked Meihua a series of questions: "Your name? Age? What's your job? Your husband's name? Where does he work?"

The last box on the form checked, the nurse finally put the pen down and asked, "Can you walk?"

"I think so." Meihua grabbed the nurse's outstretched arm. Slowly, they made their way toward the labour room, Meihua doubling over in pain every few steps.

When they reached the end of the hallway, the nurse pushed open a door, and they were immediately engulfed by the loud moans and cries of pain from several labouring women.

"Another one from the emergency room," the nurse announced. Stifling a second yawn, she handed Meihua's completed form to a second nurse.

"Lie down here," the second nurse said, pointing to a bed. Then she turned and briskly walked away.

Meihua gripped the edges of the bed, her body wracked with a contraction that she felt down to her toes. A couple of minutes later, the second nurse brought her a blue robe to wear.

"Are you Meihua Wei?" A woman doctor approached, a wooden stethoscope shaped like a long-stemmed glass in her hand. She pushed up Meihua's robe and laid the stethoscope on her abdomen. Bending over, the doctor tilted her head to listen. "The foetal heartbeat sounds irregular," she said.

Anxiously, Meihua asked, "Can you help?"

The doctor left without a word.

Meihua turned her head toward the next bed, on which a woman lay groaning. Her own pain intensified as the woman's cries pierced through the room.

About ten minutes later, Meihua was taken to another labour room. A different doctor approached her. "Do you give us your permission to perform a Caesarean section?"

"Yes, yes," Meihua replied, gasping as another contraction seized her abdomen. "Help my baby."

Several hours later, Meihua's baby safely arrived into the world.

When Meihua was returned to her hospital bed, Yao was anxiously waiting. Tearfully, she asked, "Are you all right? Is it a boy or a girl?"

"A girl. She's in the nursery," Meihua answered. "I'm fine. I just need something to drink." Her hand searched for Yao's, which she grabbed on to and held tightly,

From her tote bag, Yao pulled out a mug and a thermos filled with soup made of sweet dried dates and longan nuts. She poured the soup into the mug and handed it to Meihua. Meihua gulped the soup down right away. The warm, sweet liquid eased her dry throat and satisfied her empty stomach.

Two days later, Meihua was sitting up in her bed in the maternity ward reading the *People's Daily*. It was dated June 3, 1966. The front-page headline had caught her attention:

"Chairman Mao Calls It the Country's first Marxist-Leninist Large-Character Poster." Mao had announced his support for the large-character poster that had denounced some leaders of Beijing Municipal University and Beijing University. Mao had also branded Beijing University as a reactionary fortress that should be attacked and brought down. She sighed with resignation. It had become clear to her already some time ago that the Cultural Revolution was the largest-scale political movement in China since 1949.

She tossed the newspaper aside and then picked up the *Spring City Daily*. She turned to the second page and suddenly felt as if a cold hand had snatched her heart. The words "Behind Keming Dong's Suicide" stared back at her with a startling intensity.

Is the head of the Arts Department dead? Did he kill himself? Questions rose in Meihua as she scrutinized the article in the paper she held in her shivering hands. *Was he really guilty of a political crime?*

This shocking news, like unexpected hailstones, pummelled her body. Her muscles trembled and ached, and then she felt numb. Unable to move, she leaned back against the headboard, trying to slow down her breathing. Although her eyes were shut, restlessness had set in. Her mind wandered as if it were lost in the desert—a thirsty nomad desparate for water.

Several minutes passed, then she opened her eyes. Just a moment before, a nurse had wheeled in a cart with her baby girl inside. It was feeding time. When Meihua wrapped the infant in her arms, her heart expanded and warmth spread through her body. The infant's face was pink, her forehead slightly wrinkled, her fine hair a black, wispy cap on her tiny head. The baby's eyes were closed, but her mouth searched for food. Meihua's eyes filled with tears. *I must tell my mother about my baby girl. Why haven't I heard from her since I wrote to her a couple of months ago? Did she even get my letter?*

Cradling her daughter in her arms, she unbuttoned her blouse to let the baby's mouth find her nipple. Meihua raised her head. Her eyes fell on the newspaper in which she had read about Dong's suicide. Her mind went blank until a breeze from the window brushed her face. She drew a deep breath and focused her gaze on her nursing daughter. *My dear little Yezi, how I wish I could protect you.* Tenderly stroking her daughter's peaceful face with the tips of her fingers, Meihua prayed with all her heart: *I will hope for the best. God, please keep us safe.*

3.
WORKERS' PROPAGANDA TEAM

IN JUNE 1967, IN ACCORDANCE with Mao's directive that the working class lead colleges and universities in the implementation of the proletarian revolution and cultural rectification programs, factory workers and farmers became the authoritative voices of China's revolutionary forces. Workers' Propaganda Teams were formed and sent to colleges and universities across the country to re-educate and rectify teachers and students. Spring University also received a Workers' Propaganda Team organized by local factory workers.

One August afternoon, Meihua came home from another denunciation meeting organized by the Workers' Propaganda Team and held in the university's auditorium. She sat at the table and sipped the bowl of soup that Yao had prepared for her. She felt nauseous as she recalled that afternoon's scene on the stage. A professor of economics, an older man, was forced to confess his crime because in class he had explained the practice of life insurance in North America. A loudspeaker in his hand, the lead worker had yelled at the professor, "Why don't you admit you were brainwashed in the U.S.?" Pointing to the audience, the leader smirked. "Everybody knows 'life insurance' is a big lie! What can ensure a person's forever life?" Turning to the audience, he hollered, "I'm telling you. He isn't a professor, but a running dog of capitalists! Everybody dies even if you buy a life insurance!" He paused for a moment and then added, "No, I don't mean everybody." He clasped his hand over his mouth, with an exaggerated gesture, indicating to his audience that he had made a grievous error: "everybody" might be interpreted to include Chairman Mao. But Mao was immortal. So he shouted, "Long live Chairman Mao!" to cover his slip of tongue.

These words still echoed in Meihua's ears when she slowly finished the last spoonful of her soup. She shook her head as if to rid herself of that shameful vision. *How is Lon?* Meihua wondered with increasing anxiety. He hadn't been allowed to come home since the Chinese New Year. *Hopefully he doesn't suffer because of the denunciations. Hopefully he is not attacked because of his American wife.*

"You didn't like the soup?" Yao asked.

Meihua returned to the present. "Of course I did. I just finished it," she answered, pulling her face into a smile. "How's Yezi?" she asked. Yao was her principle caregiver now. Lon was not at home, and Meihua was preoccupied with her classes and endless political studies meetings.

"She'll be awake any minute. Her bottle's ready."

Watching Sang bite into a steamed bun and swallow big mouthfuls of scrabbled egg with tomato, Meihua smiled. *My children are healthy. That's all that matters.* But she could not help but also worry incessantly about Dahai. Like most of the high school students dispatched to the countryside, Dahai had been sent to a military farm in an area bordering Vietnam and Laos. *Hopefully he's fine there,* Meihua thought, going to her bedroom to check on Yezi. The 14-month-old baby was already wide awake, her feet kicking and hands grasping at the air. She giggled when Meihua bent over the crib to kiss her.

"Oh, my dear!" Meihua's face lit up as she picked her daughter up and carried her back to the living room. She took the warm bottle Yao had placed on the table, sat down in a chair near the room's only window, and placed the bottle in her baby's eager mouth. Wrapped in the cocoon of Meihua's arms, Yezi drank thirstily from the bottle, one hand on the bottle, the other wrapped tightly around her mother's fingers.

Yao and Meihua were started by the sound of heavy footsteps outside their door. Meihua raised her eyes from her daughter's face to see a large man push the door open and stride purposefully into the room.

Yao stood up. "What are you doing here?" she asked, a worried frown on her face.

"Who is Meihua Wei?" his voice boomed.

"I am," Meihua said.

A middle-aged woman followed the man into the room and walked toward Meihua. "You're American, right? And your real name is Mayflora Willard!"

"But I live and work for China. My Chinese name is Meihua Wei," she said firmly, wondering how they had gotten the information from her official dossier. "I have lived here for 19 years. My father is Chinese. I am married to a Chinese man."

"You are an American spy!" The woman yelled. "You—"

Shocked and afraid, Meihua watched Yezi's bottle tumble to the floor, Yezi started wailing.

Stroking her daughter's back, Meihua implored the woman, "Can you please not shout? My child—"

"Come with us! You must confess your crime!" the man barked, his thick eyebrows twisting on his furrowed forehead.

As Yao walked toward Meihua and took Yezi from her arms, she turned to the intruders and pleaded, "Don't scare the kids, please."

"We're from the Red Workers' Brigade," the man shouted, placing himself directly in front of Meihua, his heels clicking loudly against the floor. "You are under arrest for your anti-revolutionary crimes!"

"Come with us. Don't waste our time!" The woman beside him pulled Meihua's arm, dragging her toward the door.

"Mama, can I go with you?" Sang cried out, weeping as he

ran toward her and tugged her hand. "Please, Mama, take me with you! Please Mama!"

Meihua's heart constricted. She could hardly breathe; her lungs felt as though they would explode inside her chest. "My darling Sang, stay with Yao, and be a good boy. Mama will be back very soon." Turning toward Yao, Meihua gasped, the anguish in her eyes almost unbearable. "I will go with them, Yao. Please take care of the children."

"Everything will be fine," Yao said, tears streaming unchecked down her face. "We'll wait for you to come back." Yao was nodding, wiping the tears from her eyes with her sleeve. Yezi cradled in her arm, Sang's hand in her hand, Yao led them both into the bedroom. She did not want the children to be any more frightened than they already were.

"Don't wait for me. Go to bed as usual," Meihua said, her voice tight, turning to walk through the already open door.

"Let's go!" barked the man, pushing Meihua roughly out into the courtyard.

The interrogation in a factory building somewhere outside the university lasted the entire night. The workers asked her how she had become an American spy and why she supported a student anti-revolutionary organization. Since Meihua was the only American on campus, she had always aroused great attention and suspicion. Breathing deeply, she wondered what her crime was. All that she could think of was that she had recently expressed sympathy for a student who had not been accepted as a Red Guard. The reason he had been rejected was that his grandfather had owned a shoe factory before the Communist Party's takeover in 1949. This student then joined another organization on campus, later suppressed as anti-revolutionary because one of the leaders uttered a few politically incorrect words.

Meihua admitted the facts about her birthplace, her American name and education. But she did not accept the accusation of being a spy and supporting an anti-revolutionary organization. "My father is Chinese," she kept insisting although she could not answer any of their questions about where he lived. She did not know.

At dawn the tired workers stopped asking her to confess her crime and left her sitting in a chair, her arms strapped behind her. Meihua dozed off, her head awkwardly leaning against the back of the wooden chair.

A couple of hours later, the workers woke Meihua and took her to a public denunciation meeting in the city's Workers' Stadium. The Red Workers' Brigade played the ruling role for this meeting. A coarse rope tied her hands behind her back and cut into her wrists. A piece of cardboard dangled on a string around her neck. Her name, written upside down on the board, had a bold red X scratched across it—she had been marked an enemy.

Denunciation meetings like this one happened everywhere in China in 1967. The legislative system administered by Liu Shaoqi, the president of China, had been crushed under Mao's directives. The president himself had been labelled a "capitalist roader," and the commander of the bourgeois headquarters. Mao's Cultural Revolution paralyzed both the police and judicial system.

Meihua was shoved onto the stage for her public accusation. Falling to her knees, two workers with red bands on their right forearms forced her head down. In front of the stage, hundreds of people thrust their arms in the air and shouted: "Down with the American spy, Meihua Wei!" The people stammered: "She hides her real name, Mayflora Willard!"

Deafened by the clamour of shouts and screams from the crowd, Meihua could barely hear the words streaming from the loudspeaker. Vaguely she registered the cries of her American name. *How, how did they know it?* She wondered when the condemnation would end. *Hold on,* she kept telling herself: *It will be over soon. It has to be over soon.* Out of the corner of her eye, she noticed that the assembly, some in green and others in gray, with their red-banded arms jerking up and down, looked like a large, gloomy cloud spattered with blood stains, about to engulf her.

Finally, an announcement came through the loudspeaker: "Meihua Wei is guilty of sabotaging the Cultural Revolution." Wearily, she strove to understand. "She is sentenced to thirteen years in jail by the Red Workers' Brigade!" Hearing these words, Meihua felt her head spin. She fainted. At the same time, the crowd roared and repeated the war cries of the organizer: "Extinguish the imperialist if she does not give in! Meihua Wei deserves it! Down with American imperialism!"

When she regained consciousness, several soldiers had already transferred her to an open military truck. They pinned her shoulders against the front board of the truck bed as the vehicle rolled slowly down the streets of the small town. The army men forced her, like other branded anti-revolutionaries at that time, to parade in front of jeering onlookers. A loudspeaker on the truck broadcast her sentence while the crowds in the street shouted in unison: "Down with Meihua Wei!"

The truck drove through the city's main roads. The cardboard sign on her chest grew heavier; Meihua's neck burned. She tried to curl her fingers, but felt nothing. They were numb from being tied so long. Fright shook her. She wondered if her hands would still be able to hold a paintbrush.

The truck rammed onto the campus of Spring University, which was practically empty and still. Although her head remained down, Meihua caught a glimpse of the roadside out of the corner of her eye where people, young and old, gathered when they heard the loudspeaker. Suddenly Meihua heard a child's scream, "Mama, I want to go home!" suddenly reminding her of her own children. She prayed that Sang and Yao were not there, and could not see her. Her heart pounded wildly. *My babies, do you still have a home?* Despair welled up, and tears sprung to her eyes, rolling hot and furiously down her cheeks. A cry burst in her heart: *How is my baby daughter?* Her head moved in the direction of the child's squeal. She wanted to see the sobbing child.

"Don't move!" A male voice roared; a large, rough hand pushing her head down sharply. Pain spread down her back; she thought her neck had cracked. Her knees became weak, and she collapsed.

Drizzle from the overcast sky surrounded the station platform. A train began to rattle away. A girl in her early twenties in a white-and-blue shirtwaist dress rushed out of the station building toward the train, a suitcase in her hand. "Stop!" she called out. "How will I get home now?" Her desperate voice echoed on the empty platform. A teenage girl, in a white top and red shorts, ran toward her. "Sis, wait for me!" The girl with the suitcase turned her head. The suitcase fell onto the ground, spilling its contents onto the track as the train whistle blew haughtily in the distance.

Meihua opened her eyes. She was fully clothed, lying down on a thin straw mattress. She looked around and realized that she had been dreaming. The dream of missing the train was recurring one. Each time, she awoke after dropping the suitcase, her eyes fixed on her scant belongings, scattered over the train tracks.

She was in a small cell where faint light penetrated from an undersized, square window. *Thirteen years in jail!* The words flashed through her mind like streaks of lightning. Turning her back to the window, she breathed deeply. *At least I have a bed.* She was so weary and so tense after a terrifying day and a long, sleepless night.

Her body ached all over. Haunted by the unknown child's moaning, she was consumed with worries about her children, especially Yezi. Unexpectedly, a cry of "I don't want to die!" broke the silence, startling her. She jerked up in bed, her eyes scanning the dim cell. A cot, head to head with hers and covered with a quivering quilt, caught her attention. She realized she had a cellmate.

Who is it? Is she sick? Meihua hesitated. *Should I go over to her?* Then she heard another wail burst out, "I've been wronged!" As the thin blanket came away, a young woman sat up and turned to face Meihua. Her hair was matted. Her eyes were swollen and bloodshot. When the woman spotted Meihua, she gasped and stretched out her arm, as if to ensure that Meihua was actually there. "Are you an anti-revolutionary, too?" she asked.

"No," Meihua responded, shaking her head. "But they said I am."

The young woman climbed off her cot and knelt on the cement. Her hand reached into the straw under the bed sheet. She was looking for something. Finally she stood and staggered to Meihua and then pressed a packet into Meihua's palm. "Please, please get them sent," she whispered, and then struggled back to her cot.

Meihua ran her finger over the packet, which felt like paper wrapped in a small rag. She returned to her bed and sat against the window. In the unfolded rag were two handmade envelopes. Head drooping, she stared at the regular letter-sized one and identified the receiver's local address. Underneath was a larger, thicker envelope addressed to Chairman Mao and the Central Party in Beijing. The name of the sender, Ping Mu, rang a bell. Searching her mind, she remembered that Ping Mu was a former Red Guard leader. Memories of the early days of the Cultural Revolution came flooding back.

It happened a year ago. Meihua had walked past a classroom and spotted several new large-character posters tacked onto the wall next to the classroom's door. One of the posters called to complement the revolution by following Madame Mao and supporting a newly established Cultural Revolution group on campus. When several more students had gathered around the poster talking animatedly with one another, she couldn't help but overhear their conversation.

"Ha, a new fighting brigade! Have you heard who might be the leader?" asked a girl with glasses.

"I know! It will probably be Ping Mu. Her parents are revolutionary martyrs," one of the young men in the group replied. "She grew up with her aunt and uncle. Both of them are provincial government officials."

"What is the goal of this new brigade?"

"You guys talking about Ping?" Another young man chimed in. "She's in my class."

"Are you from the Spring City Institute of Engineering and Technology?" asked another young woman, joining them.

"No," the young man answered. "Are you from the Defending Mao Brigade?"

"No, but I can tell you that this new brigade is powerful," answered the young woman.

"Why? What are they doing?"

"Most of the members are from high-ranking, revolutionary families."

"Oh, yes. They even spoke to the professors at my college and persuaded them to co-operate with the Cultural Revolution."

"Do you think we should join them?"

"I don't know."

"The brigade labelled academic authorities of different universities as reactionary, bourgeoisie spokesmen. Do you think these academics are enemies of Mao?"

"How should I know?"

"Hey, don't leave. Let's read their statement," the girl with glasses raised her voice.

Later, Meihua heard on the radio that Ping's uncle had been tagged as a bourgeoisie authority; her father, a traitor to the revolution. Then Ping was singled out as an anti-revolutionary criminal. She was sentenced to death because her boyfriend had denounced her to the Red Workers' Brigade by reporting her doubts about the Cultural Revolution.

Meihua stashed the packet in the straw under her own bed sheet. An ominous presentiment surged through her as her eyes locked on Ping's. She looked like she was drowning, clutching at the straws under her mat as though they could save her. Meihua nodded at Ping until she lay back down. Her heart sank. She realized that because Ping knew her life would end soon, she had handed her final written words to Meihua.

Tilting her head, Meihua glanced at the window to be certain nobody was out there peering in at them. Then she took off her shirt and skirt and lay down. She could hear Ping whisper the words to a song written by Dong Xiaowu from *Red Guards on Honghu Lake*, an opera about a female revolutionary martyr during the Chinese Civil War in the late 1930s. In the opera, the jailed heroine sang these words to her mother during her final visit.

Bury me near Honghu Lake after my death
Dear Mother, let my tombstone face the east
So I can see the red sun rise
So I can hear the songs over the lake.

Sensing Ping's despair, Meihua burst into tears. *At the age of twenty, Ping already has to say goodbye to the world, her youth, her life, taken from her.* Ping's parents had died for the Communist Party's cause in the Nationalists' jail. *Ping never even knew her parents.* Certainly the martyrs had never expected the Communist Party would one day incarcerate their daughter. Meihua moved over to Ping's cot.

"Ping," she whispered. Kneeling on the floor, she placed her hand on Ping's shoulder. "Don't worry. I'll send the letters out as soon as I can."

"I did nothing against Chairman Mao and his Party," Ping

murmured, "but the people, who put me behind bars, are using the Cultural Revolution to disrupt Mao's authority and destroy China."

Meihua nodded and tried to smooth out Ping's tangled hair. "I believe this will be cleared up someday and we will be exonerated."

"They wouldn't allow me to carry a Mao pin," Ping muttered, unbuttoning her shirt and pointing at her chest. "Look here." Beneath her undershirt, she had pinned a dime-sized badge to her bra.

"God bless you," whispered Meihua as she held Ping's hand.

"I hope I will meet my mother," Ping said, clutching Meihua's arms. "Tell me, please. Will I meet her after I die?"

Hesitating for a second, Meihua asked, "Do you remember her?"

"I saw her in photos. I was only two when my parents sacrificed their lives. Since then my uncle and his wife have taken care of me."

"I believe you'll see your mother," Meihua said, "because souls live forever."

"Can I ask you something?" said Ping, her breathing relaxing.

"What?"

"When a girl gets married, does it hurt a lot?"

"Do you mean the first time?"

"Yes."

"If her husband's careful, there shouldn't be a problem."

"My boyfriend wanted me to sleep with him, but I wouldn't do it. Maybe he was really angry with me because of that."

"Did you refuse him because you were afraid of the pain?"

"A little bit, but the main reason was because I thought, and still think, that having sex before marriage is wrong."

"Do you miss him?"

"Sometimes. I wonder if he regrets having reported me."

"I think so." Meihua pictured the young man's hands clasping his head, bowed in sorrow.

Resting her head on Meihua's shoulder, Ping whispered, "I imagine my mama would be just like you."

Meihua kissed the girl's forehead. "Go to sleep. You need some rest," she said, covering her shoulders with the worn blanket and then tiptoed back to her bed. As she lay down she spotted something familiar on the floor at the head of her mattress. It was her old, navy blue travel bag. Somebody from her home must have brought it to the prison. *Yao knows I'm confined*, Meihua thought, holding the bag tightly as if she could feel her family's spirit contained within it. In the distance, a rooster crowed. Her eyelids heavy, she slipped into slumber.

The clank of pots and tin bowls awakened Meihua several hours later. She heard a wheezing voice outside the window: "Time for breakfast." She watched Ping pick up a bowl from the floor and make her way to the window.

"Number Seven, this bowl is for your new inmate," came the gravelly voice of an old man, who had trouble breathing. "Today, you get an extra bun, deep-fried."

The clinking moved away slowly as the old man conversed with himself, "Well, one extra bun, one more day...."

Meihua pulled a pair of sandals she found in the travel bag and slipped her feet into them. Then she took the bowl from Ping. "Thank you." Inside were a bun made of coarse flour and two slices of dark brown preserved turnip. "Where can I wash my face and brush my teeth?"

"Outside, during the break." Pointing to the only basin on the floor, Ping said, "It's empty. I haven't gone out to get water these past few days." She sat on her bed and gingerly bit into a bun.

Watching her eat, Meihua felt hungry. But she preferred to comb her unkempt hair first. As she rummaged in her canvas bag for a comb, she turned toward Ping and asked, "Would you like me to comb your hair, too?"

"Sure." Ping chewed her food slowly. Her eyes beaming shyly, she added, "That would be nice."

Meihua fingered the tousled strands of Ping's dull and lifeless hair. Some of it had turned gray, probably from malnutrition and depression.

She asked, "Can I braid your hair?"

"Yes!" Ping bit into a turnip, muttering, "As a child, I wanted to keep my hair long enough for braids, but my uncle wouldn't allow it. He said a revolutionary kid looked more vigorous with short hair." She paused. "Now I prefer my hair short, but have no scissors for it."

By the time Ping had finished eating her two buns, Meihua had woven her hair, but she had nothing to hold Ping's braids. She searched through her bag again and pulled out a pair of canvas shoes with laces. Meihua removed the laces and used them to tighten Ping's braids.

"I've been thinking about our talk last night. I believe this mess, I mean, my wrongful accusation, will surely be cleared up someday," Ping mumbled to herself. "Everything dies, but its matter remains, even though in a different form. Why should I be afraid?"

At that instant, the door jerked open, and light poured into the room. Meihua squinted and saw two soldiers with rifles standing in the doorway. "Number Seven, take your belongings with you!"

"I have nothing to take," said Ping, her voice calm. She faced the soldiers, her back straight. Before tramping toward the door, she turned to Meihua, her gaze locking on hers. A forever farewell.

The soldier pulled Ping's hands behind her back and snapped a pair of handcuffs on them. At the same time he raised his chin at the other soldier. "Go get her stuff."

The soldier strode to Ping's bed, looked around and opened a cardboard box that was sitting against the wall. He picked up the box and flipped impatiently through its contents. His voice rose, "Number Seven! Is this yours?"

Ping did not reply.

"Huh!" He tucked the box under his arms. "Let's go!"

The comb slipped from Meihua's hand to the floor. She pressed her back against the wall as she watched the men take Ping away. After the door's lock snapped into place, she stumbled to her mattress, slumping on the edge. Her eyes fixed on the dusty floor as if she had discovered the answer there to the mystery of death. She felt as if she had been frozen, encased in ice. Then her stomach growled. Her hand reached for the bun in the bowl on the bed. She bit into it mechanically. It tasted like cardboard.

When she closed her eyes, a revolutionary martyr from the film, *"The East Is Red,"* appeared in her mind. Before the hero was executed, he said he was not afraid of being beheaded, because he thought the truth was with him. Meihua wondered why truth seemed always to lead to death. She tossed the unfinished bun in her hand against the wall under the tiny window, her only link to the outside.

4.

IDEOLOGICAL REFORM

IN EARLY MARCH, THE LAND came alive again. Plants shot up, buds opened, and birds chirped and fluttered among trees. Frogs jumped into the watered rice paddies where the prisoners spent most of their days. They had been ordered to replant rice seedlings in the water field. The steam from the reeking mud and rancid grass floated in the sun. Meihua worked with another woman inmate, who introduced herself as Number Ten. Meihua responded, "I'm Number Twenty-nine." Rolling her pants up to her knees, she ventured into the cold, muddy water. A basket packed with rice seedlings on the ridge awaited her. She learned how to cut rice stalks last fall, but had not done any rice planting before. She searched her memory trying to recall any paintings or photographs she might have seen depicting rice transplanting. The only image that came to mind was that of some shadowy figures bending over a water field.

"First time in a rice paddy?" Number Ten interjected, staring at Meihua's fair skin. Curling her lips, she added, "You foul intellectuals are finally here to share the smelly air with us!" She flung a bundle of seedlings at Meihua, who studied them carefully. The six or seven inch-long, green seedlings looked like grass. Except that each one had several white roots attached.

"Watch me," Number Ten said. "Pinch a couple with three of your fingers, just like this." She stooped, her hand pushing the tuft into the water. "Press the roots into the soil, neither shallowly nor deeply."

"Why?" asked Meihua.

"They die if they are in too deep. They float up if too shallow." Number Ten rolled her eyes. "No more questions. Practice by yourself."

Meihua stepped down into the sticky, watery mud that squeezed through her toes, reminding her of pig dung. Gripping a handful of seedlings, she pressed the roots firmly into the mud and let go, but the little green tops appeared over the water's surface. She knew she had put them in too deeply, so she dragged the sprouts out. After she pressed them back into the soil a second time, they popped out of the water and drifted around. This time, she had not planted them deeply enough. Several more tries and the seedlings finally remained in the mud.

She inched her legs backward step by step and gradually reached the end of the paddy. As she raised her head, she eyed four or five lines of seedlings that Number Ten had planted. They stood straight in line, waving slightly in the breeze. Then there was the one row she had finally completed, a zigzag of seedlings wavering next to them.

Suddenly she became aware of something strange stuck to her legs. She lifted one leg out of the water and was horrified to discover several fat leeches latched onto her flesh. She screamed and pinched one of the leeches with her fingers, ripping it hard off her skin. The leech split in half, one part sliding into the water, the rest still attached to her leg. *There must be another way,* she thought, trudging to the ridge. She sat down and slapped her infested legs with the back of her palm to dislodge the remaining leeches.

"Try this." Number Ten snatched a few stalks of grass and then brushed them up and down on Meihua's leg in an attempt to brush the leeches off. Then she said, "You look like a foreign devil, white face and hairy legs. Even your eyes are different."

She stared pointedly at Meihua's face.

"A foreign devil? Do I really look like that?" Meihua asked, her mouth curving into a wry smile.

Number Ten chuckled. "I'm kidding, of course! How could you be? You speak Chinese."

"Of course," Meihua said, swiping the remaining leeches with the stalks of grass until all of them had fallen off of her legs. Relieved, she drew in a deep breath though her legs itched. At the end of the field, Number Ten pulled the seedling basket along the ridge with one hand and tossed the seedlings with the others into the paddy, bunch by bunch. Meihua stood and glimpsed the other inmates hunched over, slowly inching along in adjacent rice paddies.

Dragging herself into the mud again, Meihua caught one of the bunches and carefully untied it. She resumed planting sprouts backwards, one by one, inch by inch. Finally she completed another row. She turned around and began a new row. Her calves become numb, the watery mud slithering between her toes, row by row, she gradually acquired the transplanting skills.

The sun rose high. Meihua felt as if heavy heating pads were blanketing her back. A sharp whistle finally blew over the fields. She straightened her back, waded out of the water fields and plodded toward the elderly cook and his wheelbarrow, laden with barrels of cornmeal and cabbage. He handed everyone in line a bowl of crushed cornmeal and a ladle of boiled Chinese napa cabbage.

After lunch, Meihua's stomach was still empty, though bits of corn remained stuck between her teeth. Her torso ached, and her muscles throbbed, but she had to resume the work. The paddy resembled a cracked, rusted mirror glinting in the sun. The numerous and scattered seedlings that had just been planted were like green stars sparkling in the mirror. When she imagined herself as a paintbrush adding brilliant green strokes to the mirror, Meihua forgot her discomfort and pain.

By the end of the day, she had finished six rice paddies. Her head was heavy, and her feet were too weak to support her. It was a welcome tiredness though, as it meant she would later be able to fall into a deep and dreamless sleep.

This was the daily routine of her new life. Her legs were swollen with leech bites, and her back was a spasm of pain. At night, before sleep finally came over her, Meihua would lie flat in bed and think about her family. Since last August, she had not heard from them. During these seven months, the same questions haunted her: *Is Yezi healthy? Is Yao too tired? Has Lon been allowed to go home? How has Dahai been doing since he was sent to the military farm? Is Sang doing well in school?* She hoped some day her family would get permission to visit her. One day she would send Ping's letters out.

In April, a month later, waist-high tea bushes flourished with new leaves. The sweeping tea bushes looked like a sea of green waves rising up and down in the spring breeze. The rice paddies completed, groups of prison workers arrived in the tea fields at sunrise. Like everyone else, Meihua hung an enormous sack in front of her chest and started to pick tea leaves between two rows. The foliage smelled of morning dew. Sunshine comforted her after a night in her damp, cold cell. She pulled an offshoot, snapped the leaves off, and then placed them into the open sack. Her fingers moistened first with dew, then with green sap. As sunlight licked her forehead, her eyes narrowed to slits. Her hands moved in and out of the sack while she wriggled forward along the aisle. Her fingers soon became sore.

By the time she reached the end of the row, Meihua had filled the sack. With one hand supporting her waist, she straightened her back as she trudged toward a large, round container made of bamboo sheets. She poured the tea leaves she had gathered into it, and she asked for a slip from the armed guard as proof that she had filled a sack. Nine of the yellow slips would represent her daily workload.

She continued filling the second sack as a warm sunbeam sparkled numerous shiny threads in front of her. She looked back to the time when she was in grade ten, and known by her American name, Mayflora. That was twenty-five years ago, in 1943, when she had lived in Boston with her mother and stepfather and her half sister.

Mayflora and her friend Susan had found a summer job picking strawberries on a farm in Cambridge, outside Boston. The war was underway. Thrilled with the job they had found, the two girls commuted daily between their homes and the farm by train. Their goal was to save enough money to go to a university, even though wartime made such a dream uncertain.

They arrived before the first sunrays had cast a bright veil over the endless rows of strawberry bushes. The tender fruit, juicy and red, hid under the green or brown foliage.

"Let's see who can pick more," said Susan, bending over with a wooden basket.

"Sure, why not?" Mayflora squatted to unfold the leaves as she culled ripe berries off the stems. Soon her basket was full. When she raised her head, she saw Susan, sitting at the end of a row, beckoning to her. Mayflora waved her hand back. Then she lifted her bin and raced over to a gigantic crate. After she exchanged it for another empty basket, she resumed picking in a new row.

"I'm tired," said Susan, after gathering up five basketfuls.

"Me, too," said Mayflora, walking toward her friend. They plucked some more of the fresh strawberries from the bushes and these they munched on contentedly.

At noon, Mayflora and Susan devoured their sandwiches and then sauntered around the field. Hearing the faint peep of newly-hatched birds, Mayflora peered into the nearby shrubs and spotted a nest. On her tiptoes, she pushed a few of the branches away and peeked at the nest. "Wow! There are five really tiny baby birds here," she said.

Susan craned her head toward the branches. "Ah, they look so funny, their tiny bodies covered with only the faintest bit of down."

"They can't open their eyes. And look! They have such long beaks."

"Yeah, and their beaks are wide open. They must be starving," sighed Susan. "I wonder where their mother is."

"I have some breadcrumbs," Mayflora said, pinching some small crumbs from her sandwich bag.

They slipped the breadcrumbs into the exposed beaks of the hatchlings. Bit by bit, the chicks swallowed the crumbs and then tucked their heads under their wings to sleep.

For nearly two weeks, the two girls fed the baby birds with breadcrumbs. As the birds got older, most of their plumes gradually turned green, but the feathers on the lower part of their neck turned red. Mayflora recognized that they were hummingbirds. Each time she saw the tiny birds flap their wings, warmth flooded her heart. They even began to spring out of their nest, fluttering toward Mayflora and Susan whenever they drew near.

The strawberry season ended; so did their work. On the last day, Mayflora went to see the hummingbirds but the nest was empty, the bush silent. Gripping a branch, she gaped at empty nest, agonizing over whether they had been able to fly away, or if they had been killed by a predator.

Years later, Mayflora and Susan's dreams of going to university were fulfilled. After the Second World War, Susan went to the University of Washington in Washington, D.C., and Mayflora, the Pennsylvania Academy of the Fine Arts in Philadelphia. Meihua saw hummingbirds again in the Lancaster area during her visit to the Amish county in the summer. Accompanied by her fellow students, she hiked along a path in a sunflower field and heard a horse-drawn buggy creak down a gravel road paralleled to the path. A couple of hummingbirds swooshed past them several times, their wings glittering in the warm sunlight.

She felt as if she were one of these newly fledged birds flying across that expansive, wild blue sky.

Meihua had stuffed her fifth sack with leaves. A flock of wild geese flapping over the tea bushes drew her eyes upward. The edge of the vault of heaven looked ambivalent and obscure. She hadn't heard from her mother since she wrote to her two years ago after Yezi's birth. The Cultural Revolution had amplified China's political break with the United States, a symbol of capitalism and bourgeois democracy. As Meihua thought of her mother in Boston, her children with Yao, and her lost freedom, her eyes filled with tears.

When will I be free like these geese overhead? she wondered. Willing herself to forget the past, she shuffled to the gigantic barrel and unloaded her bag. Maybe, she thought, this toil was really helping to reform her thoughts and maybe soon she would be able to prove that she had indeed improved. Imagining her children's happy faces, Meihua rubbed her numb fingers and continued plucking tea leaves.

5.
DISCARDED NAPA LEAVES

IN 1970, THE CULTURAL REVOLUTION continued to purge the country of suspected counterrevolutionary activity. Four-year-old Yezi only saw her mother, Meihua, once a year in a distant location that Yao called a "reform-through-labour" camp. Yezi knew very little about her mother. Without the aid of some old photographs, she couldn't even remember her mother's face. The word "Mama" sounded intimate and sweet, but it was a mystery to her. When she heard her brother and Yao talking about her mother, she could not help but ask, "Why Mama not home?"

"She lives far away," groaned Yao.

Yezi could not understand why her mother had never been home. Her father also lived in a far-off place, but at least, he came home to visit several times a year. Yezi was happy her father was visiting today.

Yao was cooking their supper on the log-shaped stove made of clay that she had placed near the wall outside of their living quarters—their previous kitchenette. The family was forced to move out from their apartment after Meihua was arrested. Now their "kitchen" was in the open air. As the family members of an anti-revolutionary, they did not have the right to live in their free, furnished apartment as before, like the other university staff members did. Since Meihua had been imprisoned, they had lived in this tiny, shabby home, which was half indoors and half outdoors. Sang was in school. Yezi sat with her father at a table laid in the shade near the door. The aroma from the pot drifted enticingly around them. Yezi was reading a story from a used picture book with her father's help. Her finger pointed to the picture of a woman in the book. Yezi asked, "Do you see Mama?"

"Once a year," her father answered.

"Why are other kids with their mamas and babas?"

"You're a special and good girl," answered Lon, closing the book on the table. He hugged his daughter close. "Baby, do you like your Popo Yao?"

"Yeah, a lot."

"Well, right now, she's your Mama and your Baba."

Yezi saw the tears in her father's eyes. She was making him sad. Afraid to ask any more questions, she remained quiet, wrapping her arms tightly around her father's neck.

On June 1, 1971, Yao woke in the early morning. The two children were still sleeping soundly. The stars faded into the gray sky, but the night's veil still enveloped the yard. Soon the first rays of light would expel the darkness.

Yao's bed was actually a chair with short legs. During the day, the chair kept Yezi company. She would sit on it for meals or ride it as a play-horse. Sometimes she would stand on the chair inside their only room to look out the window at groups of Red Guards or revolutionary teams passing by. Their arms pumping up and down, they would play drums and beat bronze gongs or cymbals. Under the waving red flags, they would march and trill songs along the road to celebrate Mao's newly announced directives. Infected by their excitement, Yezi would tap on the window, or wave her hands left and right at the marching students, even though the crowds were oblivious to her existence.

At night, Yao slouched in her short-legged chair set beside the bed. Leaning her sore back against the back of the chair, she would rest her legs over a tipped stool in front of her. After napping a while that way, she would lower her head onto her folded arms on the edge of the only bed in the room. Yezi always slept sideways at one end, her brother at the other. Yao would rest her head on her own arms as a pillow, her eyes half open, in the space near Yezi's head. She had slept like this for years, ever since they had moved into this tiny home that had no room for another bed.

Since Meihua's imprisonment, the family had also been deprived of its main source of income. Yao could barely manage to feed the children with Lon's meagre salary, let alone get paid for her own work caring for the children and their home.

Curious people asked Yao why she continued to work for the family. Yao would explain that Meihua had kept her from becoming homeless some nineteen years earlier so she had made the decision to stay with the family for better or worse. "Buddha wants me to repay a debt of gratitude. These two children are under my wing. I'm going to wait for their mama to complete her 'ideological reform,'" she would answer, slapping her apron. These words were ones she had heard from Meihua during her visit to the gulag, although she was not quite sure why Meihua would need any kind of 'reform' at all. She never spoke the words aloud, but she knew Meihua was being punished for having been born in America.

Rising from her chair-bed, Yao gripped the curtain hanging from the doorframe with one hand, and rubbed around her eyes with the other. In all seasons except winter, Yao always kept the door open for her and the children to come in and go out more easily. She used the curtain to give them a measure of privacy. She reached out of the room for a short and smooth log that she had obtained from the carpenters' workshop on campus. Slumping down on it, she struck her legs and back repeatedly with her fists to relax her muscles. Her back and limbs were always stiff and sore. Her mouth half open, she breathed deeply and heavily—the outside air was better than the air inside their stuffy and cramped quarters. Finally, she felt somehow released from the night's discomfort.

She reached into a huge basket beneath the extended roof fixed by a sympathetic worker. She pulled out an apron from the stack and wrapped it around her waist. From its pocket, she drew out a broken wooden comb she had used for years. She could not afford to buy another one.

Two long braids hung on the front of her chest. First she raked the ends of her gray hair and then removed the elastic bands from the braids. As she held the comb in her teeth, she separated the plaits with her gnarled fingers. Struggling to untangle her hair, she drew the short piece of comb through the thick strands until her scalp tingled. She relished the twinges that reduced the itch at the moment. *It's time to wash my hair,* she thought.

Her long gray hair loose around her, Yao began her daily routine of gathering tinder. Some went into the stove. Several short twigs were added on top. From a pile of paper covered with a patched plastic raincoat stacked against the wall, she drew out some old newspapers. A flame started with the lit paper in a small rectangular opening at the bottom of the stove. As the wind blew in, the fire crackled through the twigs. Then she added several lumps of coal over the twigs. When the thick smoke erupted and spread over, she began to cough, her hand over her mouth. Then she laid a full kettle on the fiery stove. A tin bucket in one hand and a pot in the other, she trudged toward the communal sinks.

The sky became lighter, the sun's pale light washing over the yard. The door of one of the apartments across the yard opened, and thirteen-year-old Liang stepped into the yard. She needed to relieve herself. The screeches of a cat piercing the morning air sounded like a bawling infant, and it startled her.

Liang's heart pounded at the sight of a rotund figure, a head full of gray hair, moving around the sinks in the centre of the yard. Immediately, she jumped back inside and quickly shut the door. *There are no such things as ghosts,* she told herself. *Is this a class enemy doing something bad out there?* she wondered. What she had been told in school played out in her head.

Shaking her head, she reopened the door to peek outside and look again at what was going on. As she listened to the running water in the sinks, she glimpsed a flickering flame from the stove outside of that outcast family, and saw the smoke climb above the roof extension. Liang soon recognized the gray-haired and hefty figure, Yao, who was busily laundering and hanging washed clothes on the clotheslines across the yard. Relieved, Liang stepped out of the door and raced toward the communal latrine.

Yao poured heated water from the kettle into the pot. Then she placed the pot on the stove and began cooking rice congee for breakfast. Then she drenched her hair in the lukewarm water of a worn-out enamel basin on the table and washed it.

At 7:00 a.m. she was back in their small apartment and had pushed aside the curtain that hung in front the children's bed. She pushed Sang's arm and called out, "Rise and shine! The sun is on your butt!"

"Please don't shout. I'm getting up," the boy mumbled, kicking off the blanket. He slid out of the bed, picked up his shirt, and slipped his arms into the sleeves.

"Careful! Don't pull apart your shirt!" Yao grumbled.

"Don't yap...."

"Stop griping. Let your little sister sleep a bit longer," said Yao. Taking a bundle of meal coupons held in an elastic band from her pocket, she picked out two dark red ones and handed them to Sang. "Run and get two steamed buns at the canteen."

She went out and removed the pot of congee from the stove, replacing it with the kettle. After lifting the lid off the pot to let the congee cool, she took a worn bamboo basket that hung on the outside wall and repaired it by binding its loose edges with some old rope she'd collected from a nearby garbage dumpsite.

Sang pocketed the coupons. Behind the door curtain, he

peeked out at the sinks. *Good. Only a few people out there*, he thought. A mug, a toothbrush and toothpaste in his hand, he pulled a facecloth off a hook on the wall and went out. In the yard, Sang strode under Yao's laundry on the clotheslines; the laundry swung like various flags in the morning breeze. On the platform of the sinks, a ribbed washboard lay on the edge; an ample, cream-coloured enamel tub held the rest of Yao's laundry.

After brushing his teeth, Sang grabbed a pot with a lid and hurried to the canteen. Back with the steamed buns twenty minutes later, he joined his sister and Yao around the table for breakfast. By that time, several students had already left their homes in the yard for school.

A teenage boy named Jun walked toward them. "You dummy, aren't you done yet?" Guffawing at Sang, Jun patted him amiably on the shoulder.

"You short-lived creature! You won't see heaven if you make trouble!" Yao yelled before Sang could respond. Turning toward Sang, she added gruffly, "Eat up your food. You must get going if you want to have a chance in your next life!"

Confused by Yao's words, both Sang and Jun remained silent. They had never thought about a next life.

In the distance, Yao spotted Liang. "Sweetie," she called out, "Could you come and braid Yezi's hair later today?" she asked. Her voice was coarse, but joyful.

"Why are you fussy about her hair?" asked Liang, turning to size up Yezi.

"My little girl turns five today."

"Okay, when I'm back from school this afternoon," answered Liang. *Her birthday! What a lucky girl! Today is also International Children's Day,* she thought, waving her hand. "Be quick, Sang, if you don't want to be late."

"Let's get going," Sang said to Jun. He grabbed his book bag, and the two boys raced over to catch up with Liang.

"Goodbye," Yezi called out after them. Her eyes stayed on

her brother and the others until they were out of her sight. She plucked at Yao's apron. "I want to go to school, too."

"Not until the year after next."

"I want a book bag. And a real pencil."

"You want new stuff just like you want my life!"

"I—I don't…" said Yezi, pulling on Yao's hand.

"Let's go to the store," said Yao, one hand gripping the handle of the fixed bamboo basket, the other holding on tightly to Yezi's hand.

When they reached the vegetable store next to the large, five-storey staff dormitory, the busy hour had ended; most of the customers had gone to work. Only a few elderly people and housewives were still lining up. Occasionally a passer-by would stop to look over the prices listed on the board outside the counter, and then hurry away.

Neither checking the board nor joining the line, Yao strode toward a heap of discarded Chinese napa leaves. "Don't go anywhere," she said to Yezi as she let go of her hand. "Watch out for kidnappers!" She raised her voice as she bent down to pick through napa leaves. After tearing off yellow or rotting parts, she placed the rest into her basket. *Hopefully,* she thought, *I'll be able to get enough vegetables from what's been discarded.* She might even be able to hoard some for another day. An elderly woman came to Yao and picked one of the cucumbers she'd just bought from her basket and gave it to her.

"Thanks, Granny Yu," Yao put it into her basket and continued her work.

"That was nice of you, Granny Yu," piped a middle-aged woman walking by.

Granny Yu sighed and turned toward the woman. "I don't understand why Yao's staying with that family. Skirt Wei should confess her crime. Otherwise, she'll never get out of there."

"You don't know what you're talking about. It would be useless even if she confessed," replied the middle-aged woman.

"Skirt Wei's case is serious. And yet, she's quite lucky. Do you know our country has executed most of the active anti-revolutionaries these past few years?"

"But Skirt Wei is a good woman."

"Granny Yu, how do you know that?" asked another woman, who was from the Residents' Committee. These committees existed everywhere in China. They were formed by local residents to organize activities such as watching out for fires or burglaries, doing voluntary yard work, and road cleaning, as well as studying the ongoing directives from Mao and the Community Party. She emerged in front of the chatting women. "As a suspected American spy and anti-revolutionary, Meihua Wei should remain behind bars."

"My heavens! There are so many sinful people these days. How can we tell one from another?" said Granny Yu, turning to look at Yao. In an old, baggy blouse that had been patched with different fabrics. Yao continued to rummage through the piles of discarded vegetables. Behind her, Yezi played with ants, her fingers in the dirt. Two boys her age gathered around her.

Yezi jerked when she felt something slide down on her back. A hand-me-down adult-sized sweater, its sleeves cut off, covered her like a loose dress. Stretching her tiny white arm behind her, she scratched at her back. One of the boys laughed, while the other was busy and dropping handfuls of dirt into Yezi's dress at the nape of her neck.

"Huto, don't play with dirt," the middle-aged woman, the boy's nanny, called out. "Your father's going to come and get you if you don't behave."

The boy stopped. Running to his nanny, he buried his face in her legs and begged, "Don't tell Baba."

A contented smile on her face, Yao straightened her back and stretched. Then she covered the cucumber from Granny Yu with a couple of napa leaves, afraid one of the children might want to play with it. Relaxed, Yao craned her head and noticed there was only one customer left in the line at the front counter. "Keep an eye on my basket," she said to Yezi as she slogged toward the counter. Lifting her apron with one hand, she reached into her pants pocket with the other to pull out a packet of coins. "Chen, do you have any damaged tomatoes today? Can you sell them to me?"

"Here's a half a bushel. All yours," Chen said, sweat shinning on her plump face.

She looks happy. Perhaps her fiancé in the army will marry her soon, Yao thought. Marrying an army man was a great honour. So she said, "You lucky dog! You're going to marry your fiancé soon."

A glow of pride in her eyes, Chen teased back, "Don't spread rumours or I won't sell you anything." She turned around to drag a heavy bushel toward the doorway. "Here it is. Only fifty fen."

"Fifty fen is okay," Yao said, appraising the tomatoes. After counting the money from her packet, she asked, "Can you lend me this bushel? I'll return it to you shortly." She recounted the coins before handing them over to Chen.

"Sure, as long as you bring it back right away."

"Can you also keep an eye on my napa leaves?" Yao pointed to the basket she had filled on the ground next to Yezi. Yao had to bring the tomatoes home first and then return with the empty bushel to pick up her basket of napa. "I'll be back in no time," Yao said.

"Who wants your trashy vegetables?" Chen chuckled. "And nobody will take your girl even if you leave her here."

"Thank you. But she goes with me." Tucking the bushel of tomatoes under her arm, Yao wobbled toward Yezi. The heavy bin dragged her down. "Take the cucumber from our basket. Let's go home."

Obediently, Yezi uncovered the cucumber from under the napa leaves and gripped it in her hands. They trudged away from the market and disappeared behind the corner of gray-brick walls.

6.
LETTER FROM BURMA

THAT SAME AFTERNOON, AROUND 5:00 P.M., Liang showed up at Yezi's home, a strand of red yarn in her hand. "I'm here," she called out to Yao. "I'm here to comb Yezi's hair."

"Thanks for coming," Yao said, handing her the broken comb. She gestured for Yezi to sit down on a stool.

"Hope this won't hurt you too much," Liang said as she started pulling the comb through Yezi's tangled hair. "Don't move," she added. Holding the yarn with her teeth, Liang parted a circle on the five-year-old's head. She gripped a handful of hair and tied it with the red yarn, so that it resembled a blooming flower on Yezi's head. She then separated the hair into two parts, and Liang twisted each side into a braid. Then she fastened both ends of the braids with elastic bands.

"Wow, my girl looks pretty." Yao applauded, the corners of her mouth turning up into a wide smile. "You should say thank you to Liang," Yao said to Yezi.

"Thanks," Yezi said, shyly. Thrilled with her new hairstyle, she wiggled her head with a grin and moved toward Yao, leaning against her thigh.

"I have something for your birthday," Liang said. Fishing out two pieces of candy from her pocket, she handed them to the birthday girl.

Yezi gazed at the colourful wrapping paper, her eyes glowing. Not remembering when she had last tasted candy, she hesitated and glanced at her brother, seeking his approval. He always kept an eye on her.

"Thank Liang for the candy," Sang said.

Yezi smiled at Liang and accepted the gift. "Thank you very much."

"Not at all. Be a good girl," answered Liang, patting Yezi on the shoulder. She turned to head home.

Yezi's heart swelled with happiness as she touched her braids and then stroked the smooth paper of the candy. *This is a great birthday,* she thought.

At suppertime the aroma of food from the kitchen wafted into the air. Yao placed a bowl of cooked tomatoes and another dish of cucumber slices mixed with salt and vinegar on the table. She placed a small bowl of noodle soup with a fried egg on top in front of Yezi and then sprinkled a little soy sauce into the soup. "Enjoy your meal. It's special for you." Then she carefully tucked the bottle of soy sauce into a cabinet attached to the wall.

Watching Yezi eat her egg, Yao murmured, "You're growing. You need more food." At the same time, she spooned some tomato sauce into Sang's bowl. "Enjoy it."

In the evening Sang sat at the table, working on his homework. Yezi borrowed his crayons and a piece of paper to draw a picture. After colouring a girl's figure on the paper she had sketched, she asked her brother to jot down the words, "Happy Birthday!" for her.

Yezi hugged the drawing to her, and then tacked it up on the wall next to their bed, before climbing in and pulling the covers up to her chin. She took the second piece of candy from her pocket and carefully unwrapped the paper. She licked the candy, and then sucked on it in her mouth. As the sweetness dissolved on her tongue, she drifted off. Sang joined her shortly afterwards. Yao came to tuck both the children into bed. Then she picked out some clothes, turned off the light, and left the small room, pulling the curtain closed behind her.

On the table Yao laid out the articles of clothing. Then she perched herself in a chair. With the help of the light coming from the lamppost, a needle and thread in her hand, she began mending the garments one by one.

Eventually, darkness fell. Tranquility filled the empty courtyard. Yao had almost finished mending the last article of clothing, but her eyelids heavy. When she stretched her arms and raised her head, she noticed a figure moving toward her from a corner of the yard.

A young man's voice cut through the darkness, "Hello, are you Yao?"

"Do I know you?" she responded, rubbing her eyes to peer into the darkness.

"No," said the young man. "But can I have a glass of water?"

"Yes, of course." Rising from her chair, Yao took the kettle and tilted it, pouring some of the boiled water into a mug on the table. "It's a little bit cold. My thermos has broken." She pointed to a stool. "Sit here if you like."

The man looked to be in his early twenties, but his dark eyes were filled with a deep sorrow beyond his age. As he sat down, he reached for the mug and gulped the water down. Looking around, he asked, "Where are Sang and Yezi? Are they alright?"

"Sang and Yezi?" Yao's puffy eyes snapped open; her tiredness slipping away. Alert as a hen, she felt her wings stiffen. "How do you know their names? Who are you?"

"Me? You see…" the young man stammered. "Dahai…"

"Where is he?" Yao trembled when she heard the name of Meihua's eldest son. Her heart pounded fast. "Where is Dahai? And who on earth are you?"

"Listen," the visitor sputtered. "Dahai, he…"

"What?"

"I have here the last letter he wrote," the young man said, handing Yao a folded piece of paper. "I'm his friend, Wang."

Yao took the note and unfolded it. The only word she could recognize was "Dahai." "Could you please read it to me?"

She scanned the yard to be sure nobody was around to hear them, glad to see there were merely two windows with lights on. She also peered behind the curtain to make sure the children were sound asleep. Then she returned to Wang and said, "Please read it in a whisper."

Wang moved his stool closer to Yao, and his head bent over the page.

Burma, March, 22, 1970
Dear Yao, Sang and Yezi,
I don't have any regrets as I write this letter. I didn't choose to be born to a half-American imperialist mother. But I could commit myself to fight in the battle for the international communist revolution. That is why I escaped from the farm.

I voluntarily joined the People's Army led by the Communist Party of Burma. We are fighting Burmese government's troops to liberate the Burmese poor people. The army officers treat me like one of their people, and I don't feel humiliated because of my family background. There are five Chinese soldiers in our commando. All of us are writing letters to our families. We are making five copies of each letter. Each of us will carry letters for the others.

Tomorrow, we are going for on a special mission. If I die, this letter will deliver my last words to all of you.

My brother and sister, we didn't choose our parents, but we can make choices in life. I want to use my blood to wash away the anti-revolutionary crimes of our parents.

Popo Yao, I appreciate you for helping to raise me, and also for looking after Sang and Yezi and staying with them while our parents are confined. Maybe we are kids who shouldn't have been born to this world.

I miss all of you.
Farewell, Dahai.

After reading the letter, Wang broke down in tears. "He…he's dead," he said, finally uttering the words that had haunted him for so long.

"Nonsense!" Yao raised her voice. Shaking, her hands, reached for the corner of her apron to wipe away the tears that were spilling from her eyes. "Oh my Buddha!" she moaned. "He only just turned twenty. How did he die?" she asked, staring listlessly into the darkness.

"We stepped on a mine by accident. He died. I was injured," Wang said. Yanking his shirt up, he pointed to a large, dark red scar on the lower left side of his chest. He also pulled up his pant legs, and uncovered another scar that angrily traced the length of his thigh.

"Why didn't you come here sooner?"

"I was in Burma, recovering from wounds, and it wasn't easy get away. Please don't mention my visit to anyone else."

"Why?"

"I'll be locked up if I'm found. I sneaked across the border illegally."

"Where is your family?" asked Yao, looking at Wang more closely. "You don't sound like you're from this province."

"I'm from Bingyang, Guangxi province. My parents are dead," Wang said, his teeth chattering. He was tormented by the knowledge that his parents had been cannibalized in 1969—the year he escaped from the military farm, like Dahai, to join the army. He could not understand why some local people believed that the Five Black Categories marked for denunciation during the Cultural Revolution—ex-landowners, the rich, anti-revolutionaries, bad influencers and branded rightists—should be killed and then eaten by the revolutionary masses. "Do you think so-called enemies of the state should be eaten by the masses?" he asked, deep sorrow in his voice. His eyes darkened as he tilted his head toward Yao. "It is said that many indulged to prove their revolutionary ardour."

"What are you talking about?" Yao gasped. "I can't even

begin to imagine anyone doing that. I don't even think animals should be eaten." She rocked gently back and forth, her hand rubbing the top of her head as if she were trying to erase a terrifying image. Shaking her head, she sighed and asked, "Isn't Burma a foreign country? Why did you go there?"

"We crossed the border to join the Viet Cong fighting against the Americans, but we went in the wrong direction."

Placing her hand on Wang's face, Yao moved closer to him and asked, "Was Dahai buried in Burma?"

"Um..." Wang stammered, struggling to choose the right words. "His tomb is there. On April 5, China's Memorial Day, we commemorated him." The truth was, Wang had searched the scrubby hill after the battle, but couldn't find Dahai's body. He had found a huge mound under which hundreds of bodies were buried, but he could not tell which bones might be those of his friend. The only thing he could do was carve Dahai's name on a piece of wood and then insert it into the soil on top of the mound. Around the marker, Wang had placed a small bouquet of wildflowers.

"Poor Dahai, a lonely, homeless ghost. How can I reach you?" Yao moaned. Turning to Wang, she said, "I remember many people went to Burma during the famine in the '60s." She noticed his weary eyes and pale lips. "You must be starving. I'll cook you some noodles, okay?"

Wang nodded. He stared into the sky as if he were seeking answers to his turmoil and anguish, but heaven was a silent observer. With a deep breath, he recalled the terrible shock he had felt when he learned about his parents' horrific death on his last visit home. Even the mayor of the village had been beaten to death during the chaos. The grieving face of the school doorkeeper who had told about the tragedy was burned in his memory. The old man's deep-set eyes were like dry wells; his tears evaporated. His hands, thin and frail, had no strength; they had patted his back like withered twigs. "Never come back," he had said. His voice was as weak as the distant buzz of a mosquito, but it would echo in Wang's ears forever.

Yao appeared with a large bowl full of noodles, topped with tomato sauce, and placed it on the table in front of Wang. "I'm sorry. I don't have anything better to offer," she said, sitting back in her chair.

"This is good. Thank you," Wang said, taking the chopsticks she offered and devouring his food like a starving wolf.

After that, Wang followed Yao into the room where the two children were sleeping. He looked at their faces in the dim light from the window. He touched their heads with his hand.

"I wish for them a better future," said Wang, placing his hand on Yao's shoulder. "I'm certain it's been hard for you to look after them during these tough times. I think you're the kindest person I've ever known. And I know Dahai thought so, too." He turned his head. "Goodbye, Yao. Take care."

"Where're you going?"

"Back to Burma." Wang added, "Please remember to keep my visit a secret."

Yao breathed out heavily. "Buddha bless you," she said.

Waving to Yao, Wang sprinted out of the yard, disappearing into the dark night, a lonely sail in a boundless sea.

The thought of Dahai's death sat Yao like a stone in her stomach. Yao managed to draw a handful of paper scraps from the pile she had stacked against the wall under the eaves trough. She placed them on the ground, struck a match and lit the paper on fire. She burned the paper as ritual money for the dead. Flames quickly engulfed the bits of paper, and glowed on Yao's wrinkled face, fat tears rolling down her cheeks. She struggled to get down on her knees, and then clasped her palms together in front of her chest to pray.

The flame eventually diminished as the ashes swirled lightly in the breeze. Her eyes closed, the devout Buddhist prayed in a husky voice, "Dahai, a godforsaken soul. Rest well. I'm sending money for you to use in the world of the dead. Come back to your home when you reach your next life. Don't blame your parents. They are good people. Believe me." Yao bowed three times, touching her forehead to the ground. Her voice softened: "My Buddha, please take care of this boy."

Inside, behind the curtain, Sang rolled over in bed while Yezi whispered in her sleep, "Happy birthday. Red hair ribbon...."

At that moment every window in the yard sank into blackness. A cat meandered along the edge of a roof, meowing pitifully, as though it were reminding the world that life carried on.

7.

AMERICAN MONGREL

YEZI AWOKE FROM HER NAP in a capacious, round bamboo basket that rocked to the rhythm of Yao's steps heading toward home. Swaying up and down, the basket was like a cradle. Yao wobbled; her rolled-up pants revealed the spider veins in her legs. A pole was balanced across her shoulder blades. On one end hung a pannier filled with coal that she could not afford to have delivered home, and at the other end hung the basket that Yezi was nesting in. Too tired to walk back, Yezi had become an additional load.

The ropes gripped in her hands, Yezi kept her eyes fixed on Yao trodding along the street next to her. A bus rolled past them like a wall of peeled paint. A minute later, bicycle wheels rushed past, bells ringing.

"The Cultural Revolution—is really—really good!" a gruff voice chanted across the bustling avenue. Head craning, Yezi searched for the source of the voice in the crowd. Her eyes finally fixed on a man in ragged clothes who was marching along the sidewalk across the street. His long, unkempt hair sprang out high from his head like a proud rooster. His back straightened as if he were marching on a red carpet, and his arms jerked in the air. His tone was high one moment and low the next.

Yezi's lips were dry and hot when she heard a voice call out: "Popsicle! Four fen each."

Turning her head, Yezi shouted, "I want a popsicle!"

Yao did not respond, and only quickened her steps.

"The Cultural Revolution—" The man in rags continued to sing in his high-pitched voice, but he was not looking where he was and suddenly walked into a pole, which knocked him flat on the ground.

"Ouch!" Yezi shrieked as if her own head had hit the pole.

Yao stopped and put her baskets down. She mistook Yezi's scream as another cry for a popsicle. Her hand dipped into her pants pocket as she walked toward the vendor.

"What kind do you want, the cream or green beans?" asked the vendor.

"A four-fen one."

"Only one?"

"Yes, please." Yao nodded, handing some coins to the woman.

Yao trudged back to the baskets, a popsicle in hand. "Here you go." She stooped over Yezi. "Don't wait. It'll melt."

Yezi looked up at Yao in surprise. As soon as she grasped the stick, she licked the cool, sweet ice. Her face shone in the sun, her smile wide and happy. The noise from street vanished as she focused only on the pleasure of her juicy treat.

Yao wiped the sweat from her face with her apron. Her dry lips fought the temptation of the ice stick. She turned to face the two heavy baskets and comforted herself with the thought of all the water she could drink once she got home. She squatted and placed the pole on her shoulders. Her hands gripped the rope at the pole's ends in front and behind her, as she tried to stand. She muttered under her breath, "One, two, three!" The numbers squeezed out from her clenched teeth. Her legs were shaky, but she managed to stand and then resumed trudging back home.

Two years later, in September 1972, Yezi became a first grader at the elementary school affiliated with Spring University, where her mother used to teach. In a music class, all the students were chanting in unison: "Little friends join us in telling stories." Yezi's eyes blurred; the sheet of paper with the music score hanging on the blackboard seemed to be fluttering.

The teacher tapped on the blackboard with a pointer, catching Yezi's attention. The young voices filled the room singing the song "The Young Pioneers of China," which they had been taught by their teacher. "*We are the heirs of communism / Inheriting the glorious tradition of the forebears of the revolution/ We love our motherland and people / The crimson red scarves flutter at our chests*...." Yezi sang with the others, sluggishly watching the teacher's pointer. She was lost in thought, remembering last night's game of hide-and-seek, picking through napa leaves with Popo Yao, and a juicy popsicle on a long walk home.

In the Chinese class, Teacher Li copied down two sentences on the blackboard with red chalk. The first one read: "Chairman Mao teaches us, 'Fight against selfishness and criticize revisionism!'" It was followed by a second one: "Chairman Mao teaches us, 'Carry out criticism and self-criticism.'"

The teacher turned to face the class and read the words aloud. As she flicked the red chalk powder away from her dark-blue khaki jacket, she announced, "Girls and boys, let us follow Chairman Mao's instruction to criticize our own selfishness. Let's take turns to speak up."

The monitor, Kun, sprang from his seat. "Yesterday, after cleaning up the classroom, I dumped trash outside the window because I wanted to get home earlier."

"Kun also snitched a broom from Class 2-A!" yelled another student. "We were told off because of his bad behaviour."

"You got what you deserved!" a girl calls out, her voice shrill.

"Who saw him filching the broom?" asked one student.

"Me!" another answered.

"I saw you, Hong. You flung mud to students in Class 2-A," said a boy, attempting to defend Kun.

Wen, seated next to Yezi, placed his elbow on the desk and raised his hand high. Yezi tilted her head to watch him.

"I want to fight against selfishness and criticize revisionism." Wen stood up. "This past summer, my brother and I hung around the Red Flag Restaurant." He straightened his back. "We licked a couple of dishes left by the diners." His words provoked laughter and snickers.

Yezi could not help but laugh with the others in the class.

Unexpectedly, Wen turned to her and stomped on her foot. "You mongrel!" he shouted, indignant.

"Ouch!" Her foot ached; agony surged through her. Angrily, Yezi pushed Wen, who then punched her shoulder with his fist.

A student yelped, "American mongrel!"

Shocked, Yezi felt her face became hot and red. As Wen punched her again, this time on her head, tears began to stream down her cheeks.

"Stop it! This instance, Wen!" Teacher Li burst out. She made a beeline toward them, and placed her hand on Wen's arm.

One of the students yelled, "Don't abuse your teacher's power! You bourgeois people!"

In astonishment, Teacher Li suddenly let go of Wen's arm. As a teacher, she too was a target of the Cultural Revolution. She lowered her head, like a stooping sunflower.

Confused, Wen stopped hitting Yezi and sat down. Meanwhile several other students slapped their hands on the desks to protest the teacher.

"I'm ... I'm Chinese!" Yezi uttered these words loudly and clearly after she wiped the tears with her cuff.

An idea dawned on Teacher Li. Her eyes gleamed. "Yezi, where were you born?"

"Kunming."

"What about you, Jie?" the teacher asked.

"Beijing."

The teacher eyed the class. "Were you all born in China?"

"Yes!" All their mouths opened at the same time.

"Are people born in China, Chinese?" The teacher looked solemn.

"Yes!" The students glanced at one another.

"Then, is Yezi Chinese?"

"Yes, she is," answered Jian, a girl Yezi's age, sitting just behind her. The voices of several other students shouted out in agreement.

"Chinese shouldn't scold and hit other Chinese." The teacher's gaze fixed purposely on Wen's face. "Isn't that right, girls and boys?"

Sheepishly, Wen joined the other children, as they intoned, "That's right!"

The personal criticism resumed. But the students became friendlier to one another, as if they had just discovered they were all from the same country.

At the end of the class, Yezi handed Wen a small piece of paper sheet with a picture of a downy chick poking its head out of a cracked shell. Wen quickly opened his stationery case and gave Yezi an eraser. "Let's swap," he said and stretched his hand, shaking his little finger. Yezi accepted the eraser and then hooked Wen's finger with hers. Both chanted: "Hook on. Hook on. A deal comes along."

At the door of the classroom, her brother, Sang, waved his hand. "Yezi, let's go home," he called out.

"I'm coming." Yezi hurried away from the classroom and joined her brother on the walk home.

One October evening, Yezi and Sang were sitting around the table, working on their homework. Yezi's routine was to copy new words from her day's lesson into an exercise book. When she raised her head, she noticed Sang reading an issue of his now favourite medical periodical, *Medicine for the Masses*. "Brother, why aren't you doing your homework?"

"I finished it long ago." Sang did not look at her but said,

"Hurry up and finish. Go to bed after you're done."

At about 8:30 p.m., they washed their faces and feet, and brushed their teeth. Yezi lay down on one end of the bed against the window while Sang slid into the other end near the curtain they used as a door. This was their shared nest.

Crickets chirped in the grass. Children played hide-and-seek in the yard. Yezi listened. A child's hurried steps, the chirp of a cricket, like a seesaw, one sound rose up, the other quieted down. The youngsters chanted: "One: attention; two: hide; and three: coming!" She imagined how frantic it would be to hide from a hunting "cat." But Yao never allowed Yezi to play this game with the children in the yard. She had a good excuse: "We don't have money for the hospital if you hurt yourself, or break your bones." Feigning tears, Yao had pointed to Sang. "Look at your brother. Three stitches on his forehead! A girl can't find a husband with a scar like that on her face!" Like a hen that stretched and flapped its wings around its chicks, Yao never let Yezi slip out of her sight.

Only once, for about half an hour, did Yezi manage to slip away.

It was on Yezi's sixth birthday, several months earlier. After supper, Sang had said to Yao with excitement, "We're going to watch a movie in the auditorium." Yao was hesitant. Sang had explained, "The movie is free for kids. It's because today is the International Children's Day."

Yezi had pulled the corner of Yao's apron. "Please, Popo Yao. I want to watch the free movie. Can I go with Brother?"

"No," Yao had said, grasping Yezi's hand. "You're too little. You're not going anywhere."

"Listen to Popo Yao," Sang had said, smiling at her over his shoulder as he hurried away with his friend. "You can't tag along with us."

After Sang had left, Yezi had sat at the table, her eyes following the groups of children, hurrying past her. One called out, "Why don't you come to the movie with us?"

Yezi's heart had had skipped a beat. She had turned to look at Yao. She was washing dishes at the communal sinks. Her heart pounding, Yezi had scampered away with the group to the auditorium. After they had entered the hall, they had made their way through the crammed rows. Excited but exhausted, Yezi finally found a seat to plunk herself into.

Several minutes later, a gigantic sparkling star appeared on the screen, accompanied by lively music. The juvenile audience began clapping along with the rhythm of the melody. Yezi had trouble seeing the screen, so she knelt on her seat. The movie was about a battle. Bullets crisscrossed the smoky air, and bombs had exploded everywhere in a village. The shrieks of children resounded while squawking hens fluttered out of their coops. Barking dogs jumped over the fences.

"Japanese devils are coming into the village!" A shout had risen along with the sound of beating bronze gongs. Screaming and running, the villagers in the movie were fleeing their homes. Yezi's heart was in her throat, her eyes glued to the screen.

Suddenly, an old, gruff voice burst into the hall, "Ye—Yezi!" Trembling with worry, Yao had clucked, "Where are you, little girl?" Like a baby chick, Yezi heard the mother hen's voice and sensed the tears welling up in her eyes, but she was unsure where the hen was, in the village that was being attacked, or among the movie audience.

"Stop shouting!" A voice from the audience had cried out as the tone of Yao's voice had become increasingly frantic.

Yezi had not known what was happening until a child shoved her and said, "That's Popo Yao. She's looking for you. You'd better go." Yao was well-known to the children.

Squeezing out of the row and tumbling into the aisle, Yezi ran toward her hen, flinging her arms around Yao's legs. Yao flapped her wings with joy. "Oh little one! You almost killed me!"

Yezi had then stared into Yao's tearful face and was overcome by a sense of guilt. "I'll never sneak away again," she had said, her arms tightening around Yao's trembling legs.

The bed shook slightly when Sang turned over. The crickets had become quiet. The children's playful cries became distant, and their steps faded away. *Will I wake up early tomorrow morning?* Yezi wondered. Was it her mother's face that came to her? She was not sure. Then she fell into a sound sleep.

8.
WILDCAT VALLEY

A T DAWN, YAO ROUSED THE children and asked them to get ready quickly. As they left, the apartment complex breathed like a sleeping giant.

Following Yao and Sang, Yezi walked under the dim light of the lampposts, which outlined the shadows of fir trees along the roadside. In a cozy restaurant at a street corner, a cook kneaded dough on a wooden counter. The flames from a stove flicked.

Her hand reaching for Yao's, Yezi pranced to the rhythm of her brother's footfalls. One-two-three-four. *Going to see Mama.* She repeated the words in her head and searched for her mother's image in her memories. "Mama" made her think of a faraway figure with a beaming face and dark eyes in a yellow, faded photograph. "American spy!" echoed in her ears. That was how the Cultural Revolution portrayed her mother. She shivered, remembering the children at school who had called her an "American mongrel." *Mama is an anti-revolutionary!* The thought haunted Yezi as she struggled to keep up with Sang's footsteps.

The train station was still far, but Yezi could hear distant whistles blaring their arrival or departure. The three trudged along the road's shoulder, disturbing the dreams of small toads that one by one hopped out of the ditch as they passed by. Her feet ached. One large step, one small. She dragged herself behind Sang, Yao's hand pulling her along.

"Cheer up! March!" Yao called out. Her feet stomped on the ground in rhythm: One two! One two!

Yezi raised her head to look at the dark trees that framed the road. The nearby buildings seemed to move along with them, as if they had become alive. When she paused, they remained still. As she quickened her gait, they followed her again. Hide-and-seek. It was her own private game. She grasped Yao's hand to help her leap forward, her hair rising and falling to the motion of her steps. Then she ran into her brother's foot.

"Ouch!" Sang stumbled and stepped aside to pull up his shoe. "Watch what you're doing."

Yezi giggled.

"Yezi is strong," Yao encouraged her. "Ha! Your brother's a slowpoke," she said with a chuckle.

After walking about four kilometres in the morning dew, they finally arrived at the train station. A solitary lamppost stood by the track, its bulb glimmering in the pale dawn before sunrise. Staring at the light, Yezi watched the bulb turn into overlapping spheres. Her eyes blurred as the glinting circles expanded and merged into the ashy, gray-blue sky. A train finally rumbled toward them, a piercing whistle announcing its arrival. Sang led the way and boarded the train. Yao followed, carrying Yezi on her back. Passengers sat or stood, occupying all the space available. Making their way down the aisle of several cars, they finally found a place where if they squeezed closely together they could sit on the floor. Yezi was content to huddle against Yao and soon drifted off to sleep despite the train's constant rattling.

In her dream Yezi was a baby swallow that was hopping tentatively around the rocking car. Many children chased her. Her wings flapped, but she did not know in which direction she should fly. She could not see through the air; fog had spread through the congested car. Wanting to scream, she opened her mouth but could not make a sound, her throat dry. Fluttering her arms and kicking her feet like a swallow, she strove to flee her captors. She felt her square-ended tail droop and began to panic. Then she felt herself falling, falling....

"Yezi! Are you alright?"

Her eyes opened. She found herself in Yao's arms, a damp towel wiping her forehead. Threads of cool air spread on her hot face, but Yezi felt thirsty.

"I want water," she said, sitting up. Yao, slouched on the floor where the cardboard boxes of train supplies were stacked, picked up a mug on the floor next to her and lifted it to Yezi's lips. "Have some. You'll feel better."

Yezi drank the lukewarm water. Her dry throat was soothed. The smell from the washroom mixed with cigarette smoke filled the air and made her nose crinkle up. It stunk. She drew a shallow breath and tried to see if she could spot Sang.

At Yao's request, Sang stood by the window, keeping an eye out for their station sign. When it was their stop, he pulled a bag onto his shoulder and toward his chest. "We should get off here," he said as he made his way over to them.

"Go ahead. We'll catch up," replied Yao as she pulled herself to her feet. The strap of a patched, worn-out bag slung over her shoulder, Yao grabbed the mug with one hand and Yezi's hand with the other. With a jerk, the train screeched to a stopped. They pushed through the crowd to the door, and finally stepped down onto a narrow platform in front of a small hut surrounded by a rusty, metal fence. On a paint-peeled board, two words proclaimed they had reached "Wildcat Valley."

Yezi had been in the first grade for only two months. The first sentence she and her classmates had learned was "Long Live Chairman Mao!" She had memorized some of Chairman Mao's directives. With her brother's help, she could recognize the name of the station associated with her mother's labour camp, though wildcats seemed exotic and mysterious to her.

The station name reminded Sang of Wild Boar Woods, a place in a novel he was reading called *Water Margins*. He had been excited when he read how the Robin Hood figure,

Lu Zhishen, had rescued another hero, Lin Chong, from the woods. *Maybe I could do the same for my mother.* "Let's go," he said, kicking impatiently at pebbles on the ground.

Yao could not read any of the words, but she recognized the aged maple tree near the station. It was the sixth year she had been greeted by this old maple, which was now turning a withered orange. Staring at the fallen leaves dancing in the whirling wind and dust, Yao sighed. *I'm old.* She felt as if she were watching her own weathered skin drop to the ground.

Yezi trudged behind Yao. She asked, "How much longer does Mama have to live in the camp?"

"Not too long. Seven more years," Yao said.

Seven years is very long time. Yezi counted. *I'll be fourteen years old.* In the past seven years, neither Sang nor Yao had helped Yezi understand why her mother had become an anti-revolutionary. "Popo Yao, how old are you going to be in seven years?"

"I'm fifty-six now," Yao said, her breathing heavy. She coughed. Asthma had been bothering her for a long time, but she had no money or the time to treat it. "I don't know if I will live that long," she sputtered, and coughed again.

"Yes, you can," Yezi said, grabbing Yao's hand. "I bet you will live one hundred years."

Yao cleared her throat. "I'll try."

"Yes, you will," Yezi said firmly. She moved closer to Yao, like a vine leaning on a tree. She kicked at a tiny stone on the road. Her eyes fixed on her brother ahead of them.

After they had walked for ten more minutes, Yezi's stomach started growling. "Can we eat something, Popo Yao? I'm hungry," she whined.

Yao raised her head to locate the sun. *It must be noon.* "Sang," she called out, "let's have some lunch."

Removing the bag from her shoulder, Yao placed it on a flat stone at the edge of the road. Then from her bag, she drew out a package bound in cloth and unwrapped it, revealing several plate-sized pancakes. She picked one up and gave it to Yezi. "Eat," Yao said. She raised her hand to beckon to Sang.

Joining them, Sang took a pancake and sat down on a patch of weeds next to Yezi. Yao passed a canteen to Yezi to drink from and then handed it to Sang. After that, she, too, ate a pancake and had some of the water from the canteen.

Lunch finished, they continued along the dusty path, an endless snake winding through the woods up to a hill. At what would be the head of the snake, they could see a courtyard walled with electric barbed wire. Beyond the yard was a wide field that resembled a dark green lake.

Yezi asked, "What is that?"

"Tea bushes," answered Yao, reaching for Yezi's hand again. "Let's make our way down the slope. The camp's there."

They reached a shelter-like post at the gate with a rectangular placard on the door. The words on it read: "Wildcat Valley Labour Camp." At the window, Yao drew out from her pocket a requisition letter stamped with the round, red seal of the Residents' Committee that oversaw civilians who did not have a job assigned by the government. Passing it to the guard, she said, "Comrade, please read the letter and let us in. We are here to see Meihua Wei."

A hand stretched out from beyond the window, took the letter, and then placed a form on the sill. "Fill this out first."

Yao pushed Sang forward. "You do it."

Sang carefully completed the form and returned it through the opening. Then he was given a slip of paper, with a large red stamp on it: "The pass must be returned before 3:00 p.m."

The gate opened. Knowing where to go, Sang strode toward a two-storey concrete building in the compound. Yezi quickened her steps when she watched her brother enter the building. Her mother was waiting inside. Yao could not help but grumble, "Why are you walking so fast? Hurrying up for your next life?"

By the time Yao and Yezi had stepped through the entrance, Sang had already asked the guard to get his mother. He was sitting on a bench in the lobby and flipping through a back issue of *Medicine for the Masses*. Yezi and Yao slid next to him on the bench.

"Sang, how long do we have to wait?" asked Yao.

"They said about twenty minutes," answered the boy as he glanced at the clock on the wall. "It's 1:15 now."

Quietly the three waited for their turn. Thirty minutes later, a uniformed guard finally escorted them to the visiting room. Yezi saw their mother first, sitting on a bench in a far corner of the room.

Meihua looked pallid and thin, but her eyes lit up as she saw her family come toward her. Another long year had passed. She hugged them one by one. Then she draped her arm gently around her daughter's shoulder, and asked, "How is everybody? Where is your father?"

"We're okay. Everything's fine," answered Sang. "

Yao told Meihua that Lon had come home the week before, but a heavy rain that had lasted all day long prevented them from taking the trip to Meihua's gulag. Yao added that Lon might come to see her if he could get some time off in the next weeks.

Uncertain of what to say, Yezi was quiet, although she had so much she wanted to tell her mother.

"I'll tell you something," Sang said, his tone conspiratorial. Scanning the room to be sure that nobody was listening to them, he lowered his voice and added, "I saw a documentary about President Nixon's visit to China in February 1972."

"Oh, really? That was eight months ago." Meihua's eyes beamed. "Any other news?"

"A classmate of mine, Liang, said her uncle from the States would come to visit," said Sang. Excitement filled his voice. "Now people don't say 'American imperialists' any more. Now they say 'American friends.'"

"Son," Meihua was whispering. "Be careful of saying 'American friends.' You need to read more of Chairman Mao's Red Book." Meihua was fearful of his enthusiasm, worried that he might let those words out at the wrong time, to the wrong people. The Cultural Revolution was not over and her heart froze at the thought of harm coming to any of her children.

She turned to Yezi and stroked her hair "You're taller than last year," Meihua said, smiling at the little girl. "Do you enjoy going to school?"

"Sometimes I do," said Yezi, who liked being petted by her mother's tender fingers. She remembered how in thunderstorms she always curled up in bed, wrapped in a blanket, where she felt safe and warm even though the roaring thunder had silenced the world, and the wind and rain threatened to come through the roof and walls. In her bed, snuggled under her blankets, she felt safe from the storm raging outside. Now her mother's hands made her feel the same way, and she finally relaxed against her mother, seeking refuge in her arms. "Popo Yao made this for my birthday," Yezi said, fingering her dark green blouse.

"I made it out of old curtains," Yao said with broad smile. "I don't have any windows to cover."

"My children depend on you. What would they do without you? I am so grateful to you, Yao," Meihua sighed, and looked up at Yao with a weary smile. "Have you had any news about Dahai? I am always so worried about him."

Yao hesitated. Then she said, "Maybe he's been too busy on the farm to write. I hope we'll hear from him soon."

"I know these children are a huge burden on you. I feel so bad that I haven't been able to pay you a single fen all these years." Meihua lowered her head to hide the tears that were welling up in her eyes.

"You gave me a home when I needed one," Yao said. "I will always be grateful for that. Things will get better when you get out of here. Now you need only to take care of yourself,"

Yao spoke as she handed a package to Meihua. "This is for you: some biscuits and a sweater I knitted for you with some used yarn."

"It's too much work for you." Meihua sighed, her eyes filled with anguish.

"Your life is harder than ours. We get money from Lon every month. We manage fine."

Meihua placed her thin hands on Yao's arms. "Please take care of your own health." Having spotted the guard striding over to them, Meihua wrapped her arms around her children once more. "Both of you do whatever Yao asks you to. Sang, help Yao more with family chores."

The guard barked, "Time is up. Time is up!"

"Okay, we're leaving." Yao dried her eyes and drew Yezi close to her. "Reform your thoughts well. You'll be able to come home sooner if you get pardoned," she said, using the words she had heard were the right ones to speak.

As the three left the Wildcat Valley Labour Camp, gray clouds rolled in, veiling the sky. They returned on the same path across the field and trudged back to the station under the gloomy overcast sky.

After they had disembarked from the train and were on their way home, a torrential rain caught up with them. Carrying Yezi on her back, Yao wobbled through the downpour with Sang. By the time they had reached their apartment, they were drenched. Yao put Yezi down, and dropped her bag to the floor. Sang pulled his bag off his shoulder and carefully hung it on the wall.

"Sang, change your clothes," Yao urged as she dragged a box from the corner and picked out some clothing. "Yezi, let me help you change into something dry."

Outside, the rain poured, streaming down the windowpane. Wrapped in a warm blanket, Yezi quickly fell asleep.

She dreamed that she was on the back of a giant swallow

soaring over a high wall where her mother in ragged clothes stood alone behind the barbed wire, waving. Yezi longed to hug her, but the swallow did not slow down. Yezi pulled back its wings, but they continued to flap, causing a swirl of air. As the wind whistled and pushed open a path, the swallow shot through the air like an arrow leaving its bow. Eyes squinting, Yezi saw her mother's shoulder-length hair falling over her face. Yezi longed to touch her mother's hair, but the swallow swooped over the wall and above the human figure. Yezi was close enough to notice the flash of hope in her mother's deep-set eyes. Yezi wanted to sing: *I'm a flying swallow*. Her mother's silhouetted face against the lit sky stayed with her through that rough, stormy night.

9.
ANTI-REVOLUTIONARY SLOGAN

IT WAS 1974, AND YEZI was almost at the end of Grade Two. One June morning, as the students were preparing for their math class, the head teacher, Huang, stepped into the room. "Girls and boys: please get a sheet of paper and pencil ready." She looked solemn. In a firm voice she said, "Eyes on the board. Please copy my words. Write each sentence over and over until you fill all the lines."

One of the students raised his hand, but Huang scowled. "No questions. Just finish your work and hand it in. Make no corrections, please."

Turning to the board, Huang said, "Let's start." Slowly, she wrote: "Long live Chairman Mao!" and "Down with capitalism!"

Yezi completed the entire sheet with carefully copied characters. She was proud of her neatness.

After submitting the page to her teacher, she joined the other students in the hallway outside the classroom. A girl whispered, "Will they find out who did it? You know, the person who wrote the anti-revolutionary slogan?"

"Sure," a boy said with a mysterious tone. "My brother said the City Public Security already sent people here."

"Do you think they can still identify the handwriting even if the person fakes it by using a different style from his own?"

"Sure they can. They must have a special way to figure it out."

Yezi finally understood why the teacher had asked them to copy the sentences. *What did the anti-revolutionary slogan say? Who wrote it?*

After school she met her classmate, Jian. Jian's father was a medical doctor. The family lived in one of the buildings that were in a walled yard across the road from Arts Paradise. Numerous branches with palm-sized leaves, trimmed from a huge plane tree, were piled against the wall. The two girls decided to build a lean-to that they could use as a hideout with the twigs. They pulled one of the larger tree limbs out of the stack, set its end on the ground two steps apart from the yard wall and let it go. When it fell, its top reached over the wall. One by one, they placed about ten twigs side by side. Long branches full of leaves closed off one end of the lean-to. They chose two short but large branches with more leaves and tied one over the other to cover the entrance at the other end. They could lift the branch door and place it aside easily when they wanted to go in or come out of the hideout. Running back to her home, Jian later returned with two small stools. "Let's hide in our hut," she said. "Now open the door for me, so I can bring these inside."

Yezi carefully held the tied-together branches and moved them aside as Jian hunched over to creep in. As Yezi followed her in and stooped into a corner, Jian lifted the branch door and pulled it over the entrance from the inside. "We can hang around here after school," she said, giggling and admiring their new paradise.

"We can almost see through these," Yezi said, touching the light green leaves between the twigs. "Look at this." She pointed to a delicate butterfly on a leaf, glistening in the sunshine that reached through the gaps between twigs. "So pretty," she murmured.

"If I can catch it, let's make it a specimen," Jian said, squeezing her two fingers together, inching her hand toward the butterfly.

"How?"

"You sandwich it in a book 'til it's dried out." Jian's eyes glowed like a cat in the dark as she raved about the specimen. "Wait here. I have to get something to show you."

"Get what?" asked Yezi.

Jian did not answer but scrambled out of the lean-to. A few moments later, she reappeared with a thick, brown dictionary. She flipped open a page. A dragonfly lay there flat, its twisted head and two eyeballs drooping to the sides. Its screen-like wings gleamed a blue-green. Jian said, "Take a look."

Yezi examined the dragonfly. As she flipped to another page, she saw another insect with an oval-shaped body and small beige wings. "What's this?" she asked.

"A moth. It changed from a silkworm after spinning its silk."

"Really? Have you ever raised any silkworms?"

"Not yet. But I'd like to. Maybe I can get some eggs."

Yezi said, "Oooh! I want to feed silkworms." She felt exhilarated when she imagined the soft, glossy silken threads spun by corpulent worms. Her light brown eyes glinted. "But I am afraid of worms," she added with a shrug.

"Hey! Do you know these words?" asked Jian, her finger pointing to words on the page.

Yezi shook her head, as she examined the book in Jian's hand. "No. They're foreign."

"I thought you would know."

"Why?"

"Your mama's American," Jian said, not noticing Yezi's embarrassment. "This was my father's English dictionary, but he said books in foreign languages are no longer of any use. When he sold his English and Russian books to a recycling guy, I begged him to keep this big one for my specimens."

"But I can say a couple of English words," Yezi said, her hands up with excitement.

"What are they?"

Yezi stumbled over the words a little bit. "*God bless you.*"

"What does that mean?" asked Jian, a puzzled look on her face.

"It means, *shang-di bao-you ni*. Do you get it?"

"Yeah. It sounds superstitious, but I like it anyway. Say it in English again."

The two girls repeated "God ... bless ... you" over and over, giggling in their hut.

"Where are you, Yezi?" Yao's voice was close, her tone stern. "You little rascal ... don't make me look for you!"

"Time for supper," Yezi told her friend as she pushed open the twig door.

"Remember to keep our secret from others," said Jian.

Yezi nodded. "See you soon," she said and hurried away.

After supper, Yezi and her brother did their homework at the table. As she unfolded her exercise book, she remembered what she had copied from the blackboard that morning.

She picked up her pencil and wrote down the characters, "Chairman Mao," on the page. Yezi's eyes focused on the script. Then she scribbled "down with" next to "Chairman Mao" without thinking. As she scanned the sentence silently, she was shocked: *that's an anti-revolutionary slogan!* She erased all the words immediately, but the strokes of the characters were still recognizable. Frightened, she furiously drew a group of stars over the faint traces. Carefully, with an eraser, she then rubbed out the stars. She felt as though she were a thief hiding something she had not stolen.

"What are you doing?" Sang asked her. "You haven't written a single word."

Heart pounding against her chest, she answered, "I will." She opened the Chinese textbook, but her mind lingered on the invisible words she had erased.

The following morning, Yezi was called to the principal's office during recess.

What have I done wrong? she wondered, as she made her way to the office, her feet dragging. She thought anxiously about the words she had written last night. *Did they find out?* Trembling with fear, she knocked on the door.

The middle-aged principal, Xiuming Wu, behind the desk raised her head. "Come on in," she said, gesturing for Yezi to move closer. Her short hair was almost gray; her eyes showed concern. "Tell me where you went last Friday after school," she said.

"Last Friday?" Yezi stood in front of the desk. Her eyes looked down to her shoes. She was puzzled and tried hard to remember what she had done that Friday. Then, she remembered. "I hung around the playground," she answered, her eyes still fixed on the tops of her shoes.

"What did you do there?"

"I watched other students play ping-pong."

"What else did you do after that?"

"I waited for my friend, but she didn't show up."

"Did you see anyone else around?" asked the principal, who was looking at Yezi intently.

"Some boys were there."

"What did they do?"

Yezi searched her memory. "They seemed to be running after one another."

"When did you leave there?"

"After I read a story."

"What story?"

"*A Poor Boy Saved*."

"Do you love Chairman Mao?"

"Yes," Yezi said, feeling her chest tighten.

"Why?"

"He brings happiness to the people. He's our saviour," she recited what she had learned in her Chinese class.

Principal Wu got up from her chair and approached Yezi. She smiled at her benevolently. "If other people ask you these questions, give the same answers. Will you remember?"

"Yes, I will." Dismissed, Yezi left the office.

She returned to the classroom, but was troubled. Back at her desk, she did not even hear what Jian had asked her until she felt a nudge on her arm. "Where have you been?"

"I — I went..."

"I saw you come from the principal's office," said Jian.

"What happened?" asked a boy sitting behind her.

"She must've done something wrong!" another boy next to Yezi shouted. "Tell us what you did!"

A girl said, "It must be related to the anti-revolutionary slogan."

"It was not me!" Yezi raised her voice in answer to her classmates, most of who were now looking at her with suspicion. She buried her head under her arms on her desk like an ostrich with its head in the sand. She whimpered, "I did nothing wrong."

"Who did it?" several voices questioned.

Jian answered for Yezi in a firm tone, "She didn't do it."

Yezi was comforted by Jian's voice, but the boy next to Yezi yelled, "Yes she did it, she did it!"

"No! You're the one who played around the ping-pong table that day!" Jian protested. Like other students, she had heard the gossip about the slogan having been written on the ping-pong table.

"How dare you say that? I'll beat you up!" the boy screamed.

At that instant, the teacher of political studies entered the room. "Time for class! Be quiet!" he roared.

Then, he stared at Jian and another student who were still arguing. "You two get out of here!" His hand pointing to the door, he ordered, "Go to the office of the workers' leader right now." Then he scanned the class and stared at Yezi, asking impatiently. "What are you crying about?"

"She was the one who wrote the anti-revolution slogan on

the ping pong table," another student said.

"What?" the teacher gasped. "Yezi! Stand up and confess your crime!"

"I did not do it." Yezi insisted, her legs trembling. She stood, wiping her tears with the back of her hand. Her face paled. Strands of hair stuck to her wet cheeks.

The teacher slapped the desk. "Who did it?"

The children looked at one another, confusion and fright in their eyes. But, at that moment, the words of Teacher Li echoed in their minds: "The Chinese shouldn't scold the Chinese." They answered in unison, "We don't know."

The teacher raised his eyebrows. "Yezi, go to the leader's office! Do you hear me?"

"Yes," Yezi answered, collecting her book bag. She left her seat, her face red, her eyes still full of tears.

The teacher said, "Let's read Chairman Mao's directive on class and class struggle. Open the Red Book. Turn to page ninety-nine and look at the second paragraph."

When Yezi stepped out of the classroom, she heard different voices reading Mao's words aloud behind her: "We should support whatever the enemy opposes and oppose whatever the enemy supports."

Who are our real enemies? Yezi wondered, gripped with fear.

At home, Sang was finishing his lunch. After peering up and down at the road again, Yao asked, "Are you sure you didn't see Yezi on your way home?"

"Nope. I already told you twice."

"I can't wait any more. I must try to find her," Yao said, wiping her forehead with a corner of her apron. She walked along the road toward the school filled with anxiety.

On her way to the school, she checked every corner of every garden calling in each direction: "Yeeh-zee! Where are you?" Her gruff voice reverberated around the campus. As she reached the elementary schoolyard, her legs were weak, and tears and sweat poured down her face.

Peering into every door she passed, Yao found only closed classrooms with empty seats. Suddenly Yao detected a woman's shout from inside an office. "Do you hear me? You must confess if you want to go home!"

Yao dashed toward the room. Through the window, she recognized the solemn face of a middle-aged woman, the Workers' Propaganda Team leader, sitting behind a desk, her face stern, her lips pursed in anger. The frightened Yezi sat on a chair in front of the desk, her head bent low over her lap. Her shoulders were trembling. *My God! There's my baby!*

Yao knocked loudly on the door and pushed it open before the leader had time to respond. Darting toward Yezi, she pulled her from the chair and enfolded her in her arms. "Little One! What're you doing here?"

Startled by the action of the heavy-set, gray-haired woman, the leader's eyes widened. She asked, "Who on earth are you?"

"Yezi is my girl. I look after her. Who are you?" Yao responded.

"I'm the workers' leader. She did—"

Yao had heard that the workers' leader could give orders to the principal, because the working class under Mao was of a higher rank than educated people. She also knew that as a peasant during this revolution she would not be questioned. "I'm from a poor peasant's family," she said loudly, puffing her chest out and standing as straight as she could. She knew it was also important to praise Mao. Her gruff voice rose, "Chairman Mao is our savoir. How can you become a leader without Chairman Mao?" Yao wanted to remind her that both of them were from the same class, and she knew these were words she could utter without fear of reprisal.

Flabbergasted, the leader asked, "What are you talking about?"

Yao's mind went blank, not knowing what else to add. Determined to get the child out of there, she tried again. "Because of Chairman Mao, I've lived a better life. Now Yezi needs to come home and eat her lunch."

"Her mother is an anti-revolutionary!" The leader scowled.

"But the child is not. She has grown up with me." Yao was firm, her eyes glaring at the leader.

"Why are you loyal to this anti-revolutionary family?" asked the leader, standing up. She drew in a breath. "Your loyalty to the family is wrong."

"I don't know that," answered Yao, trying to hide the tremor in her voice. "This little girl has been living with me since she was an infant, and she's done nothing wrong."

The leader came face to face with Yao, her finger jabbing at Yao's shoulder. "Do you read Chairman Mao's work? He teaches us, 'Mercy to the enemy means cruelty to the people.'" Gripping Yao's arm with her hand, the leader hissed, "Don't you think you are cruel to people like me from the proletariat class when you pity and stand beside the enemy?"

"I'm illiterate. I can't read Mao's great work. But what if this child were your daughter—"

"She's not my daughter," the leader sputtered.

"If she were yours, I'd take her under my wing, too." Yao turned to the leader. "I beg you— I'll get down on my knees if you wish," she said and stooped.

"What are you doing?" The leader shook with anger as she tried to pull Yao up, her teeth chattering.

"Please let her go. She's a harmless child." As Yao pulled Yezi toward the leader, she motioned for her to kneel down beside her. Yezi's eyes were fixed on the small sparrows that were hopping on the window ledge behind the leader's desk. They looked as though they too were apprehensive and not sure what to do.

The leader trod back to her chair and exhaled. "Fine! I'll let her go. But you must know that her parents are our enemies!"

The workers' leader could punish any person hired by the school, but she was unsure what she could do to this unlettered old woman from a poor peasant's family, a member of her own class.

"Thank you. I'll pray for you and ask Buddha to bless you," Yao entwined her hands, raising them up and down, and then bowed her head to show her appreciation. Then she pulled Yezi's arm. "Thank the mistress."

"Thank you," Yezi mumbled.

Holding back tears, Yao looked down at the crying girl, and pulled her gently to her feet. "Come on, little one, let's go home."

10.
SECRET HIDEOUT

YEZI FOLLOWED YAO OUT OF the office into the sunny yard. The sunlight blinded her drained, red-rimmed eyes. But other senses overwhelmed her: hunger and weariness, embarrassment and fear. *Did my mother feel like this, too?*

On the way home, she encountered several students returning for afternoon classes. Afraid of any gossip about her detention, she evaded them by walking behind Yao.

"Let's get a move on," Yao said, pulling Yezi's hand closer.

It was 2:00 p.m. when they sat down at the table for lunch. Still dizzy, Yezi ate little. "I don't feel like going back to school, Popo Yao. I only want to sleep."

"Don't worry. I'll tell your teacher you're ill."

Yezi climbed into bed and closed her eyes. Her heart thudded painfully, and a scene from the last year played out in her mind.

During their visit to the Wildcat Valley Labour Camp, Yezi could not help but ask her mother, "Are you anti-revolutionary?"

"What do you think?" her mother had replied, and smiled, her voice weak.

"People say you are, but I don't want you to be."

"Neither do I, but..."

"But what?"

"It's hard for me to answer your question. But you should know

Taking the bowl, Yezi bit into her first egg in many weeks. She was hungry and it tasted so good.

Later, after school, Jian came to see her. Eagerly, she asked Yezi to come with her to their hideout.

Delighted to see Jian and happy to be invited to play, Yezi felt much better. She nodded, clasping Jian's hand. "I can't go right now, but I'll see you there tomorrow. I'll show you some pictures I've drawn," she said.

Sang overheard them talking excitedly. After Jian left, he asked, "Where is your hide-out?"

Joining him at the table, Yezi said, "I can't tell you because it's our secret."

He looked solemn as he said, "Be very careful. Have you already laughed away the incident of the ping-pong table?"

"It's not a real hide-out," she frowned. "It's only a small lean-to we made with a bunch of branches. They were cut down in Jian's yard."

"What do you do there?"

"We sit there, and talk, and look at insects and share pictures."

"Okay then. I heard about the leader's talk with you. Even though she knows you had nothing to do with the anti-revolutionary slogan, you still have to be careful." Sang took his sister's hands in his, and said, "I am going to tell you a secret. It will cheer you up. Mama might be discharged before her sentence expires." He was elated. He couldn't stop the grin that swept over his face.

"Really? Oh my," Yezi gasped. She could not believe her ears. "Oh! That would be so great!"

"Yeah! Mama is innocent, you know," Sang said. His eyes beaming, he placed his hands on her shoulders, and leaning close, he whispered, "The people who put her behind bars have fallen out of power now. Mama will be home very soon."

Grasping her brother's arm, Yezi looked at her brother and pleaded, "This is true, right? It's true!"

"It's true, yes, but we will have to wait and see."

The next Sunday, Yezi got up early to help Yao with chores. From behind the door, Yao dragged out her treasures: a basketful of split tomatoes, leftover red peppers and green beans she had bought at a discount price. She cut away the blemished parts, and placed them in the large pot that Yezi would take to the communal sinks. Yezi then washed the vegetables in an enamel basin and when she returned, she placed each in different containers as Yao instructed.

Yezi told Yao what she had heard from her brother, but Yao just said, "I know, but I won't believe until I see it. I've been waiting for that news for a long time." She didn't lift her eyes from the vegetables she was chopping.

An hour later, when everything was ready for cooking, Yezi asked, "Can I go hang out with Jian now?"

"As long as you don't stay out too long." Yao nodded, and then set one of the pots on the stove.

Running across the road, Yezi headed to their hideout and slipped in quietly. Jian was already waiting inside, using a stack of bricks as a stool. Yezi found a couple more bricks and stacked them together for her stool. Jian pointed to another pile of bricks that was blanketed by a large piece of white paper trimmed with scalloped edges. "This is our table."

"Wow! That's fantastic," Yezi said, placing the heap of drawings she had brought with her on the makeshift table. Then she proudly presented them one by one to Jian.

Unexpectedly, a boy's voice called out, "Jian, where are you?"

"Shhh!" Jian placed her finger over her mouth.

They both stretched their heads toward the gaps between the branches and spied a boy about thirteen loitering in the yard. "Ha! He doesn't know where we are," Jian whispered delightedly, as the teenager turned and started walk away. Impulsively, she shouted, "Ming!"

Ming turned his head, scanning the yard. He turned his head from one side to the other, and spotting no one, continued on his way. Yezi giggled and decided to play the same trick by calling out to a girl who had just come out of one of the nearby units "Yes, who is this?" the girl responded, eyeing the area. Not seeing anyone, she left the yard, baffled.

When Jian's mother stepped out of their unit with a tote bag in her hand, Jian tried calling out to her. But her mother was not easily fooled and quickly located her daughter's voice from the shelter. "Jian! I know you are there!" Her mother trotted over to them.

"No, Mama. I beg you." Jian laughed. "I am not here!"

"Okay," replied her mother, turning to stride out of the yard. "But you must finish your homework before going anywhere else."

Suddenly, Ming's voice burst out right next to them. "I am going to take down your shack, you troublemakers!"

The door crashed, and Ming appeared in front of the two girls before they realized what was happening. He laughed. "Ha! You two rats are hiding here." His hand levitated over the twigs, and he made a pulling gesture. "I'm going to tear this nest to pieces," he growled playfully.

"Please don't destroy it," Jian begged. "Please. I'll lend you my chess book anytime you want."

"A done deal!" Ming stretched his head inside and said to Jian. "Your brother told me you were looking for silkworm eggs. If you can beat me in a chess game, I'll find some for you."

Jian promised to play chess with him after finishing her homework, and then asked him to leave them alone until then. As soon as Ming left, she told Yezi she would ask her brother teach her some tricks in chess so she could win the game.

Yezi was excited at the thought that her friend might get a few silkworm eggs as a reward. Remembering that dinner was probably almost ready, she told Jian it was time for her to make her way home.

That evening, Yezi asked her brother to teach her a song in English. "Which one? Why?"

"The one you learned from our mother," she said. "That one that goes 'Row, Row, Row Your Boat.' Jian and I would like to learn to speak English." She was looking at him intently, her hands placed firmly on her hips.

"No, I'm not teaching Jian anything. I might be accused of spreading bourgeois ideas. I don't need that." He drummed his fingers on the table as though he were solving a difficult mathematic equation in his head. His face softened as he leaned toward her. "But I will teach you some English if you can promise to keep it secret."

Yezi nodded emphatically. "I promise. Brother, I promise."

"Okay, repeat after me. *Row, row, row your boat...*" He sang quietly under his breath.

Yezi happily repeated the words, picturing herself and her mother sitting in a boat that floated along a bubbling brook. The sun was shining, and she and her mother were holding hands while they sang. She continued to sing the song with her brother until she had memorized all the words and it was time for bed.

The next morning, she met Jian on her way to school. Yezi asked if she had beaten Ming in the chess game. Jian shook her head. "Not yet. But I will beat him some day soon." Grabbing Yezi's hand, she said, "Remember, we're going to our hide-out after school."

"Of course," Yezi smiled. "Of course."

They didn't notice that one of the children in their classroom was following closely behind them and had heard them speaking. "Where are you going?" he asked. "Tell me," he insisted.

They both grinned, but did not answer. It was their secret. And he was simply annoying.

In gym class, Yezi and the other students played ping-pong on the playground. One of the concrete ping-pong tables in the school yard seemed somehow different from the others.

The surface of one corner had been mended with cement. Yezi trembled uncontrollably when she saw it. That must have been where the anti-revolutionary slogan had been scribbled.

After school, when Yezi got home, she plunked herself down at the table beside the door and started to work on her assignments. Moments later, Jian rushed over to her. "We've lost our hideout!" she shouted in a desperate voice.

"What?" Yezi could not believe her ears. She stood up and grabbed her friend's arm. "How? Why?"

"It's gone! No more hide-out!"

"Who would have done that?" Yezi asked, her lips trembling.

"Maybe the gardeners took it away along with the other branches." Jian's eyes were brimming with tears.

"This is awful," Yezi sighed, sitting back on her stool. "What should we do?"

"I guess we will have to wait until next time they trim the trees," Jian said, wiping her eyes. "Then we'll build another one."

"Yeah, we'll do that." Yezi slung her arm around her friend's shoulder, trying to comfort her. "Stay here, with me. We can do our homework together."

"Why don't you come with me?" Jian said, sniffling. "The table at my home is bigger..."

"Go where?" asked Yao, who had just returned from the communal sinks with a pot in her hand.

"Can I go do my homework at Jian's home," Yezi asked. "Please, Popo Yao? Please?"

"Okay," said Yao. "Only to do your homework. Be back on time for supper."

"Great!" Yezi stood and gathered up her things. Arm in arm, the girls walked away, their heads almost touching. Yezi breathed deeply. The cool evening breeze carried the scent of lilacs as it brushed past them. The fading sunlight danced between the shadows of the locus trees that lined the street. The two friends bounced across the road like butterflies fluttering over a garden. They had forgotten all about their hideout.

One Saturday afternoon at the end of June—several weeks after the anti-revolutionary slogan had been found on the ping pong table in the school playground, the principal called all the students to assemble in the yard. The Workers' Propaganda Team leader announced their success in locating the student who had scribbled, "Chairman Mao" on the ping-pong table and then carved three X's over it. Yezi took a deep breath. A pitiful feeling arose in her for the guilty student, the boy who stood on the stage, his head lowered, his arms dangling at his sides. When the announcer's voice thundered from the loudspeaker, Yezi could not help but shiver even though she was standing in the steamy sunlight of an early June afternoon. "Now we can prove that 'a hero raises a revolutionary son, and a reactionary father, an anti-revolutionary bastard.' Guo Li's father is anti-revolutionary. That is why he wrote the anti-revolutionary slogan and committed this crime." The speaker wiped her agitated face with a handkerchief and then barked loudly, "Guo Li has been suspended from school for a year! If he doesn't improve, the revolution will reform him as it has his father!" Her hand slashed the air as if she were cutting off the head of a criminal.

The sunlight was hot on Yezi's face, but a chill surged in her heart. She did not know what the suspended student felt like, but she guessed his legs were weak, and his hands numb. Gloom and dread pressed down upon her. Finally the workers' leader demanded that each class hold a political meeting to denounce Guo Li's anti-revolutionary crime. As she banged the loudspeaker on the table, someone shoved the young boy down the steps, pushing him onto his knees on the ground below the platform. Craning her head, Yezi stared at the boy, whose dark hair, licked by the sunlight, looked like a patch of dry grass on fire. When she blinked, several sparkles danced in front of her eyes. She felt as if she were the one being pushed down from the stage. Her legs buckled, and she forced herself to keep standing, willing her legs to hold her steady.

11.
THE READING ROOM

AFTER FINAL EXAMS, THE 1975 summer break started. Like birds freed from cages, Yezi and the other children scampered contentedly around Arts Paradise, playing hide-and-seek. The sun shone. The yard came to life with their play and babbling. As the days passed, the exuberant children expanded their territory, hiding in places outside Arts Paradise and then, even farther out, so that the "cat" would sometimes take hours to catch a "mouse."

One such afternoon, while the cat counted to one hundred, Yezi along with two other mice ran toward some remote buildings about ten minutes away. As they passed through a garden, Lan, Ming's twin sister, decided to hide among the bushes, but Fu, her little brother, who was running with them, kept going. Yezi decided to follow Fu. They finally reached the entrance of a library, a large and imposing building made of dark gray bricks. They climbed up the stairs and headed toward a large window facing the road to the entrance. Fu slouched down on the low windowsill. "I'm going to stay here," he announced. "I can see the cat before he gets here."

Yezi, standing beside him, was intrigued by the double doors across from the window. She could see they led to a spacious room where several people were sitting at tables reading. People came and went, past the woman doorkeeper who seemed not to pay attention to any one in particular. Curious, Yezi tapped Fu on the shoulder and, pointing toward the room, said, "I'm going inside to take a look. Call me if you see the cat."

Nobody stopped her as she entered the reading room. She tiptoed around the shelves, captivated by the rows and rows of books of different sizes and colours. Her eyes fell on several rows of journals and magazines and finally rested on an issue of the *People's Pictorial*. She pulled it down and slowly thumbed through its pages, full of photographs, each one with a different story to tell.

"What are you doing here?" a familiar voice asked, startling her.

Yezi raised her head and was surprised to face her brother. "Why are you here?" she asked.

"I'm studying—"

"Ha! You're not a university student."

"Neither are you." With a mischievous wink, Sang motioned her to a seat at a nearby table. He rested his hand on a stack of periodicals and papers on the table and said, "I've been reading all of these."

"You have an English newspaper." Yezi picked it up and scrunched her nose at the words in large, bold type. "What does it say?" she asked.

"It's *The Morning Star* from London. There are more newspapers over there," Sang said proudly.

"Do you understand English?"

"A little bit," he said, fingering a thick book. "This dictionary helps me."

As she glanced at it, she said, "It's the same as Jian's."

"Jian has an English dictionary?"

"Yes. Oh, no, it was her father's." Excited, Yezi's voice became higher-pitched.

"Shh. We are supposed to be quiet. We can be thrown out for making too much noise." He waved his hand, fanning her away. "Go look around, *quietly*."

Yezi slunk toward the newspaper rack and flipped through the different English newspapers. She grabbed the first newspaper rod she could reach easily and examined the front page of the newspaper it displayed.

A young student next to her turned and asked, "Do you read English?"

"No, but I know it's English."

"What's this?" asked the student, pointing to a word with a pen in his hand.

"I don't know. Can you teach me?"

"Sure. *Times.*"

"What does it mean?"

"It's the name of a newspaper published in England."

"*Times,*" she repeated the word. "Thanks. I'm going to read it through," she said matter-of-factly. Turning around, she carried the paper rod like a flag in her arms.

The amused student smirked. "Good luck."

After reciting the word in a whisper, Yezi carefully laid the newspaper on a table. She inspected the spelling of the word, *Times*, and searched through the dense text to see if she could recognize the same word somewhere else. Examining the photographs on some of the pages, and running her fingers through lines of text, she finally spotted the word "time" again. Wondering why the word did not have the "s" character at the end and why the first character appeared a little different, she raised her head to question the student that had spoken to her earlier, but could not find him. Instead, she replaced the paper on the rack and returned it to the stacks. She decided to walk around some of the tables so she could see what the university students were reading.

At an unoccupied seat, she found several issues of an English magazine. Kneeling on a chair, she thumbed through the pages to look at the photographs. The people in other parts of the world looked happy and were dressed in colourful clothes. Delighted, she spotted a photograph of a little girl, her age, with a wide smile and a violin in her hands. Fingering the photograph over and over, she could almost touch that girl and her instrument. She looked at all the other smiling faces in the magazine and felt her throat tighten. *I want to smile like all these people*, she thought. *I want my mama to smile like this too.* She couldn't wait tell with Jian about the English world she had found in the reading room.

Light-hearted, she left the table and strode past the entrance. She grinned at the doorkeeper, who did not smile but nodded back. She realized then that looking happy was not difficult, and people seemed to like it. Remembering her playmate, she headed toward the windowsill. Fu had fallen asleep. His head, leaning against the window, was bathed in the late afternoon sunlight.

"Wake up," Yezi said, gently shaking his shoulder.

Fu jumped up, a puzzled look on his face. "Why am I here?"

"We were playing hide-and-seek. Did you see the cat?"

"The cat?" he asked with a shy smile. "I forgot to look. Maybe he hasn't gotten here yet."

"The game's over. Let's go home."

"Are you sure? Maybe the cat is still looking for us," Fu said, following her glumly downstairs.

Outside, the sun hung westward, making everything on campus golden. The sky was an endless pale blue. Eyes narrowing to a slit in the bright light of the afternoon sun, Yezi said, "Everything looks so fantastic."

"What?" Fu perked up and then glanced at her. "You look happy," he said.

"Yes, I am," she answered, thinking about the child violinist in the photograph. "You should be happy, too." She laughed and looked up into the clear sky, enjoying the feeling of having discovered something wonderful.

Just as they were nearing their courtyard, the song, "The East Is Red," blasted through a loudspeaker, a signal on campus for suppertime. Waving goodbye to Fu, Yezi ran the rest of the way home.

"Where were you this afternoon?" Yao bit her lip when Yezi drew close to the table.

"I was at the library."

"Library? How did you get in? It's not a place for kids."

"But I did. So did Sang," she said, her eyes glowing.

"Are kids allowed there?" Yao took a breath.

"You can ask my brother." Joining Sang at the table, Yezi said, "I'm hungry now."

"You poor starving creature." Raising her eyebrows, Yao filled a bowl with steaming rice and shredded cabbage.

"It's delicious," Yezi said, smacking her lips.

Surprised, Yao said, "But you don't like cabbage. I cooked some tomatoes for you."

"From now on, I like everything," Yezi said, grinning. "Well, now, what has changed you?" Yao asked, staring into Yezi's smiling face. "Books?" She remembered what she had heard as a child: if people had an education, they had a chance of being hired by the emperor. She was told that reading books could make people officers. *Maybe Yezi will be hired by the emperor.* She felt suddenly very proud of her young charge.

After supper, with Yao's permission, Yezi pranced across the road into the yard, and walked over to the large, four-storey, brown brick building that faced her apartment. She climbed the stairs two at a time until she reached the top floor. She stopped in front of the first door and knocked.

Jian opened the door with a welcoming smile. She gripped Yezi's arm and pulled her inside. "What's up? You look so happy."

"Guess what? I discovered some English newspapers."

"Where?" Jian asked, as they scrambled onto chairs at the table where Jian's younger sister, Kang, was playing with a mound of toy blocks.

Yezi told Jian about what she had found in the reading room of the main library. Jian told her that she had spent the afternoon playing chess. She had won the chess game and would soon be getting some silkworm eggs from Ming.

"I'd like to see those newspapers. Let's go tomorrow," Jian said. "Then we can go for a walk along the lakeshore. There are mulberry bushes there and we can pick some leaves for our silkworms to eat." Her arm shook in the air as if she had already grabbed a few branches.

Yezi pictured worms crawling on green leaves.

"Can I come?" Kang whined, pushing her blocks away.

"We're not going anywhere right now," Jian said to her sister. "Come on. I'll help you build a house."

When Yezi got back home, she was still thinking about her discovery of the newspapers in English. "Do you know *Times*?" she asked her brother.

"You mean *The Times*, the newspaper?" Sang raised his head from his book, looking at her with surprise. "What about it?"

"Guess what?" she said, grinning. "I found a misspelled word."

"How? You don't even read English." Sang was dismissive.

Yezi placed a piece of paper on the table and wrote the words '*time*' and '*Times*.' She thrust the paper toward him. "Do you see the difference between the two?" she asked.

"I sure do. This is its singular form." Her brother laid his finger at the end of the word '*time*'. "There's no 's' here."

"Well, look here. There's something else that is different," Yezi said, pointing to the letter, 't.'

"It's in the lower case, but the letter in the title is capitalized."

"Oh! English is confusing," Yezi said, puzzled. "Why do they write the same character in different ways?"

"Look here." Pointing at a Chinese character he had written, Sang asked, "Read it."

"Sun."

He added a stroke to it. "Now read this one."

"Eye."

"One more stroke made a different character. This is the way of written Chinese."

"I see." She laid her finger on the English word. "So that is the way of written English."

"Smart girl," Sang said, clapping his hands. "I'll teach you the English alphabet if you want."

Yezi nodded emphatically. "Yes! I want to learn."

The next morning after breakfast, Jian found Yezi sitting at the outside table and reading a book. "Are you ready to go?" she asked.

"Yes," Yezi said as she got up. Turning toward the communal sinks, she raised her voice, "Popo Yao, I'm leaving." Without waiting for Yao's response, the two girls headed for the library hand in hand. The campus was empty. Most of the students had already gone home for the summer. They were accompanied only by the twittering of birds hopping along the side of the road looking for worms.

In the library, once they reached the double doors, Yezi was surprised to find a different doorkeeper. A middle-aged man was sitting in the chair in front of the doors. He put up his hands to stop Yezi and Jian from entering the room, stating in a firm voice, "Children are not allowed here."

"We are students," Jian protested.

"You aren't university students yet," the man said, waggling his fingers. "So, please go away now."

Tugging at Jian's hand, Yezi whispered, "Let's come back another time."

Disappointed, the girls left the library and decided to head toward the lakeshore and the mulberry bushes. As they walked along, Yezi looked up into the clear sky and thought, *next time, we'll be lucky*. As they strolled past the gardens, a boy's voice suddenly rang out from behind the hedges, making them both jump. "Stinking Ninth! Evil American!"

Yezi turned around and spotted a teenager from their courtyard. It was Tao, the neighbourhood bully. He squeezed himself out from behind a series of hedges, puffing angrily toward them.

Jian pulled Yezi back, wondering what to do next. Number Nine referred to intellectuals who were ranked below the eight undesirable categories of people that were regularly denounced during the Cultural Revolution. Jian whispered to Yezi, "Ninth refers to my father because he's a doctor, and American to your mama." Suddenly, she turned toward the boy and screamed, "Don't call me Stinking Ninth. You are nothing but a big bully!"

Yezi stomped her feet and yelled: "And don't call me Evil American, either!" Then she burst into laughter when she saw Tao bounce back and dash away. Relieved, she said, "Maybe we should go to the mulberry bushes another time."

"I agree," said Jian, letting out a big breath. "Let's go home before he comes back. We can do our summer homework."

Later that afternoon, fortified by a hearty lunch, they decided to walk over to Lake Dianchi where swimmers floated or splashed in the water. The air reeked of fish and waterweeds. The bushes swayed in the warm summer breeze, beckoning to them.

Jian stretched out her hand to touch the leaves on a nearby bush. "This *is* a mulberry bush!" she squealed.

Yezi plucked a leaf and sniffed at it. "Are you sure? I have no idea. I've never seen mulberry leaves before."

"My bother calls this the oily mulberry." Jian pulled a branch of the white mulberry bush and picked two leaves that were oval in shape. "I'll ask my brother to take a look and tell us if they are okay for the silkworms."

As the two continued their inspection of the lakeside bushes, they found another kind of mulberry bush that Jian called maple mulberry since its foliage looked like maple leaves.

They picked a couple more leaves to give to Jian's brother

for further verification. Suddenly, they heard, *whoosh*! Tao jumped at them from behind the bush, snapping a branch in the air as if it were a whip. "Stop it!" he yapped excitedly.

"Why? These are not your bushes!" cried Jian, raising her arm in front of her face to avoid Tao's branch.

"I found them first," the bully shouted lashing his branch again in the air.

"Let's leave." Yezi pulled Jian's hand. "We'll come back another time."

The two girls darted away, leaving the boy's laughter to resound in the bushes and dissolve into the whispers of the lakeshore waters.

12.
MULBERRY LEAVES

SEVERAL DAYS LATER, JIAN ARRIVED at Yezi's home with a big infectious grin on her face. "Guess what I have?" she said, carefully pulling a lump of toilet paper out from her pocket.

Yezi blurted out the first thing that came to mind. "Candy?"

Jian shook her head. "Try again," she giggled.

Yezi paused. "Hmmm ... silkworm eggs?"

"You got it!" Jian said, unfolding the toilet paper to reveal a cluster of tiny gossamer eggs. "I'll give you this part," she said, cautiously tearing the toilet paper in two. She handed one piece to Yezi. "Check it every day. When you see a tiny black dot in an egg, a worm is ready to bite its way out."

"Wow!" Excited, Yezi carefully examined the eggs, imagining what she should do when all the eggs turned into black points. Her hand became sweaty and itchy as if the silkworms had already crept onto her palm. She could picture the worms spinning tiffany silk that would glint in the sunlight. "How long will it take them to hatch?"

"Maybe a week."

"Where should we keep the worms?"

"I'll find some empty needle boxes from my father's clinic and give you one."

"Great," responded Yezi, folding the toilet paper into a careful square and pocketing it with caution.

"It's Friday. Let's try getting into the library's reading room again," Jian said, eagerly tugging on Yezi's hand and pulling her out the door.

"Okay, okay," said Yezi, grinning.

The woman doorkeeper was back. *Lucky us*, Yezi thought. "I'll go first. When you pass by, make sure you smile at her," she whispered to Jian. Yezi took a deep breath and headed toward the doors. Her heartbeat quickened as she muttered a breathless "hi" to the frowning woman. The doorkeeper looked at her, but did not stop her from entering the room. Yezi headed straight for the newspaper rack. Then she turned to look over at Jian, who was hurriedly following another student into the room.

Yezi gestured at her to come over to the newspaper rack. Together, they lifted the rod of *The Times,* and crept silently to a nearby table. Yezi pointed to the title of the paper and then searched for the word '*time*' in another part of the dense text. It took some time, but she was proud to have found one that she could show her friend. Later, they managed to locate the copy of the magazine Yezi had looked at during her previous visit. They looked closely at the little girl in the photograph holding her violin, and Jian joked that the girl looked like Yezi. Then they pulled down a few issues of the *People's Pictorial* and were flipping through the pages when they heard gruff whisper approaching from a distance, "Wheeree arrre youuuuu?"

Yezi recognized the voice. "Popo Yao is looking for me. I've got to leave now." She sighed and hurried to the doors. She did not want Yao's strident voice to spread throughout the reading room.

She stumbled downstairs and ran into Yao. "Please don't yell," she begged, pulling her arm.

Surprised to see Yezi, Yao swallowed the words, "You—" She began coughing as she rumbled, "Why didn't you tell me you were coming here?"

"I'm sorry, Popo Yao," she said, her tone pleading.

"I'm okay now," Yao said, holding tightly onto Yezi's hand. "I'm glad I found you. Let's go home."

On their way home, Yezi fished the wad of toilet paper out of her pocket and held it up for Yao's inspection. "These eggs will be silkworms pretty soon. When they are ready, I'll use their silk to make a handkerchief for you."

"That's so kind of you," Yao said. "But it would be better if you didn't run all over the world and worry me to death."

As they walked, Yezi noticed that her head now reached the height of Yao's ear. Her gaze fell on Yao's long gray braids. *She is old and tired. I should take care of myself,* she thought. She withdrew her hand from Yao's and said, "You know, I can go home by myself, and I can do my own laundry, too."

"I believe that," Yao said with a big smile. "Hopefully you'll do my laundry when I can't move around." Talking with the girl made her happy. Like a crumpled handkerchief that had just been ironed, a radiant glow smoothed her wrinkles away.

A week later, Yezi discovered that several of the silkworm eggs were marked with the much-anticipated black dots. Exhilarated, she reached for a box that she had perched on the windowsill just for this occasion. The lid of the box had numerous holes punched in it for ventilation. She lifted the lid from the box, and carefully placed the toilet paper with the eggs inside. From a small plastic bag on the table next to her, she withdrew one of the mulberry leaves she and Jian had collected and then wrapped in a wet rag so that they would remain moist. She laid the leaf in the box adjacent to the eggs.

"Bedtime, Yezi," Sang called, as he leaned against the headrest. He was waiting for her to climb into the bed behind another makeshift curtain that now divided the bed into two parts.

After returning the box to the sill, Yezi asked, "Do you think the baby silkworms will come through?"

"Certainly. They can survive better than human beings."

"Are you sure?" she asked as she clambered onto her part

of the bed. She was so excited she could hardly sleep. It wasn't long though before her dreams were filled with delicate webs made of silk fibres.

The following morning, she sprang out of bed and ran to the little box on the windowsill. Inside, she found two tiny, dark brown silkworms on a partially eaten leaf. "I've got two!" she shouted.

"Get yourself dressed before playing with the worms," Yao's voice sounded from outside the room.

Yezi dressed and ate her breakfast faster than usual. She couldn't wait to show the box to Jian. When she was about to leave, Jian surprised her at the door, a similar box in her hand and a wide smile on her face. "I've got some worms," she said, brightly.

"So have I!" Yezi replied exalted, holding out her box for Jian to see.

"Wow! We both have silkworms now."

"We should go and get some more mulberry leaves," Yezi said gravely, taking the box from Jian's hand. "Leave your box here with mine," she said, gently placing both boxes side by side on the windowsill. The two friends bounded out to the yard, excited to pick mulberry leaves.

A week later, fifteen worms crept inside Yezi's box, devouring mulberry leaves and leaving tiny black pellets. Day by day each grew the length of a single grain of rice.

Yezi and Jian collected mulberry leaves every other day; soon the mulberry bushes along the lakeshore became bare. They needed to find a new source. When they heard that a group of children from Jian's yard planned to go to Hundred Step Islet, they decided to join them to try and find more mulberry bushes.

On a Tuesday afternoon, Yezi left with Jian for the shore to meet the other young adventurers: Ming and his twin sister, Lan, Jian's brother, Keyu, and Benben. The group walked along the lakeshore for a while before they reached the stepping stones in the water that led to the islet.

"Watch out and take big steps. The stones are far apart." Keyu, about to enter the seventh grade, resembled a commander with a stick in his hand. "You can hold onto my stick if you are afraid."

"Someone can hold the handle of my net, too," said Ming, waving his butterfly net.

"No, sir. I'm not chicken," Benben, the youngest, responded.

When Yezi approached the stone steps, her heart pumped fast. She was afraid of the water and nervous about making her way across the stones without falling. Jian pulled at her blouse, and said reassuringly, "Don't worry. I'm with you."

Yezi eyed the space between the first stone and the second. They were about twenty center metres apart. The water seemed to run fast. The gap appeared to widen. Yezi was terrified.

Benben pushed his way in front of Yezi and sprang to the first stone. "I'm okay, everybody." Then he leapt to another one. Yezi sucked in a breath and tried to raise her right leg. Hesitating, she stepped onto the first stone.

From behind her, Jian was encouraging. "You are doing fine. Keep going. I right behind you."

Yezi moved on to the second stone and then the third. She found it hard to concentrate on each step. Two of the children had already made it to Hundred Step Islet, and were gleefully running along the shoreline. Benben, on the stone in front of Yezi, turned around and said, "I'm coming to get you."

Ming yelled, "Benben! Don't ..." Before Yezi realized what was happening, Benben had already stepped onto her stone, but he lost his balance and toppled into the water. Frightened, Yezi shuddered, and tried to catch Benben's hand. She leaned forward, but was also caught off balance and fell into the water. Benben and Yezi's heads bobbed to the surface. They were coughing and flailing as water surged around them.

"Help!" shrieked Jian.

Time seemed to have stopped. Yezi was keenly aware that her body was getting lighter as the water swelled up to her chest, then her shoulders. Soon it reached her mouth. *Am I going to die?* Managing to open her eyes, she screeched at the top of her lungs. Under the hazy water, she could see strands of her hair floating around her and feel the heaviness of her clothes as they clung to her skin. The water was cold, penetrating her flesh, and then her bones. Her hands clenched, but there was nothing to hold onto as she felt herself sinking downward.

Before her feet touched the lakebed, two hands grabbed her arms and lifted her out of the water. She was light-headed and gasped for air, but relieved to feel her hand graze the warm stepping stone. Jian grabbed her from behind and helped her sit up on the stone.

Keyu stood in the water, his hands on Yezi's knees. "Are you okay?"

Yezi nodded. "Many thanks."

Meanwhile, Benben, who had also been pulled from the water, was now sitting sheepishly on the next step. Ming was behind him, holding his back upright. The sunlight was warm on Yezi's skin, and the air smelled fresh. *I'm okay,* she thought. Soothed, Yezi let her feet dangle in the water that no longer menaced.

"Maybe we should stay in the water," Keyu said to Ming. "We can help everyone along the stepping stones."

"Sure. I can even carry Benben to the islet," said Ming, relieved. But suddenly he turned and shouted, "Where is my net?"

"It's down there!" Lan had reached the islet and was pointing to a brown spot further downstream.

Yezi stood up. "Let's go."

"Hold my hand," Keyu said, wading beside the stone steps. "I'll walk with you to the shoreline."

In front of her, Benben was holding Ming's hand tightly as he stepped onto the next stone. Finally, the whole team gathered on the islet and flopped down on the grass. Yezi, Benben, Ming and Keyu were drenched. Pants and shirts off, the three boys were in their underwear and laid their clothes on bushes to dry. Yezi preferred to keep her clothes on. She could hear Yao's stern words: "Do not take your clothes off anywhere except at home!"

"Your clothes will dry faster if you take them off. You don't want Yao to see you in wet clothes!" Jian said, removing her T-shirt, under which she wearing a tank top. Handing the T-shirt to Yezi, she said, "Put this on."

"Okay, I'll find a place to change," Yezi said as she slipped behind some bushes.

She changed into Jian's top, but kept her wet pants on. She did not want to walk around wearing only her panties. Yezi's blouse joined the other clothes hanging on the bushes.

Ming found a Y-shaped branch, upon which he tied his handkerchief. The substitute net looked crooked, yet might be useful for capturing dragonflies and butterflies. Keyu pulled a coiled fishing line from his pocket and attached it to his own stick. He intended to fish for small turtles lurking behind rocks in the water.

Yezi and Jian searched for and examined all the bushes around Hundred Step Islet hoping to find some mulberry bushes. An American song her brother had taught her sprang to Yezi's mind: "*All around the mulberry bush, the monkey chased the weasel...*" Jian followed her lead, skipping behind her and humming the tune. "*The monkey thought 'twas all in fun. Pop! Goes the weasel!*" A breeze whispered through the trees; the water gurgled sweetly along the shore. Altogether, the two girls identified five mulberry bushes. They hung circles of willow sprigs on each bush as markers for their next visit.

Then they wrapped the mulberry leaves they had picked into a handkerchief. As the group gathered, Keyu showed them the three fist-sized turtles he had managed to catch. He promised

to give one to Benben. Ming's plastic jug contained three butterflies that had red spotted wings, and two dragonflies with
blue-black heads. Lan was holding a huge bouquet of daisy,
honeysuckle and blue flag, their individual scents mixing to
create an intoxicating aroma. Before making their way back,
Ming offered to help carry everyone's treasures, while Keyu
helped the others across the stepping stones by wading into
the water that reached his chest and guiding their steps. He
reminded everyone to keep their adventure a secret; tattlers
would be excluded from future explorations forever.

Back at home, Yezi used a piece of wet cloth to rewrap her
mulberry leaves so that they would stay moist for four or five
days. Lying in bed that night, she replayed in her thoughts the
events of that afternoon and resolved to learn to swim.

Two days later, Yezi and Jian, followed by Yao, arrived at the
swimming area of Lake Dianchi. Many of the neighbourhood
children were already there, in shorts or bathing suits, playing in the water or lying on the beach. Yezi and Jian, wearing
shorts, joined several girls standing in the sun.

"Ha! Look at these white-skinned piglets!" A boy nearby
laughed as he pointed at them.

Looking down at her body, Yezi realized that her skin was
pale. Jian's skin looked white too, but Yezi suddenly became
aware that her skin was fairer than anyone else's.

"White-skinned piglets, from dark pigsties!" Two other boys
joined the chant.

Neither girl dared to answer back, so they hid themselves
among other girls.

"Brown pigs!" howled Yao, stamping her foot. "Dare you
confront me? If I catch you, your lives will be short!" Her
strong voice swept over the shore and eventually frightened
away the boys who had been teasing them.

"We should get suntans." Yezi clasped Jian's hand. "Then
they won't call us names."

"Yeah, but let's follow other kids into the water first." Jian moved along with several older swimmers.

"Wait a minute." Yao pulled Yezi's arm, drawing her close. She tied one end of a long rope around Yezi's waist and gripped the other end. "You can go into the water now," she said.

Yezi plodded into the lake with Jian. Each time she squatted down into the water, Yao would yank her up. Yao's rope drew attention from children, who giggled and pointed at Yezi's awkward bobbing motions. Yezi didn't protest. She knew Yao would keep her safe. She hadn't forgotten falling into the water on their way to the islet. And she was still a little bit afraid of the water.

As Yezi and Jian waded out further, other swimmers played noisily around them, splashing and laughing under the hot sun. Yezi couldn't keep her eyes open because of all the splashing water. She simply flapped her arms, which made Jian laugh and scream. In the end, an older girl volunteered to show them how to hold their breath underwater.

A month passed. By the end of the summer, Yezi had learned to float and could swim with her head under the water.

In the meantime, Yezi's silkworms shed their skins a second time. They grew longer and fleshier so that she had to move some of them to a bigger box. One more moulting would make them mature eough to start spinning silk threads.

On a Friday afternoon, just before the start of the new school year, Yezi and Jian sneaked into the library's reading room one last time. The two eager readers explored the library for a couple of hours, searching the stacks and devouring any books that caught their attention. On the way home from the library, they noticed several boys squatting on the sidewalk, a few marbles scattered around them. A list of figures was scribbled in chalk to record each player's points. When Yezi accidentally stepped over a chalk mark, a sly voice yelled, "Hey! You white skinned-piglets!" Scowling, Tao, the bully, shouted, "You are on my territory."

"We are sorry," Jian answered.

Tao grabbed a handful of dirt and angrily tossed it at them. "Get lost!"

Linking her arm with Jian's, Yezi pulled her away and said, "Ignore him."

"You won't get away with this!" Tao said, snatching a branch from a hedge to attack them. He hollered, "Stinking mongrels!" One whip of the branch struck Yezi; another hit Jian.

Yezi's neck ached from the blow, but her fury surged. Turning her head, she propelled her body forward, ready to pummel him with her fists. Shocked by her sudden reaction, Tao leaped back. His branch dropped. Yezi picked it up and screamed with anger, "Touch us again and I'll beat you up!"

His hands over his head, Tao turned around to flee, but not before howling, "American mongrel!"

Yezi ran after him, forgetting he was teenage bully that most of the children feared. All she wanted was to catch him and hit him with all her strength. The other children who had stopped to watch cheered her along: "Go! Go! Get him!"

Taller and faster than Yezi, Tao dashed into the auditorium. Yezi, the mad warrior continued to chase him although she knew she would never catch up with him. Jian's voice, calling, "Stop it, Yezi!" grew distant.

By the time Yezi reached the entrance to the auditorium, Tao had already reached the first row of the seats, and was still running. Tossing the branch away, she picked up a fist-sized stone she had spotted at the door and flung it into the empty hall. Its thumping echoed. Tao got away from her by running out another exit. She kept pumping her legs as fast as she could, making her way through the rows of seats. By the time Yezi emerged out the other door, Tao, panting like a dog, had escaped.

For the first time, Yezi felt strong. All her fear and anger vanished. Jian darted toward her and grabbed her arm. "You really scared me," she said, breathing hard from her own frantic dash to the auditorium.

Wiping tears and sweat off her face with shaky hands, Yezi chuckled, "I'll never be afraid of him again." The next instance, she felt a searing pain in her elbow; she had knocked it several times against the auditorium's hard seats.

That night she fell fast asleep. In her dream she saw her mother watching her from the distance, a glint in her eyes. *Mama knows everything. She saw me falling into the water. And she saw me fighting with the bully.* Yezi tried to speak to her mother, but could not make any sounds.

13.
FAMILY ENTERPRISE

ON THE MONDAY MORNING, SEPTEMBER 1, 1975, Yezi went to school to show the teacher all the homework she had done over the summer. After waiting in line for a while in the classroom, Yezi got her turn. Teacher Huang browsed through Yezi's exercise books and then ticked her name off on the roster. "Well done. Hand in six yuan tomorrow for the tuition fee." She returned the exercise books to Yezi and nodded to the next waiting student.

Yezi walked home alone, wondering why Jian was not at school. A girl's voice rose from behind her, "Hey you!"

Fang, her classmate, who had had repeated the same grade last year, walked toward her. Taller than her, Fang easily draped her arm around Yezi's shoulder. "We're going in the same direction."

Yezi found Fang's arm heavy, but she was too shy to decline the friendly gesture. The older girl led her into a garden and motioned to Yezi to join her on a stone stool under a large French plane tree. "Can I take a look at your exercise books?" she asked, taking Yezi's bag before Yezi could even respond.

"No problem," said Yezi, surprised and flattered by Fang's friendliness.

Fang unbuttoned Yezi's bag and reached inside for the exercise books. She quickly thumbed the pages of one of the books. "Can you wait here? I need to go to a washroom right now. I'll read your books on my way there," Fang said, pulling a piece of candy out of her pocket and handing it to Yezi. Then she walked away. Yezi sucked happily on the hard candy as she waited for Fang in the garden. The candy finished, Yezi roamed the small garden, admiring the blooming flowers: wine-red peonies, yellow-hooded foxgloves and purple catmint. But her new friend never reappeared so, puzzled, she decided to go home.

The following morning, when Yezi got to school, Teacher Huang called her to the office. "Where are your assignments?"

Yezi told her what had happened the day before.

"Here they are." Drawing the two books from a pile on her desk, the teacher said, "Don't lend your books to anybody again, okay?"

"Yes," Yezi dutifully replied, but did not understand how her books had ended up on the teacher's desk.

After that, Yezi never saw Fang in class, but learned from her brother that Fang had tried to claim Yezi's summer homework as her own.

On Saturday night Yezi and her brother went to bed earlier than usual. Yao had told them she would need their help the next morning with what she called a "family enterprise" to ensure their basic survival. Yezi was excited just thinking about using her reward for helping to buy treats like candy, gum, sweet and sour olives or ice cream. She could already smell the aroma of sweet and sour olives, and it made her mouth water in anticipation.

After breakfast, Yao loaded a borrowed cart. "Sang, hold onto this so I can tie the rope."

Frowning at the crumpled paper and cardboard in different sizes packed tightly in the cart, Sang asked, "What are you going to do with this junk?"

"We need cash for food." Yao knotted the rope tautly around the stacks as she steadied her knee against the load. To make ends meet, Yao had to sell all the recyclable waste she had collected. "You hold tight. Yezi, push here."

"But you just got money from Baba last week," Sang said, pressing his hands on the pile. "I don't need anything new for school."

"That money was used to pay your tuition fees. Besides, I borrowed three yuan from Ling some time ago, and I still haven't paid her back."

"But you told me she said you didn't need to pay her back."

"It doesn't matter what she said; I don't want to owe anybody. A Buddhist doesn't keep anything that doesn't belong to her" said Yao, locking the door behind her. She shoved the chairs and stools under the table beneath the eavestrough. "Let's go. You two push on the back of the cart if I get stuck."

Sang hesitated for a moment, and then strode purposefully toward Yao. Taking the handle from her hands, he said firmly, "I can pull the cart."

"Are you sure?" Yao asked, a smile of relief playing about her lips. "Okay. But please put these gloves on," she said. As Sang pulled the cart, Yao helped push it to the side as they plodded along the road.

At the recycling depot where used newspapers, cardboard, bottles and cans were collected and stacked, the dusty air and stale odours made them sneeze. Yao sold the cartload for 9.24 yuan, from which she gave 24 fen to Yezi and 50 fen to Sang. "Go get your treats. Then we'll go and get some coal."

"I don't need anything right now. I'll stay here with you," answered Sang, pocketing his coins. He intended to save them for a book he wanted to buy. "Yezi, you go get your stuff," he huffed proudly, and waved her away.

Yezi ran happily into the street. Bicyclists passed by shoppers clutching baskets or handbags. Some people crowded around vendors; others came in and out of the stores that sat amid the houses along the alley. A number of trees provided some welcome shade for the crowds. After spotting a sign for ice cream, Yezi dodged the gaggles of shoppers and reached the ice cream stand, panting.

"What would you like?" asked the vendor, popping her head out from the opening. "Twenty fen for a cone. Do you want one?"

Yezi fingered the coins in her pocket, trying to make up her mind. "Does an ice stick cost four fen?"

"You don't have enough money for ice cream?" asked the vendor, a lopsided grin on her face. "How about getting two ice sticks?"

"Yes, and sweet and sour olives. Is five fen enough for a packet?" she asked, passing twenty fen to the vendor, who nodded. She took her treats along with the change, and like a baby bird that luckily caught itself some worms, Yezi flew down the street.

Her face was red and bathed in sweat when she handed the ice sticks to Yao and her brother. "My treat," she said grinning.

"I'll pay you back," said her brother.

She shook her head. "You don't have to." Contentedly she opened her tiny packet and placed a tasty olive in her mouth.

An hour later, they returned home with the coal-laden cart. Exhausted, Yezi plopped down on a chair, her legs spread out in front of her. She noticed that her brother had a few blisters on his hands, but in a whisper, he asked her not to tell Yao.

Yao prepared a rich lunch for them: tomato soup with scrambled eggs, steamed rice and stir-fried pork with green peppers. It was a meal Yao only prepared on special occasions. "If I can pick up another load of cardboard to sell," she said, "we'll have enough cash."

Sometimes, after school, Yezi and Jian would pick mulberry leaves. Their growing silkworms needed to be fed twice a day.

One evening, Yezi discovered a sleek but stiff worm inside her box. "Is this one sick?" she asked her brother, a worried frown on her face.

Raising his head from the book, Sang looked into the box. "Ha! It's ready to spin silk."

"Really?" Yezi was surprised. Clapping her hands, she asked, "What should I do now?"

"I'll give you some straw," said Yao, who overheard them. "Do you have an empty box?"

"No," Yezi replied, turning to her brother. "Could you find one for me?"

Sang went into their only room and returned with a worn metal box he had used to keep his marbles and screws in. "Is this okay, Popo Yao?"

"That's pretty good," Yao said. She pulled a long stalk of straw from under the children's bed. Then she picked up a pair of scissors and cut the straw into several sections, placing them in the box. She guided Yezi in settling the worm into its new nest, where it lay motionless for a while before it finally lifted its head.

The next morning, Yezi jumped out of bed and looked into the box. "It's making a cocoon!" she squealed, imagining an expanded egg-shaped cocoon glistening in the sun.

After school that afternoon, on their way to the lakeshore to pick more mulberry leaves. Yezi and Jian noticed a crowd by a billboard in front of a classroom on campus. "Let's go see what's happening over there," said Jian, quickening her steps.

As they ran toward the building they heard Yao's husky voice say, "I won't leave them." The warm air smelled of dust and the musty paste stuck on the bulletin board.

"You don't get paid, but you're making money for them?" asked a worker in overalls. Pulling a flyer off the board with his hand, he added, "Are you crazy? You could get a lot of money for your hard work."

"They're good kids. I won't abandon them!" Yao said, sitting on the ground, wiping her brow with her apron. "I grew up an orphan. I know how hard life is without parents."

"I will never understand you." The worker stooped to gather the torn paper. Like a professor surrounded by students, he said, "You've chosen to stay there, with them, until your next life. Look! Who is going to help you when you're too weak to walk even now?"

Yao's voice trembled. "My next life will be better. I don't worry about that." Rubbing her eyes with her sleeve, she added, "I'll be able to go home by myself after I have this little rest."

Yezi pushed through the crowd and reached out her arms for Yao. "I'm here to help you," she said, her voice breaking.

"Yao's face lit up when she saw Yezi. One hand gripping Yezi's arm, Yao struggled to stand up, her other hand holding her hips.

Jian stepped toward them and grabbed Yao's other hand. "Let me help."

Yao stood, staring at the basket full of used paper and cardboard. She moved toward it. "Would you put it on my back, young fellow?" she asked the worker.

He walked over to the basket and gripped its straps to lift it. "It's too heavy for you. I'll bring it to you when I finish my job here."

"Are you sure? Thanks a lot," said Yao. Laying her hands on each girl's shoulder, she wobbled home with them.

Yezi clasped Yao's sweaty hand tightly. At that instant, Yezi felt closer to Yao than anyone else in the world.

The following day, more cocoons appeared in Yezi's box. Jian also had a few cocoons. The silvery or golden-orange pupal cases thrilled them. Their eyes glowed with joy.

One afternoon in the last week of September, before suppertime, when Yezi and her brother were doing their homework at the table beneath the eavestrough, a middle-aged staff member from the road approached them. "Are you Sang?"

The boy answered, "Yes, I am." Looking up at him, Sang rose from his chair.

"Go to the Security Office right now."

Surprised, Sang asked, "Why?"

"You'll know when you get there," the man said with smile. Before walking away, he added, "The office is in the administration building."

Sang told his sister, "Tell Popo Yao I'll be back soon."

Yezi watched the man as he walked away, and then her brother as he headed in the same direction for the Security Office. Not sure what it all meant, she raced over to Yao, who was washing vegetables at the communal sinks and told her what had happened.

Yao took hold of the enamel basin. Quivering, she asked, "Are they gone?"

"Yes," Yezi said as she held onto the basin's other side and helped Yao carry it home. After they sat at the table, Yezi asked, "What will happen now?"

"I don't know. I hope no more disaster." Yao lowered herself slowly to the ground. On her knees, her hands clasped, she spoke softly, "Infinitely Merciful Buddha, please bless us. I'll burn lots of joss sticks for you when I have money to buy them."

God bless us! Yezi also prayed, as she watched the glossy sunset paint the road, trees and buildings a burnished gold.

"I've tried my best," said Yao, rising slowly to her feet.

Yezi said, "Here, Popo Yao. Have something to drink." As she passed Yao a mug of boiled water, her hands trembled but her eyes lingered on the sunset, her feeling of dispiritedness diminished by the glorious view.

Yao sipped the water slowly. "Are you hungry? I'll cook now. We must eat after all." Placing a pot on the stove, she began preparing their supper.

After Yezi had set the table, and Yao had placed the pot of

rice and vegetables on the table, Sang dashed in. He was elated, and thrust his hands up in the air as he jubilantly announced, "Hurrah! Mama is coming home!"

"What?" Yezi could not believe her ears. "Now?" It was as if the dark metal bars over the tiny window in her mother's cell had suddenly fallen into a heap at her feet. Her heart wanted to jump out of her chest.

"Good heavens!" Yao gasped. "When?"

"They said before October 1, National Day," answered Sang with a broad smile. "They'll allot us an apartment and help us move next week. The director asked me what furniture we want. I told him we needed all the things other people have."

"We need more beds," Yezi and Yao squealed, grinning at each other.

Stroking Sang's arm, Yao asked, "Tell me what else the director said to you."

"Let me think." Sang sat down. "He said we could go to him any time if we have any difficulties."

"We need money for bedding and other stuff," Yao said. Taking a deep breath, she added, "This coming Sunday, we can sell another cartload of cardboard, but we still won't have enough cash for what we need to buy."

"Let's borrow some money." Sang clasped his hands in front of his chest. "I have a classmate whose father got his back pay after his release from the camp. Mama will probably get her money back for those years, too."

"What's the name of the director? I'll talk to him tomorrow," Yao said as she passed each of them a bowl of food. "Enjoy your meal."

The next day, at lunchtime, Yao took a note from her pocket and handed it to Sang. "When I spoke to the director earlier today, he said yes. We can borrow fifty yuan. He wrote this note for us. You need to take it to the financial sector and sign for the loan."

Sang placed his bowl on the table and stood. "I'll go right away."

"Wait till 2:00p.m.," Yao said, pulling him back onto the stool. "Nobody is in the office right now, and you need to finish your lunch first."

"Okay, I forgot the time."

"I'll go with you. I can bring the cash back right away so I don't have to worry about you losing it."

After listening to their conversation, Yezi said aloud, "I want a sheet with flowers for my bed."

"Okay, we'll go shopping on Sunday." Yao's face lit up, her gray-haired head nodding. She suddenly looked younger, and less tired. She held her bowl up to her mouth. "We will be able to get everything we need before your mother gets home."

14.
EGG TREE

THE FOLLOWING DAY YAO, YEZI and Sang went to visit their future home, a two-bedroom apartment on the second floor of a five-storey building that faced a basketball court, about a seven-minute walk from Arts Paradise. The director had said that the university would allot them a three-bedroom apartment as soon as one was available.

Yao told Sang, "Write to your father about it. He won't have to sit in a chair all night when he visits." She didn't say, *and I won't have to sleep in a chair anymore either.*

"Yes, I can draw a map for him, so he can find our new place. I'll also send a letter to my brother. He can use my bed whenever he returns. I don't mind sleeping on the floor." Not hearing Yao's response, Sang raised his voice. "Can you find Dahai's address? Even if he doesn't answer, I'll go to the farm to find him. Everything will be okay when Mama is out of the camp."

"Yes, I'll look for it," Yao sighed, wondering if this was the right time to tell them about the long-hidden letter that Dahai's friend, Wang, had delivered four years earlier.

Several days later, around noon, a group of workers came to help the family move. Within two hours they had transported all their belongings to the new location.

Coming home straight from school, Yezi ran up the stairs to their new apartment. After she passed the apartments' communal room and doors to several other apartments on their floor, she found the one to her new home. Turning the knob, she opened the unlocked door and stepped into the living room. Sang was unpacking scattered cardboard boxes. Yao was busily arranging items in the kitchen.

Yezi went to inspect the bedroom prepared for her mother. A desk sat under the window. On one side of the window was a double bed, and on the other side a bookshelf had been placed against the wall. The room seemed empty, especially with that bare bookshelf. She couldn't wait to see her mother fill it with her own things.

The other bedroom, for Yezi and Yao, had two single beds that flanked each side of the window. One of the beds had only a pallet on it. The other was covered with a floral bed sheet that Yezi had chosen when shopping with Yao. She hung her book bag on the doorknob and plopped on the bed.

"I'll do laundry in the communal room." Yezi heard Yao say outside her bedroom door. Yao then appeared in the doorway, a basin full of dirty clothing under her arm. "Yezi, you should help Sang tidy up the living room."

"Okay, in just a minute," answered Yezi. She touched the sheet, feeling content. *Finally I have my own bed!* Joy flooded her heart as she stretched her limbs out. She would never again live in the cluttered, gray-looking room that was the only home she remembered. She missed it, but hated it. She stared at the shiny window and the newly plastered walls in the roomy space. *This is real, not a dream!* She rubbed her eyes and pinched her arm. She smelled the light odour of limestone in the air and marvelled at the dappled sunlight on the walls.

Suddenly, Sang cried out, "Damn it!" Then Yezi heard him weeping. She jumped off the bed and hurried into the living room. Sang sat on an unrolled pallet on the floor, a sheet of wrinkled paper in his hand.

"Yezi," he sobbed, thrusting the paper at her. "Our brother is dead! These are his last words!"

"What?" Shocked, Yezi's eyes widened. She took the page from Sang, her hands trembling. As she read it, tears drenched her face. Her eldest brother, who had only appeared in her dreams, had vanished from this world before she could meet him in person.

Just then, Yao walked through the door. Sang asked her, "Why did you hide this from us?"

"Hide what?" Bewildered, Yao stared at Sang's tearful face. "What are you talking about?"

"Dahai is dead!" cried Sang. Taking the letter back from Yezi, he shook it in front of Yao. "Have you forgotten this?"

Yao's face paled. "Of course not!" Tears slowly trickled down her face. "I saw your brother grow from a baby to a young man just like I've watched you grow up. But…" she stammered, wiping her face with her hand. "I didn't want to scare you with this terrible news. You were both too young."

"Does Baba know?" asked Sang.

"I told him, but I just couldn't bring myself to tell your mother."

"You should've told us earlier," Sang lowered his voice.

"Why?" Yao went into the kitchen and set a pot on the stove. "It wouldn't have brought him back to life. I burn paper money for him every year so that he is happy in his next life."

"You are too superstitious," Sang muttered.

"This is what I know and what I can do," Yao protested.

"I don't want to argue with you." Sang placed the letter on a nearby table. He then continued the arrangement of the living room—his temporary bedroom. His eyes darkened, as different images of Dahai ran though his head. Dahai's face twisted with pang and anger; Dahai's eyes filled with horror. Such images haunted Sang. He collapsed on the bed. His throat tightened with a soundless cry.

That night, Yezi slept on her comfortable and spacious bed. However, she dreamed of a smoky explosion and, once the smoke had cleared, a bloodied body lying on the ground.

Although she could not recognize the face, she knew it was her eldest brother.

Yezi had gathered eleven oval cocoons from her silkworms. Seven were yellow, and the other four were silver. Each cocoon had a hole on one end where the moth had bitten its way out.

She picked out a small, dry branch and a piece of wood from Yao's junk collection, and then glued them together. One silvery cocoon capped the top of a twig, a yellow one another. Yezi decorated the sprigs with all of her cocoons, which now looked like a plant in bloom. When Jian saw the decorated branch, she coloured some of her cocoons red and added them to the makeshift arrangement. Yezi placed the final version on the desk in her mother's bedroom. They called it "Egg Tree."

Several days later, Yao hand-sewed cotton curtains and hung them over all the windows in the apartment. The material was light blue with white polka dots, the nicest design they had been able to find in the stores. When Yezi woke in the morning, she enjoyed looking at the dotted shadows on the wall, cast by the first rays of sunshine penetrating the curtain. Yao also worked all day long on a cotton pad for Meihua's bed, as she said Meihua had suffered for a long time and needed a decent place to sleep. The other beds would not be furnished with pallets until sufficient money and ration coupons for cotton became available.

Despite the fact that the living room was cramped, Sang looked at his bed with satisfaction. *I can easily turn over in bed now. Also, I can read my books under the light from the living room lamp.*

The kitchen was so crowded that they had to eat their meals in Yao's and Yezi's bedroom. But it did not bother them. In contrast to their previous "apartment," a small kitchen was anything but a problem. Yezi thought they now lived in a palace.

During those days, Yezi expected her mother and father to come home any time. Smiling in front of a mirror became her daily practice. She noticed that Sang and Yao seemed to happier, too.

Every evening, Yao boiled water after supper as if Yezi's mother were there for tea. Yezi frequently went outside to look for any sign of her mother returning, but found no one.

One day after lunch, Yezi heard steps stop outside their door. As soon as she heard a knock, she rushed to the door and flung it open. There stood woman clad in an olive green uniform. She asked, "Is this Meihua Wei's home?" *Meihua Wei?* The name sounded familiar yet distant to Yezi. She hesitated. She tried to say "yes," but found her throat too dry to make a sound. Instead, she nodded.

"Yes, yes," said Yao, who had stepped out of the bedroom. "Army Comrade. Where is she?"

Seeing no one behind the soldier, Yezi froze. *Where is Mama?*

"Come with me. She is in the jeep," the woman said, turning from the door to go back downstairs.

"We are coming. Thank you," Yao said as she stumbled down stairs.

Yezi raced out fearing her mother would disappear if she had failed to reach her in time.

The soldier walked to the jeep parked on the roadside and opened the passenger's door. Yao threw herself into it. "Meihua!" Her shaking hands clasped a woman's shoulder. The woman looked up and smiled. Yao took Meihua's hands and helped her out of the jeep, then stepped back. "Oh my! Here is Yezi." Yao pulled the girl over and pushed her toward Meihua.

"Mama!" Yezi wrapped her arms around her mother, but could not find any words to say.

"Let's go home," said Meihua, her voice feeble, but her mouth curved in a smile.

Sang signed a form provided by the soldier. Then following her directions, he reached into the jeep and took out his mother's travel bag.

Yezi and Yao grasped Meihua's arms from both sides and helped her walk to her new home.

After they entered the apartment, Sang laid the bag on the desk in Meihua's room. "This is yours, Mama."

"I can stay with you this afternoon." Yezi helped her mother sit in a chair in her bedroom.

"No. You can't miss school." Meihua looked serious.

"Well, okay. I'll go if you want me to." Yezi went into the kitchen and returned with a mug. "Here's some jasmine tea. Popo Yao is making noodle soup for you right now."

Meihua sniffed at the mug, her soft brown eyes glowing. "What a treat to smell tea!"

When Yezi carried in the noodle soup, she found her mother dozing in the chair.

"Don't wake her. She needs to rest." Yao beckoned for Yezi to come out of the bedroom. Then she closed the door. "Go to school now, little one. You can be with your mother after school."

At suppertime, Yezi sat at the table close to her mother, who wrapped an arm around her. "I've looked forward to this day for so long," she said, stroking Yezi's hair.

Snuggling against her, Yezi caressed Meihua's hand, which was rough and hard. She thought her mother must have starved at the camp. "From now on you'll eat Popo Yao's food every day. You will get healthy."

Two days later, Yezi's father, Lon, arrived. It was September 30, the day before China's National Day.

After supper, he opened his bag. "I have brought some gifts for everyone. I haven't done this for ages...." His voice was filled with cheer.

Lon handed Yezi a doll that had moving eyes, the same doll she had admired when she and her father had walked past the display window of a department store a year earlier. Yezi had not dared to ask for it because she knew her father could not afford it.

"Thanks, Baba. I love her. I can't believe you remembered."

Lon then motioned over to Yao and placed her gifts in her lap. "I hope you like the colour of this sweater. And, here's some Vaseline. You can put it on your hands after you do laundry."

"I like everything. It's very kind of you." Yao accepted the gifts, her hand caressing the soft sweater. "Thank you very much."

Yezi wondered about her brother's gift. Sang's eyes brightened when he opened a rectangular metal box.

"Thanks, Baba." He carefully pulled out a long needle. "Acupuncture needles! How did you know I wanted these?"

"I know you wish to become a barefoot doctor in the countryside next year," Lon said with a grin. "But you don't look like a doctor yet. And, I don't want you to try one of those needles on me."

"I'll try them on myself," Sang replied, his eyes bright and happy.

"Don't worry." Lon laughed. "You can try them on me, too! Tomorrow, okay?"

"Where's Mama's gift?" asked Yezi.

"I already received mine," Meihua said happily, stepping out of her room. "Look at me." She wore a creamy white blouse and pale gray skirt.

"Mama, you look great." Yezi clapped her hands. She seldom saw women in skirts.

Lon then made an announcement, "Tomorrow we are all going boating in Broadview Park. Is that okay with everyone?"

"Yes!" Yezi jumped up with excitement.

"Do I need to prepare anything for it?" asked Yao.

"No, no." Lon shook his head. "You need a break. We'll eat in the restaurant to celebrate our family's reunion."

"If only Dahai could be here. Have you contacted him?" Meihua looked at Lon, then at Sang.

Lon's gaze dropped to the floor while Sang closed his eyes.

"What's going on?" Meihua's voice faltered. "Tell me. Tell me the truth."

Yao walked to Meihua and took Meihua's hands into her own. "It's my fault."

"What's your fault? Why hasn't Dahai been home in all this time?" Meihua turned, searching Yao's eyes.

"Dahai is unable to come home—" Yao sobbed.

"Why?" Meihua gasped. "Is he—"

"He died a hero," Yezi said in a low voice.

"Tell me how!" Meihua's eyes widened. "What on earth happened?" she asked, her face ashen. She sank into a chair and wept.

Lon placed his hand on Meihua's shoulder stroking her arm with the other. "I'll show you his letter." He led her back to the bedroom.

The next morning, Meihua appeared in black clothes. Her eyes were swollen. Lon framed a photograph he had found of Dahai taken on his sixteenth birthday. He decorated the frame with a piece of white silk and hung the photograph on the wall. The family remained at home instead of going to Broadview Park, to mourn Dahai's passing. From the others, Yezi learned about her brother as they shared their stories, and remembered him with love.

Yezi listened to the storties attentively, wishing that she too had one that she could share. She did not understand why Dahai had believed their parents were sinful.

Several days later, the family decided to go to Broadview Park after all. They all boarded a rowboat; Lon and Sang took turns rowing. They competed with each other and laughed. Yezi sang the song, "Row, Row, Row Your Boat." Her ability to sing in English amazed her mother. Yezi's long-time dream of riding in a boat with her mother had finally come true. She could hardly believe it.

The lighthearted chatter coming from other boats floated over the lake. When Yezi noticed that Yao had tears mingling with the sweat on her face, she handed her a handkerchief. "Don't weep."

Taking the handkerchief, Yao wiped her face and smiled. "No weeping today. I'm so happy." Finally she covered her face with her hands and sobbed.

"I'm so thankful." Meihua stretched out her hand to stroke Yao's shoulder, murmuring, "I don't know what disaster would have befallen my poor children if you hadn't been with them. We are all so lucky to have you as part of our family."

Tears flooded Yezi's eyes, but she tried to smile like the merry American girl in that photograph she had seen in the magazine at the library, holding her violin tight.

15.
3,000 YUAN

YEZI WAS ECSTATIC ABOUT HER family reunion. But the celebrations ended quickly. Her father returned to the mine with a promise to come home once a month, if allowed. Meanwhile, Meihua rested and slowly eased her way back into her life. She went to the Arts Department at the university and requested her teaching assignment from the Party's Secretary. Instead of getting a clear answer, she received, according to the Party's policy, compensation for her financial loss during her prison term. When she finally stepped out of the payroll office, she carried a heavy handbag stuffed with 3,000 yuan in bills, equivalent to what her salary would have been for three years. Heading for home, she found herself repeating the same mantra with each step: *3,000 yuan for eight years! Two thousand, nine hundred and twenty days and nights in jail!* The memories of that time haunted her. She wanted to fling the bag into the air. *Let the bloody money go with the wind*, she thought.

Home. She was back in her sweet home. She asked Yao to come to her room. Then she handed her a bundle of banknotes. "This 1,500 yuan is yours, Yao."

"I don't need the money," Yao said, as she gazed at the bundle, wondering if it had rained yuan. "You need it more than I do."

"You haven't been paid a single fen for all these years. You have taken good care of my children, and you deserve it," said

Meihua, a smile on her face. "From now on, it seems I will be paid even though I won't be teaching."

"Didn't they—"

"They said I need time to prepare for next September's classes. I have been told to study Chairman Mao's directives and the policies of the Communist Party that I've missed over the past years. In any case, I'm paid from now on."

Yao held the money in her hand and went to the bedroom she shared with Yezi. Yezi was lying on her bed, working on her homework. As Yao wrapped the bills in several handkerchiefs, she grinned at Yezi and said, "I'll buy you a skirt when we go shopping."

"You don't have to 'cause Mama already said she'd buy me new clothes," answered Yezi, raising her eyes from her book. "But you can buy me an ice cream cone."

"I can get you a hundred ice cream cones if you want." Yao chuckled and placed the money in her pillowcase.

The following day, when Yezi came home from school, her mother was sitting in her wicker chair, her head leaning on its back, her hand on her forehead. "Mama, are you okay?" she asked, trying to hide the worry in her voice.

"I'm completely overwhelmed." Meihua shook a letter in her hand. "Look at this."

"It's in English." Yezi gazed at it. "Who wrote to you?"

"It's from your grandmother. My mother."

"My grandmother?" Yezi caught her breath, an astonished look on her face. She had never thought about her grandmother's existence before. "Where is she?"

"She lives in the United States."

"Is she a foreigner?" Yezi picked up the envelope from the table and examined the stamp.

"Foreigner? She's my mother." Meihua looked into Yezi's eyes. "Is that something regretful?"

"No. I like the faces of happy foreigners in the magazine."

"What magazine?" her mother asked with surprise. "Where did you see this magazine?"

"It's an English magazine I found in the library's reading room. I don't know what it's called."

I don't know my daughter that well, Meihua thought ruefully. "Do you know how to read in English?"

"Only a couple of words." Yezi asked eagerly, "What did my grandmother say?"

Meihua scrutinized the page and interpreted it in Chinese. "Dear Meihua, Lon, Dahai and Sang, as well as the youngest if he/she exists...."

Yezi was dismayed. "Why doesn't she know me?" she asked.

"I wrote to her about you in September 1966. It seems the letter never reached her." Meihua continued reading the letter.

This is my fifth letter to the same address, a copy of which went to your provincial government. I've been trying to locate you since 1972 when the relationship between the United States and China was normalized.

In May 1966, I mailed you a parcel and a letter, but never heard back from you. I even contacted the Chinese Central Committee of Education in Beijing after I failed to get any reply, but they advised me to wait due to the ongoing Cultural Revolution.

I never anticipated the wait to be this long.

If any of you get this letter, please answer me as soon as possible. I'm 71 years old and longing to hear from my family.

"Where did her other letters go?" Yezi asked, dropping to her knees next to her mother's chair.

"Maybe they were disposed of because people were afraid of anything coming from outside China." Meihua took a long breath. "But things are getting better now. At least this letter got to me."

In her reply, Meihua did not tell her mother in detail about what the family had gone through; however, she did give her the heartbreaking news of the death of her eldest son.

A month later, as if carried by a pigeon that flew freely across the Pacific Ocean, another letter from Yezi's grandmother safely landed at their door. She expressed her joy about the family's reunion, and also told them that Meihua's stepfather had passed away the year before. She enclosed a photograph of herself and asked for one of Meihua's family.

Yezi gazed at her grandmother's face and identified that foreign but familiar expression she had seen in photographs in the library's foreign magazines. She couldn't quite put her finger on it, but it was a kind of happiness that she had never seen on Yao or her mother's face, despair having lingered within them for so long. Looking up at her mother, Yezi realized she wanted to know more about her. "Why did you leave your American mother for my country?"

"Your grandfather, my father, is Chinese. I came to look for him after I finished university." Meihua began to draw, for Yezi, an intelligible picture.

"Did you find him?"

"No, but I met your father, so I stayed."

"How did you get here?"

"By ship. It took around twenty days."

"Is the United States that far?"

"Yes, but today it would take only a day by air." Meihua smiled. "You have so many questions."

"Is it inappropriate?" Yezi was eager to find the answers to all her questions. "My teacher always says 'Don't ask too many questions. Good students always listen.' Popo Yao says the same thing. What do you think?"

"Some students learn by asking questions."

"I'm interested in lots of things. Me and my best friend want to learn English from you."

"Who is your best friend? And why do you want to learn to speak English?"

"Jian. You saw her yesterday. We've been hanging out and raising silkworms together." Pointing to the cocoon-decorated tree branch on Meihua's desk, Yezi said with elation, "Look at this Egg Tree. Some of the cocoons are from her as well as me."

"Let me think about it."

"We won't tell others about it, Mama. I promise."

"When do students begin to learn English in school?"

"Grade seven."

"Can you find an English textbook?"

A week later, Jian joined Yezi for their first one-hour-per-week English lesson. Meihua corrected their pronunciation of the alphabet, which Sang had already taught them. They practiced saying, "Long Live Chairman Mao," the first sentence from a textbook Yezi had brought home, which mostly consisted of Mao quotations such as, "the working class is the leading class," and "the children are the flowers of our motherland." Meihua also taught them how to greet people. Yezi practiced saying "hi" to Jian, and they shook hands with each other giggling, and practicing the words, "how are you?"

In November, Lon came home and surprised them with a black-and-white television. Yezi and Sang were thrilled. Yezi did not need to go to cinema; she could watch people move and talk on the magic screen on weekends, like other children did. Meanwhile, the family had a photograph taken for Meihua's mother. Yezi wore a new, dark green skirt, a popular colour that reflected China's military power. It was the only colour of skirts they could find in stores. Her mother wore the pale gray skirt that Lon had given her. In the photograph, her hands rest on Yezi's shoulders. Yezi's smile is exuberant, like the girl in the magazine. Yezi was certain her grandmother would be able to feel her delight.

The family gathered just before the new year of 1976. After dinner, they discussed Sang's future; he had, as they all knew, a keen interest in studying medicine. But, according to Mao's recruitment criteria, universities only accepted applicants who had worked as workers, peasants, or soldiers for at least three years. Too, applicants had to be recommended by the authorities of their work units. Like most other high school graduates, Sang had simply one option: to settle down somewhere in the countryside and receive re-education from peasants.

"I've been attending a free workshop at the hospital. It lectures on basic medical aid." Sang showed his parents his handouts and reading materials.

"Where are you going to go for your re-education?" asked Meihua.

"Our head teacher said we should find our own places, instead of making arrangements through the school."

Yezi asked, "Can you go to the countryside near home?"

"Why don't you ask me to open up the land in the yard and grow vegetables here?" Sang laughed.

Lon was also concerned about the location. "Where do you plan to go, son?"

"I'm thinking of Xishungbanna where the native people really need us."

"The Dai people have a tough life." Yao had heard about their arduous living conditions. "You don't even know their language. How can you survive there?"

"I'm not afraid of hardship because I've already gone through it. I don't know their language, but I'll learn." Sang looked into his father's eyes. "Don't you agree with me?"

"On the one hand, you're right. It might be an interesting place." But Lon wanted Sang to be open to other possibilities. "You will need to find out if the government has any special policy for the area, because it borders Vietnam, Laos and Burma."

"I don't want to lose another son," said Meihua. The thought of Dahai's death pieced her heart like a needle.

Frightened, Yezi shook her mother's arm. "Brother won't

leave us. Isn't that right, Baba? "

"Don't worry, Meihua." Lon feigned a smile to lighten the mood of the room. "He may not have to go that far. And even if he does go there, it's still in Yunnan Province."

"I may be able to find him a closer spot," Yao said, thinking about the village she came from. "It's closer, so Sang could come home once a month."

"Where is it?" Yezi jumped up. "Tell me."

"In Yuanmou."

"Yuanmou? The fossil of early man was found there." Excited, Yezi clapped her hands. She considered Yuanmou the most important place in the world.

"Can you get in touch with someone there?" asked Meihua, relieved at the thought that her son might not have to go too far to receive his re-education.

"I'll try," said Yao, "even though I've been out of touch with my relatives for a long time now."

Busy with the upcoming Chinese New Year celebrations, Yao needed Yezi to shop with her. According to the Chinese lunar calendar, the Chinese New Year, or Spring Festival as it was commonly called, would fall on January 30, 1976. She joined one line-up for groceries and asked Yezi to wait in another line. Yezi disliked this kind of chore, but she had to help Yao. Sang was buried in basic medical training, and Meihua could not stand long because of her sore back.

Every family had ration coupons intended for the holiday: pork, peanut oil, eggs, sticky rice, bean noodles, sugar. Even bars of soap and yards of cloth were rationed.

The last day of January 1976 was the first joyful Chinese New Year in Yezi's life. Both parents were home, and they had lots of food to eat and celebrate with. She and her mother helped prepare the ingredients while Yao cooked the many dishes that would be eaten over several days. Yao planned to visit her home village with Yezi on the second day of the Chinese New

Year, the day on which people traditionally visited relatives or close friends. She intended to organize Sang's placement in the village she was from. Yezi had begged to go with her, and her parents had consented. They felt Yao might be able to use Yezi's help during the trip.

Lon purchased two bus tickets for them after waiting in line for five hours the night before. Early the next morning, Yao dressed Yezi in Sang's thick jacket, worn-out work pants and a faded cap. As she tucked Yezi's hair under the cap, she said to Meihua, "Look, nobody will notice she's a girl. She'll be safe from any potential mishaps."

"How long will it take to get to your village from the bus stop?"

"About two hours; the same time that took us to walk to your camp from the train station."

"Have you stashed your money properly? Once you lost money on the train," Meihua reminded her.

Excited, Yezi imagined the home of Yuanmou Man, who had lived there one million, seven hundred thousand years earlier. "Don't worry, Mama. We look so poor that nobody will rob us." She looked into the mirror. Face to face with her was a familiar-looking boy in ragged clothes, standing next to an old woman in sack-like clothing. Yezi snorted and laughed. "How about if I put some coal dust on my face?"

Everybody laughed.

Yezi and Yao boarded a long-distance bus to Yuanmou County. Many of the passengers carried so many bags and pieces of luggage that it seemed as though they were moving houses. Nudging their way through the crowd, Yezi and Yao finally reached their seats. All around them were large sacks of belongings and over-filled baskets with sturdy handles. Yao had to shove their handbags under their seats. The bus departed from the city and passed adjacent fields covered with wheat seedlings, carrot tops and climbing peas. Through the open window, Yezi breathed air that smelled of fresh-cut hay and manure. Drenched in water, endless rice paddies were ready for planting. Four hours later, the bus pulled into a depot. The driver announced a half-hour stop for passengers to buy some food and use the washroom.

Yezi and Yao left the bus. "Do you need a drink?" asked Yao.

"No, I want to look around." Yezi walked past a row of vendors that had vegetables and live fowls displayed on tables. She watched the caged chickens and ducks while Yao kept an eye on her.

"My god!" an old woman from their bus exclaimed. "Where is my wallet?" She looked astounded, her hand reaching into her pocket and coming out empty. "I must've lost it when I bought that bun."

"Look over there," said Yao, pulling on Yezi's hand.

In the middle of the yard, a young man in a dark blue jacket, about ten steps from them, had grabbed a teenager's wrist. "Give me back my wallet!"

"Let go of me! I don't have your wallet!" the teenager shouted. He used his other hand to slap the man in the blue-jacket. The two men began pushing each other. To everyone's surprise, a middle-aged woman raced over to pull them apart. The teenager darted away.

"Oh my!" Stunned, Yezi also caught sight of the old woman who had lost her wallet, now standing in front of one of the vendors. She was gaping at the scene, shouting that the teenager probably had her wallet, too.

Frightened, Yao gripped Yezi's arm. "Let's get back to the bus." Back in her seat, Yao sat back and took a deep breath. The bus was safe. At least the thieves were outside.

Meanwhile, a woman sitting behind them muttered, "These thieves are so well-organized that we can't do anything about it."

16.
YUANMOU MAN

WHEN THEY FINALLY DISEMBARKED AT a place called Red Soil, Yezi asked, "Why didn't we get off at Yuanmou station?"

"From that station, we would have had to walk two kilometres more to reach my village," Yao explained, as they began their walk down the road that led to Xiaohe Village. The sun warmed their faces while a cold wind blew over endless fields.

"How did you find me in Kunming?" Yezi asked.

"Not you, your parents. It's a long story." Yao recalled the day she had sat on a dusty roadside for hours, her legs crossed. She had been trying to find a job so that she could make the five silver yuan she needed to bury her mistress, an elderly Buddhist nun who had passed away several days earlier. "Your parents were on their way to Kunming. Their bus stopped for a rest. After they listened to my story, they decided to help me and offered me a job. So, after I buried my mistress, I followed them to Kunming."

"Where were your folks?"

"They died young. The nun took me under her wing."

"Where was I?"

"Nowhere. Even Dahai was still in your mama's belly."

"Why did my folks come to Kunming?"

"They got jobs, so they moved there."

As Yezi listened to Yao, she scanned the area. A red, dirt road wound up the empty, sloping hill ahead of them. "Where would the Yuanmou Man be?" She was determined to find some fossils that she could bring home to Sang and her parents.

"Everywhere in this area." Curious, Yao asked, "Why do you want to see them?"

"They aren't alive. I can't see them. I want to find their bones!"

"Why on earth do you want the bones of dead people?" Yao was mystified.

"Because they are the Homo Erectus who lived here a long, long time ago."

"How do you know that?"

"My textbook said that archaeologists found two tooth fossils of Yuanmou Man in 1965."

"What's the use of the teeth? They can't give you food to eat."

"All you think about is food," Yezi chided Yao playfully. "Yuanmou Man fossils are way more important." Yezi ran toward a pit surrounded by rocks and bushes. *This looks like the foundation of an old hut. I might come across something,* she thought, taking a knife from her pocket to dig in the soil.

"See if you find any fossils." Yao huffed as she perched on a rock by the roadside. It was time for a short rest.

Yezi picked a pebble from the soil and cleaned it with her fingers. She also found several others, but none of them were fossils. Yezi pulled Yao to her feet and told her that they would probably find something further along the road. Half an hour later, Yezi spotted a mound of soil next to the roadside. *That must be something.* "Wait for me." She raced toward it and squatted in front of it. She scraped away at the soil with her knife, creating a hole in the process. Hollowing out dirt and sand, she thrust fast. Soon her knife grated against something hard. "I got a bone! A real bone, Popo Yao!" Her enthusiasm made Yao smirk.

Yezi jumped on the mound with the bone, trying to dislodge it. At the same time a horse-drawn wagon stopped in front of Yao. "Do you need a ride?" a young driver asked. "Where are you going?"

"Xiaohe Village," answered Yao, who motioned to Yezi. "Come! We have a ride."

Yezi stuffed the bone into her pocket and then flung their bags into the wagon. They clambered into the wagon and then slouched against the boards. "Thank you very much, young man," Yao said. "Do you live in Xiaohe?"

"No, but I pass by it." As the driver pulled the reins and whistled, his horse began to gallop. "What about you?"

"We're going to see my cousin's family. How's life in the country?"

"Tough enough, you know. We must sell our rice and other food we grow at low, fixed prices to the government. So, we never have enough money."

"Is this your horse and wagon?"

"No. They belong to the brigade. I'm only a handler."

"But they pay you, don't they?"

"About a hundred yuan a year, in addition to my ration of grain." The horse handler added, "Most of the people in my village only get about twenty yuan a year."

Yezi sniffed at the bone she had managed to pull from the mound and tapped it with her knuckles. She compared it to the bones in her own hand and foot and wondered if it came from Yuanmou Man. Then the horse-drawn wagon stopped in front of several small houses, and Yao asked Yezi to jump down.

"Is this your cousin's place?" asked Yezi.

"Yes, dear. Now help me get out of the cart, as well." Yezi helped Yao step down and then watched her pull out a crisply folded man's handkerchief from her handbag and hand it to the driver. "Please keep this little gift from us with our thanks," she said.

The young man thanked her profusely and drove his horse-drawn wagon away.

Yezi trudged with Yao along a muddy, gravel path full of shallow puddles. They passed several clusters of houses made with earth walls and thatched roofs, surrounded by vegetable gardens and fences. The smell of fermented pigweed and composted manure spread throughout the village. Smoke with the aroma of cooking food floated lazily around the houses.

When they paused in front of a house in a mud-walled yard, a dog at the doorway growled. Yezi leaped behind Yao. Bending for a stone that she could throw at the dog, Yao shouted, "Anybody home?"

A boy of thirteen stepped out of a double door in the centre of the house. Petting the dog, and holding him still, he asked, "Who are you looking for?"

"You must be Dabao. Is your grandfather home?"

"How do you know my name?" the teenager asked, staring at Yao. He sized her up, and then turned his head back toward the door calling, "Grandmother, we have guests."

A woman in her late sixties appeared on the stoop. Yao recognized the wife of her cousin, Ah Xiu. The woman exclaimed, "Oh, my heavens!" Her hands flapped on her apron. "What has brought you here, Yao?"

"It has been a long time. Is my cousin home?" Yao pulled Yezi with her toward the house. "This is Yezi, the daughter of my mistress."

"She's so cute! Please come in." Yezi stepped over a high wooden threshold and then sat down at a table in a hall-sized living room. The hostess raised her voice toward a side room where Dabao's grandfather was resting. "Laotang, come! Your cousin, Yao, is here." Picking up a rag, she wiped the table. "We ate just now, but I'll cook something for you," she said as she went into the kitchen.

The door of the side room opened. An old man shuffled out, a cane in his hand and a towel on his head. "I haven't seen you in ten years, Yao. I thought you'd forgotten us." He coughed as he spoke. "I'm not so well these days."

Rising from her seat, Yao walked over to her cousin and helped him to a chair. "Laotang, I had a tough time these past years," her voice trembled. "I couldn't come to see you until now."

While they chatted, Ah Xiu prepared a meal of steamed rice, and slices of smoked pork, boiled cabbage and carrots in a chilli sauce. Hungry, Yezi wolfed down the food. Yao drank a cup of rice wine and continued her long chat with her cousin. As the room darkened, the hostess lit an oil lamp; the light of the flames flickered over the table. Yezi gazed at the shadows of the human figures in the room trembling slightly on the walls, reflections of the flickering lamplight. Bunches of white or orange ears of corn, braids of white garlic and bundles of yellow tobacco leaves hung on hooks attached to the smoke-stained, dark brown ceiling beams. A ladder leaned on one side wall, above which was an open attic used as a storage room and guestroom.

Suddenly, steps could be heard outside. Dabao entered the room with several children. "Hello," he called out. "My friends want to meet the city boy."

"Me?" Yezi stood.

"Aren't you a city boy?" Dabao raised his head, a puzzled look on his face. Yezi no longer wearing her cap. Two long pigtails rested on her shoulders. "You are—"

"I'm a girl." She laughed and swung her shoulder-length hair.

"Why did you dress like a boy?"

"Popo Yao wanted me to. She thinks a girl in the countryside is vulnerable."

One of the girls pulled Yezi's sleeve. "Do you go to school?"

"Do you...? I mean do boys like you play basketball?" A boy made a face at her, pointing at her braids and laughing. Dabao grinned and scratched his head.

Yezi giggled and answered their questions. Yao gave each

of the children a gift: hairpins to the girls and a pencil and sharpener to the boys. They pulled Yezi outside for a quick game of hide-and-seek.

At bedtime, Yao held an oil lamp in her hand as she gingerly climbed the ladder to the attic. Yawning, Yezi followed her to the upper floor and fell onto the double bed that awaited them. Yao placed the lamp on what looked like a table. Yezi was shocked to notice that the table was actually a black coffin stacked on top of another coffin, its surface reflecting the glare from the flame. Eyeing the casket in the dim light, Yezi shivered and pulled the blankets up to her chin.

Yao turned around and said, "I should have told you about this earlier." She sat down beside Yezi and stroked her shoulder. "Don't be scared, little one."

"Why on earth do they have coffins inside the house?" Yezi asked, shuddering.

"Here every family keeps one or two for their elderly parents," Yao said, as she climbed into the bed beside. "You must be tired. I am. Let's go to sleep."

Curling up next to her, Yezi wrapped her arms around Yao's arm. "Stay with me, okay?"

"Okay." Yao said and blew out the lamp.

The next morning, Yezi got up early and followed Yao to the ladder. Carefully they made their way down. Dabao was sitting on a bench, carving a piece of wood.

Yezi took the bone from her pocket. "Look! Do you know what this is?"

He looked up from his carving and gave the bone a cursory glanced. "A pig's bone."

"What?" She did not believe him. "Isn't this a human bone?"

"What are you talking about?" Dabao snickered. "I can find tons of these bones if you want."

"Do you know where Danabeng village is?"

"About eight kilometres away. Why?"

"Have you heard of Yuanmou Man?"

"Never. Who the heck is he?" Forgetting the carving he had been working on, Dabao stared up at her, his eyes wide. "Okay, tell me more."

Yezi told him about that she had learned about Yuanmou Man in school. Amazed, Dabao wondered how a girl two grades below him could know so much.

After breakfast, Yao and Ah Xiu dismantled a door and set it across over two benches as a makeshift table, on which Yao cut patterns and hand-sewed several shirts with the fabric she had brought with her, a gift to her cousin and his wife.

Yezi resolved to try her luck at digging for a tooth of Yuanmou Man. Dabao went along to help. Dabao led Yezi to a path alongside the house. Two of Dabao's friends caught up to them and asked them where they were going. Eager to help with the expedition, they followed Yezi and Dabao and crossed a field blanketed by green wheat swaying in the early morning breeze. A large mound surrounded by bushes and trees came into sight. Dabao and his friends used to play around the area and had once discovered several bullet shells. He led the way to the mound. They thrust a hoe into the sandy soil and began to dig. Yezi acted as the archeologist and inspected the loosened dirt.

She uncovered numerous grassroots and cocooned insects, then handfuls of pebbles. But she found no bones, nor a single animal hair. After grubbing in the dirt for an hour, the boys felt sweaty and hot. They took off their jackets. Dabao's face was flushed and shone in the sun. He hunkered down on the ground and checked everything they had pulled from the mound. "I don't think we are going to find any bones."

Yezi selected two pebbles and pocketed them. "Let's try another spot." They traipsed to another mound but discovered nothing significant.

Later, Dabao took Yezi to his family's vegetable garden

behind the house. This time, she had a basketful of treasures: carrots and radishes. "Try one." The boy scraped off a carrot and handed it to her. She bit into the crunchy, juicy root, and inhaled its fresh soil scent. Satisfied with their loaded basket, they went home.

The house soon filled with the pleasant sounds of children's babbling and adult chatter. Another door was dismantled to become a makeshift table for Yezi and Dabao to help his siblings with their homework.

Then, Dabao's uncle and his family from the next house joined them for supper. Yezi was thrilled by all the other children at the table. She had never been at such a massive gathering before. After dinner, the three men smacked their lips on long-stemmed pipes and puffed on lit tobacco leaves, filling the hall with hazy smoke. Rice wine flowed down the adults' throats, and more words and sighs of relief found their way out of the drinkers' mouths. Meanwhile the children drank mugs of water sweetened with sugar and giggled about nothing as they passed around numerous meat and vegetable dishes.

Yao spoke to Laotang's family about Sang's accommodations. Laotang confirmed that Sang could live with them. Also he demanded that Dabao's uncle, one of his sons, get permission from the brigade's leader since he worked as an accountant, an important position within the brigade. This would secure Sang's position in the village.

Along with Ah Xiu, Yao visited many families in the area, some of whom she barely remembered. She had left the village when she was ten years old, but everybody knew she was here visiting and wanted to see and greet her. The villagers did not have telephones to pass on the news, but their eyes and ears collected all the news they needed about each family in the village. Yao's visit was an honour and her gifts were an eye-opener to everybody. Yao gave the women buttons and threads for their needle work, who were amazed by the oval or diamond shapes of the buttons in various sizes and colours.

The men received cigarettes and nylon socks. Some sniffed at those not handmade rolls, and some pulled on the nylon socks to see how far they could be stretched. Children were excited by colourful head bands and hairclips or pencils and erasers in the shape of animals they had never seen. A brown plastic cup was a completely new surprise to each family. In the countryside, such things were rarely seen.

Yao gave a hundred yuan to her cousin. She said, "Don't decline it. We're family." Two days later, after a tearful good-bye, Yezi and Yao left to make their way back home. Half of the villagers walked them out to the road. A cart waited for them to climb in. Sitting down, Yao positioned a basket full of fresh eggs in her lap. Yezi held onto a string bag; a chicken with its legs tied was shivering inside. Two young men pulled the cart to the bus station.

Meihua's shelf was gradually filled with books from stores and libraries while folders and files slowly piled up on her desk. Sometimes, she stayed up, plunging into her painting until a newly finished canvas joined the others of various sizes against the wall. She would gaze at these paintings for hours at a time, her brown eyes glowing with satisfaction.

June 1, International Children's Day, arrived. Yezi's school held a celebration. Students from each class performed on the school stage. In the evening, Yezi's mother placed a black case on the desk and said, "Happy Birthday!"

Yezi was ten years old, but it the first time she had ever received such an important gift. "A violin!" She gazed at the child-sized instrument case glimmering under the lamp light. Meihua knew Yezi admired the girl with the violin in the magazine photograph. They had talked about the photograph many times. The gift of a violin was a real surprise to Yezi. Eager to reach the case, Yezi almost stumbled over a chair. She opened it and fingered the smooth surface of the violin. The strings seemed to be whispering, "Play me!" The image of the

American girl ran across her mind, making her shiver. For a moment, she felt as if she were becoming that girl.

"I have great news." Her mother's voice brought Yezi back to the present. "My mother plans to visit us in August."

"Really?" Astonished, Yezi ran to Sang, who was testing acupuncture points on his legs. She shook his arm. "Can you speak English with our grandmother?"

"Don't push me. I have needles in my legs." Remaining motionless on his chair, Sang said, "I'll try. But I'm going to the countryside. I won't even be able to find any English papers or magazines there. In fact, I won't need English there at all."

"But I want to practice English with you before our grandmother comes."

"Okay, but you can also practice with Mama and Jian." Sang pulled one of the needles out of his leg. "I'm good at needles now. Hopefully, I'll be able to help the peasants with their aches and pains."

That night, exhilarated about the violin and the news of her grandmother's visit, Yezi tossed and turned in bed. She imagined the moment she would meet her grandmother. She couldn't decide whether she should say, "How do you do?" or "How are you?" She decided to ask her mother the following morning. She closed her eyes and willed herself to sleep.

17.

A FOREIGN GRANDMOTHER

WAITING FOR FURTHER NEWS FROM her grandmother became Yezi's main interest. One day in late June, Yezi returned home from school. Before walking into her bedroom, she popped her head into her mother's room. "Any news?" Yezi wanted to be informed of all details about her grandmother's visit.

"Not yet. It takes time for them to make a decision," said Meihua, raising her head from her book.

"Why do we need to get permission from the university?"

"Because your grandmother is a visitor from the outside of China."

"Hmm. Do you remember Liang, Sang's classmate? Last year, her uncle came from the States."

"Right. I don't foresee any problem. We just have to be patient."

"Do you still need me to model for you tomorrow morning?"

"Absolutely. Do you have any other plans?"

"Jian got a kitten. I'm going over to her place to see it, but I'll be your model first."

The next morning, Yezi put on the worn-out clothes she had used for her trip to Yuanmou. She placed the cap on her head and let her hair hang loose over her shoulders. She sat in a chair, clutching a stick in her hand, adopting what she hoped was a good pose for her portrait. Meihua sketched out Yezi's portrait; she tentatively titled it "Tomboy." She peered at Yezi constantly from behind the easel, dipping her brush into the paints, her strokes rapid and sure.

"Has Grandmother visited us before?" asked Yezi, her head full of questions.

"No."

"What does she do?"

"She's a retired nurse." Meihua gestured to Yezi with her paintbrush. "Don't move."

"How long do I have to remain still?"

"Not too long. By the way, what colour is Jian's kitty?"

"White and beige with a brown tail, but I haven't seen it yet."

"It must be cute." Meihua added the final touch. "I had a tabby long ago; it was brown with black spots." Finally she laid the paintbrush on the tray. "It's done."

Yezi leaped past the easel and turned her head. "Wow! It's me. But why do the eyes have no colour?"

"I'll add colour soon. Your brown, deep-set eyes look like mine. You also have a tiny, high nose, just like mine."

"Are my eyes brown? Not black?" Walking toward the closet, Yezi looked into its full-length mirror.

"That's right, tomboy!" Her mother laughed, her eyes narrowing at the painting.

"Bye, Mama. I'm going to see the kitten!" Yezi left the room and raced over to Jian's home.

Yezi watched her mother paint portraits of each family member. Yao dozed in the armchair during her portrait sitting over several evenings. During his turn, needles in acupuncture points on his legs, Sang remained motionless for hours in order to test their effectiveness. Meihua entitled the painting "Barefoot." When Lon returned home, after helping Yao clean the apartment, do the laundry and go grocery shopping, he also posed in a chair as a model, sipping the tea from a cup in his hand and enjoying a moment of relaxation. Weeks later, Meihua had finished a portrait for everyone except herself. Yezi wondered how her mother would paint her own picture until one Sunday morning. In front of the closet mirror, Meihua sat with the easel beside her and sketched on the canvas by observing her reflection in the mirror. When she was done with the sketch, she started to add colour with her oil paints. Her self-portrait depicted an artist whose eyes were sharp and thoughtful.

Yezi began checking the campus mailroom frequently, anxious for a letter from her newly-discovered grandmother. At last, in mid-July, a letter from the U.S. arrived. Yezi ran home and rushed into the apartment, waving the envelope at her mother. "Grandmother's letter! It's here!"

Meihua opened it. As she read it through, her eyes clouded over.

"What happened?" Yezi shook her mother's shoulder.

"She didn't get the visa."

Yao came in with a cup of tea. "Have something warm to drink. It will help you calm down. The sky won't fall."

"What is a visa?" asked Yezi, her hand pulling at her braid.

"She needs a visa to enter China. It's like getting permission. But they didn't give it to her." Meihua dabbed her eyes with a white handkerchief.

"It's okay. We can wait for her as long as we're alive," said Yao, a wry smile on her face.

"Thanks, Yao. You're right." Meihua lowered her voice, "I can wait. It is nothing compared to eight years in jail." She thought back to the wild geese that flew over tea bushes at the camp. Now the warm tea soothed her heart. *Yao's right.*

Shocked and saddened, Yezi couldn't understand why the visa people rejected her grandmother's application.

Sang graduated from high school in late July of 1976. During the Cultural Revolution, there were no graduation ceremonies that parents could attend as education was not valued. But Meihua was proud and she and Yao prepared a special dinner so they could celebrate with him at home.

Since his grandmother's visit was postponed, Sang decided to leave earlier than planned for Xiaohe Village. Meihua sobbed as if it were the last time she would ever see him, even though Sang had promised her monthly visits home.

"Don't worry. My cousin's family will look after him," said Yao, patting Meihua's back.

"I know. But Dahai's..." Meihua pulled her handkerchief from her pocket. "I just couldn't bear to lose another son."

"Mama, you know what? If I delay going there, it will hurt my chances of getting a recommendation for a university."

"Can't you wait for your father to come home?" asked Yao. "He'll be back soon. And I know he will want to accompany you to the village."

"Okay, but I'm definitely leaving next Monday, even if he hasn't made it back home before that." Sang sat on his bed, staring at his stacked luggage. "I'm old enough to do this by myself."

Lon arrived just in time to accompany Sang to Xiaohe Village. With the help of his father, Sang was able to take all his personal possessions with him.

Yezi reminded her brother to search for a fossil of Yuanmou Man in his spare time. Sang grinned. "Absolutely. If I find one, it's yours!"

The summer break arrived at the beginning of August. Yezi and Jian continued practicing their swimming in the river; Yao still watched over them from the shore. When Yezi opened eyes under water, she could see the shiny surface above. But each time she tried to lift her head above the water, her body sank. Jian and the other girls encouraged her to keep trying so she could learn to swim with her head above water.

Every Sunday evening, Yao accompanied Yezi to her tutor's

home for violin lessons. The tedious practicing helped Yezi come to appreciate that one minute's performance from a violinist was based on more than one hundred times in practice. The image of the happy American girl playing her violin always cheered her up and motivated her to practice.

By the end of August, Yezi had learned to swim with her head out of the water, and she was as tanned as all the others. Her fear of water, and of being called "white-skinned piglet," faded. To Meihua's delight, she had also learned to play a couple of simple pieces on her violin.

In September of 1976, Yezi entered the fourth grade. Her mother returned to her teaching post after a nine-year absence. Like a paintbrush, time had coloured Meihua's hair gray. But her face brightened when she stood in front of her students.

September 9, Yezi's teacher announced in class that Chairman Mao had died. Yezi could not believe her ears. *Is he really dead?* She had thought that "Long live Chairman Mao" meant he would live ten thousand years. Uncertain whether she should feel sad or relieved, she lost herself in thought. *My brother was eighteen when he died.* The idea of death stirred in her heart. *I don't want Popo Yao to die, nor Mama or Baba.* She sobbed; so did the other students.

When Yezi got home, the door to her mother's room was closed. She overheard Ling, her mother's best friend, speak. "Don't think about it too much."

"When will they trust me?" asked Meihua. "I've never complained about anything."

"They don't trust anyone who isn't from a family of poor peasants or factory workers, but I don't really care," replied Ling, her voice firm. "My background remains only with me. I don't have kids who could be affected."

"Why didn't they allow us to attend the meeting?" Meihua's voice sounded desperate. "It was just a memorial service for Chairman Mao."

"It's okay," sighed Ling. Yezi did not see her, but could imagine her caring eyes. "Things will change in the future." Ling's voice had a soothing effect just as her words "take care" had in the past. That phrase had always made Yezi feel warm inside. She always said it, as she was leaving, whenever she had dropped by their apartment to bring Yao some food.

Mao's death marked the end of the Red Terror; Deng Xiaoping's rehabilitation brought fundamental changes. A year later, in October, 1977 when both Lon and Sang returned home for China's National Day, Sang informed them that entrance exams for universities would soon be re-established. He had heard from his high school teacher that exam scores would be the only criteria for acceptance; recommendations regarding an applicant's politics were no longer required. Looking at his father, then his mother, Sang asked, "Do you think it's possible?"

Lon answered, "Quite possible, but who knows when?"

Meihua was happy; entrance exams meant that all qualified applicants could go to university without having to rely on a recommendation from a unit authority. "I think Sang should start preparing for possible exams," she said.

Sang opened his palm and then closed it tightly as if he had caught something called opportunity and did not want it to slip away. "I'll borrow a couple of books and get started."

At the end of October, the *People's Daily* announced the re-establishment of entrance exams. After receiving permission from his brigade, Sang returned home to prepare for the exams. It was a battle all the youth who had missed the opportunity for higher education in the past ten years were willing to entertain.

Each time Yezi saw Sang bury himself in books, she felt hope for him. His dream would come true. He would become a university student. Yezi could not help but ask, "Brother, will you study at Mama's university?"

"I don't think so. You should ask me which program I'm going to apply for," said Sang.

"Okay. Which one?"

"Medicine," he said, imagining himself in a white uniform helping patients. "I'll go to a medical university if I'm accepted."

"Is that far from home?"

"Depends on which university. We can talk about it when I finish my exams." He waved his hand. "Don't you see I'm busy right now? Leave me alone."

Yezi wondered what she should do when her time came.

In early February of 1978, winter jasmine was just starting to spread around the lakeshore again when an acceptance letter from the medical university in Kunming arrived at their door. Sang returned from the countryside. The new admission requirements generated a light-hearted atmosphere at colleges and universities all over China. It was a promising time that benefited from Deng Xiaoping's policies.

By then, Yezi was half way through the sixth grade. She was busy preparing for two sets of exams: final exams for elementary school and entrance exams for junior high school. She spent most of her spare time working on assignments, completing quizzes and pre-tests.

One Saturday evening at the end of February, Meihua announced, "Great news! My mother is arriving in two weeks!"

"Are you sure?" Yezi paused in the middle of her homework. She leaned against the back of her chair.

"Certainly. I got her letter today. She wrote to confirm her arrival date," said Meihua happily.

"Wow! This time Grandmother is coming for sure!" Yezi clapped her hands.

"Is she coming by air?" asked Yao, coming out of the kitchen, a cup of tea in her hand. "I'd be scared in the sky."

"It's nothing to be afraid of," Meihua said. "You are fine if you just think of yourself as sitting in a big room full of people." She chuckled, "Even though I was afraid the first time I got on an airplane."

"When did you do that?" asked Yezi and Yao together.

"When I was twenty-one," said Meihua. "I flew with my mother to Halifax for my grandfather's funeral."

"Where's Halifax? Is that as far as the United States?" asked Yezi.

"Do you mean from the United States to Halifax or from China to Halifax?" Meihua asked.

Yao snorted. She also wondered where these places were. "This little one always asks difficult questions."

"Well, Halifax is located on the East coast of Canada. Boston is on the East coast of the United States." Meihua went to her room and returned with an atlas. She opened it to a page that had a world map. Then, she pointed out two tiny dots: Halifax and Boston. "It's a two-hour flight from Boston to Halifax. And from Boston or Halifax, China is about the same distance. It would be about a twenty-hour flight."

Yao's eyes widened in disbelief. She couldn't imagine being high up in the air for such a long time.

"I have another question." Yezi checked the map, her eyes glowing with curiosity. "Why did your grandmother live in a country different from your mama's?"

"A good question."

"Is that because your grandmother was sent to live in Canada like you were sent to the camp?" Yezi reasoned this based on her experience, expecting her mother's answer to be "Yes."

Meihua frowned at the memory. "That's not the same thing. Nobody was dispatched anywhere." Her eyes roved over the map as her mind wandered away. "My mother had decided to move to Boston before I was born."

"Then you decided to live in Kunming—"

"Enough questions." Yao tugged at Yezi's sleeve. "Let's talk about what we should do to get ready for your grandmother's visit."

"I've reported it to the leaders," said Meihua. "They said she can stay in the campus guesthouse, because we don't have enough space to accommodate her here. They'll also arrange an interpreter to show her around."

"Do you mean Grandmother won't stay with us?" asked Yezi. "Why not, Mama?"

"They said they'd take care of her. They want to leave her with a flawless impression of China." Not wanting to disappoint Yezi, Meihua explained the situation in what she hoped was an optimistic tone. "Anyway, we can join her whenever we want. The guesthouse isn't far. Yezi, you can still practice your English with her."

"That's good," Yezi breathed a sigh of relief. "As long as nobody stops her from coming to see us."

18.
SWEET POTATO CONGEE

TWO WEEKS LATER, MEIHUA DRESSED up after lunch. Then she waited for the car dispatched by university that would take her to the airport.

Yezi heard a knock as she was about to leave for her afternoon classes. She pulled the door open and saw a young woman standing in the doorway. "Are you Yezi?" the young woman asked. "Aren't you coming to meet your grandmother?"

Yezi smiled and showed the young woman her book bag. "I'd like to, but I've got to go to school."

"No, you don't have to." The woman smiled. "I already told your teacher you'd be going to the airport."

Yezi looked at her, puzzled.

"Teacher Wei," the woman called out, looking over Yezi's shoulder at Meihua. "I'm Zhong Wang, the interpreter from the Office of Foreign Affairs at the university. My director asked me to arrange things for your mother, Mrs. McMillan, and your family."

"My mama speaks English," Yezi murmured. "We don't need an interpreter."

"You can come with us." Meihua smiled broadly at Yezi and then turned toward the young woman. "Thanks, Miss Wang. Shall we go now?"

The interpreter led them downstairs. It was Yezi's first time in a car. In the back seat next to her mother, Yezi listened attentively to the conversation in English between her mother and Miss Wang. "Teacher Wei, please don't mention anything unnecessary to your mother. You represent China and must think about the dignity of our country."

Meihua, confused, asked, "What do you mean by 'unnecessary?'"

"For example, you don't need to tell her about your time the prison camp—that sort of thing. You're in a teaching position now. Your son is going to university. You'll know what to say if you think positively."

"Why would I tell my mother about my past?" replied Meihua, scowling. "I'd erase it from my memory if I could."

"Agreed," the interpreter sounded relieved. "I don't want any trouble on my first assignment with a foreigner."

Yezi knew they were discussing her grandmother's visit, but only caught a few sentences. The conversation ended. She looked at her mother and noticed her mouth was twisted into a tight knot.

They got out of the car at Wujiabar Airport. Yezi followed her mother and Miss Wang into a roomy hall with enormous windows. Rows of chairs lined the walls. Many passengers strode past, carrying suitcases or dragging luggage on wheels. They were better dressed than the passengers Yezi had ever seen at any bus or train station. Amazed, she spotted an airplane outside taxiing past the windows. It glided to a runaway, and then zoomed up high into the air. *It's just like in the movies!*

Suddenly, she felt her sleeve being tugged. She looked away from the distant airplane and saw her mother hurrying over to an elderly woman. They embraced, their heads in each other's hands. At the sight of her mother and grandmother together, Yezi envisioned the two dots on the world map merging into one. Not wanting to disturb them, she stood silently beside Miss Wang.

Meihua turned around and said to Yezi, "This is my mother, Agnes McMillan." Then, pointing to the woman from the office, she said, "This is Miss Wang, an interpreter from my university." The elderly woman looked at Miss Wang, puzzled. Hesitantly, she stretched out her hand. "How do you do?"

Miss Wang shook hands with Yezi's grandmother. "I'm from the Office of Foreign Affairs. I will look after you during your visit here."

"Thank you very much." The elderly woman's gaze fell on the little girl. "Yezi? Please come here. I have so longed to meet you."

Miss Wang interpreted what Yezi's grandmother said.

"Grandmother," Yezi said only one word as she approached and stood before her.

Agnes wrapped her arms around Yezi and whispered in her ear, "You are a beautiful young woman." Yezi felt her face grow hot, but she couldn't stop the wide grin that was sweeping across her face.

"I'll take you to the guesthouse, Mrs. McMillan." Aware of Agnes's bewilderment, Miss Wang continued, "We will all go there together. Supper is ready. The driver is waiting for us." She led the way outside to the car.

Upon their arrival at the guesthouse, Miss Wang asked them to make themselves comfortable in the chairs placed around the table in the dining room. She went to the kitchen. Soon after, two servers carried out dishes, bowls and plates heaped with food. "Help yourselves," Miss Wang said. "This is a welcome treat from the university." She passed a dish to Agnes. Then she picked up a pair of chopsticks for herself.

Miss Wang began to talk as she ate. Meihua seldom spoke; she merely sipped her soup slowly. Yezi had a lot to ask, but did not dare. Agnes's brow furrowed, but she listened politely to the interpreter rave about Spring University and Kunming's attractions. The meal ended quietly. Finally, Miss Wang handed Agnes a sheet. "This is a list of sightseeing spots you might be interested in. After you have selected some places, please let me know. I will accompany you. My phone number is on the paper. Goodnight, everybody."

"Goodnight." Meihua said, holding her breath. When the interpreter hesitated at the door, her hand on the doorknob, Meihua quickly added, "We will leave soon as well."

After the interpreter finally left them alone, Meihua and Yezi walked Agnes to her room on the second floor. "Where's your home?" Agnes asked scrutinizing the guarded looks on her daughter's and granddaughter's faces.

"My apartment's a little crowded. They want you to stay in the guesthouse here, near my home."

"Where are Lon and the others?"

"They may be on their way home."

"Can I see them?"

"I'll bring them here tomorrow night if you like. Sang commutes daily to his university. Lon should be coming home tonight. Tomorrow morning I'll meet with my substitute teacher to discuss the lessons she will be teaching during my absence."

"I have lots to ask, Flora," said Agnes. "First of all, I wonder if you can take a trip with me."

"To where?"

"Chengdu. You know I lived there for half a year. I'd like to revisit it."

"I don't think that will be a problem. But I will have to ask permission."

"Please book two round-trip tickets as soon as possible." Agnes's eyes beamed. "I'll pay for the trip."

Yezi was watching her grandmother carefully. Her short blond hair shone under the room's dim lights. Her silver oval earrings shimmered when her head moved. She wore a light pink sweatshirt over dark brown sweatpants.

"Grandmother, what does Chengdu look like?"

"Oh my, Yezi! You can speak English, can't you?" Agnes asked, so astonished to hear her, and so pleased, too, a broad smile on her face.

Shyly, Yezi grinned. "A bit. And I can sing some songs if

you'd like to listen," she said, managing to utter that whole sentence with only a little help from her mother.

"My sweetie! I bet you can sing beautifully." Agnes placed her hands on Yezi's shoulders. "Why didn't you speak earlier?"

"I didn't like to be watched by Miss Wang," Yezi said in Chinese.

Meihua relayed to Agnes that Yezi thought since Miss Wang was not part of her family, that it was best not to say anything.

"Flora, I'm proud of your daughter, a smart and sweet girl." Agnes smiled. "I'll let you go home now to prepare things for tomorrow. If Yezi wishes, she can stay with me. I have an extra bed here."

"Me? What?" Yezi caught only enough words to know they were talking about her.

Meihua interpreted what her mother said.

"Yes, I'd like too very much." Yezi nodded enthusiastically.

"So you stay here, Yezi," said Meihua, turning to hug her mother. "I'll come over tomorrow after my morning meeting."

"Grandma? Is it okay to call you Grandma? Why did you call my mother 'Flora'?"

"Of course you can call me Grandma. And, in answer to your question, your mother's American name is 'Mayflora.' 'Flora' is a short form."

"What does it mean?"

"'Flora' means 'flower.' And 'Mayflora' means 'flower in May.'"

"Her Chinese name can also mean 'beautiful flower,'" said Yezi. "I have so many questions for you." Yezi's English was halting, but somehow they managed to understand each other.

"I'll try to answer all of them. Why don't you sit here?"

Agnes said, pointing to the only armchair in the room. Her suitcases were poised against the small sofa. She reached for one, opened it, and took out a small package. "This is for you. I hope you like it."

'What is it?" Yezi held the package in her hands, uncertain what to do with it.

"Open it. You'll see."

Yezi unwrapped the package. A bright yellow dress with a floral print tumbled out. A look of surprise crossed her face, then she gave her grandmother a wide smile.

"You can try it on in there." Agnes pointed to the door of the bathroom.

Yezi ran to the bathroom and later swirled out with the dress on. "Thank you for your lovely gift, Grandma." She spun, and the dress swept around her like flowers thrown into the air.

"What are some of your questions?" Agnes sat in the sofa, a look of contentment on her face.

"Do women in your country carry these?" asked Yezi. She sat close to her grandmother and touched her earring with her finger.

"You mean earrings? Yes, we do. Don't Chinese women wear them?"

"Only rich women in ancient times wore them."

"How do you know that?"

"I have seen them in picture books about ancient times."

"Do you read a lot?"

"I do now, but I didn't have any books before my mother lived at home."

"Where did she live before?"

"In the camp."

"What did she do in the camp?" Agnes looked baffled, and then her voice low, she asked, "Was it a prison camp?"

"Prison?" Yezi did not know the word. Unable to say yes or no, she tried to explain, "It was a reform-through-labour camp. She lived there until two years ago."

"Really?" Agnes's hand was shaking when she placed it on Yezi's shoulder. "Whom did you live with?"

"Popo Yao took care of Sang and me all those years when Mama wasn't home."

"Do you know why your mother was in the camp?" Agnes's face darkened as if a black cloud had passed by the window.

"They said she was an anti-revolutionary." Yezi's voice grew quiet as gloomy memories came flooding back. She pictured her own tearful face in the office of the workers' leader, the shout of "American mongrel" resounding in her head.

"Poor little girl, you must've had a hard life," sighed Agnes. In an attempt to lighten the mood, she asked in her best perky voice, "Now tell me, how did you learn to speak English?"

"I started studying with my brother a couple of years ago." She looked at her grandmother's face. "I like your smile. Can you speak Chinese?"

"I still remember some. *Ni hao ma?*" Agnes replied.

"Fine, thanks. I understand you," Yezi giggled. "Where did you learn Chinese?"

"I learned Chinese from my tutor over fifty-four years ago in Chengdu," answered Agnes in Chinese. The past shimmered in her mind: Mei interpreting Agnes's instructions to the middle-aged woman when she delivered the baby; the pilgrim's desperate leap to Buddha's Glory at Mount Emei; and, the accident with horse-drawn wagon in the field that dark night during their trip back to Chengdu.

"In Chengdu? Are you going back to visit your tutor?" Yezi's question pulled Agnes back to the present.

"I don't know where he is now," Agnes said, the words in Chinese slowly coming back to her. "But I'd love to see Chengdu again." In her mind, the missionary compound on White Pagoda Street still shone in the sun, and Mei, Mayflora's handsome father, was still in his twenties.

"Why did you go there?"

"I was a missionary—"

"What does *missionary* mean?"

Agnes replied in Chinese, "*Chuan jiao shi.*"

"I've heard these words somewhere. People said…"

"What did you hear?" Agnes held Yezi's hand, curiosity in her eyes.

Yezi hesitated. "I heard people say missionaries had tried their drugs on Chinese babies."

"Do you believe that?"

"I don't know." Yezi shook her head, her puzzled eyes searching her grandmother's face for an answer. "What did missionaries do, anyway?"

"They spread the gospel to people," Agnes said, holding Yezi's hand.

"I don't know what *gospel* means," Yezi said, caressing her grandmother's hand. "But I'll learn."

"Sure. As you grow up you'll learn and come to know many things. I'll tell you more about me and my time in China, and I'll learn a lot from you, too." Agnes kissed Yezi's cheeks. "Bedtime! You have to go to school tomorrow morning."

"Okay," Yezi answered, stifling a yawn. She still had so many questions. *They will have to wait until tomorrow.*

Yezi woke up and found her grandmother sitting by the window. Sunlight was streaming through the window, filling the room with a golden light. Agnes's head looked as though it was outlined in golden threads. "Good morning, Grandma. You are up early."

"Yes, I have jet lag." Agnes turned to smile at Yezi.

"What *leg*?"

"Jet *lag*, not *leg*." Agnes chuckled. "Did you sleep well?"

"Yes, I did."

"Why don't we take a walk in the fresh air?"

"Sure. I'll take you to my house."

"Yes. I'd really like to see it."

Several minutes later, Yezi led her grandmother downstairs,

and they headed for home. The sunshine glinted over the gardens as they walked along the road. Several joggers passed by. Agnes took a deep breath of the air mixed with the scent of winter jasmine and said, "It's spring here. Back home, we had a terrible blizzard two weeks ago."

"Kunming is called Spring City, because of its nice weather all year round; no hot summer, no chilly winter," Yezi said in an elated tone.

"I love spring," said Agnes.

They approached the apartment on the second floor. Yezi tapped on the door.

"Ah, you're back." Yao opened the door, her eyes wide with surprise. "And you too, Grandmother! Please come on in."

"Popo Yao's making breakfast," Yezi explained. "What would you like to eat, Grandma?"

Agnes answered in Chinese, "Sweet potato congee."

"What?" Yao could not believe her ears. "How do you know that? From a book? Sit here, please." Yao motioned at them to sit at the dining table.

"Don't make anything special for me. I'll eat whatever you're cooking," Agnes responded, chuckling.

Agnes pulled a stool up to the table, while, Yezi made her a cup of tea.

Just then Meihua walked in, sheafs of paper in her hands. "Mother! You're here," she exclaimed, her eyes gleaming with joy. She set the papers down on a table near the door, and walked over to give Agnes a hug.

"I wanted to see your home." Agnes looked extremely happy. "I am so glad you are close to the guesthouse. Yao is making breakfast for us."

"I'm making fried buns." Yao sliced some of the buns that Sang had gotten from the canteen earlier that morning and fried them in a pan. "I'll cook sweet potato congee for Grandma next time."

"Here's soymilk, Mother." Meihua placed a bowl in front

of Agnes and another one in front of Yezi.

"Where's Sang?" Agnes asked.

"He's gone to his university," Meihua answered, taking the plate of fried bun slices from Yao and placing it on the table. The aroma of food wafted through the room, calling everyone to the table.

"He was accepted to the medical university," Yao added proudly as she joined them at the table.

Unable to lift a slice with chopsticks, Agnes used her fingers instead. Yezi found it funny and decided to use her fingers, too. Yao darted a stern look in her direction. "Don't forget your table manners."

At that moment, Yezi heard a knock on the door. *Is this Baba?* Bouncing from the chair, she dashed out of the room to open the door. But it wasn't Lon.

19.
STONE FOREST

WHEN YEZI OPENED THE DOOR, a frowning Miss Wang brushed past her impatiently. "Is your grandmother here?"

Startled, Yezi stepped backward. "Y—yes," she said, stepping aside to let her in.

Miss Wang strode into the room, barely acknowledging Yezi. When she approached the table, she forced a smile on her face. "Good morning, Mrs. McMillan. I didn't expect you to be here this early."

Agnes stood to greet her and noticed Yezi's silence. "Sorry about that. I dropped in to surprise my daughter's family. It was irresistible. Don't you relish surprises?"

"Yes, I do," Miss Wang said, a note of irritation in her voice. "But my duty is to make sure you're all right, and that things are not out of place."

"But how can things be out of place when I am here with my daughter. That is the reason I am visiting," Agnes said, her voice and smile coyly sweet.

Returning to her chair, Yezi glared at Miss Wang. "My grandmother enjoyed a breakfast of tea and soymilk. She likes sweet potato congee, too."

"Really?" Surprised to hear Yezi talk, Miss Wang laid a hand on her shoulder, nodding to indicate encouragement. "Our Chinese food is the best in the world, don't you think so?" Wang's face was strained, her lips pursed.

"Any food is good for me." Yezi grinned. "Chocolate especially."

Raising her eyebrows, Miss Wang abruptly withdrew her hand from Yezi's shoulder. "You're ignorant."

Agnes gasped. But before she could say anything, Yao stood up and said to Miss Wang "Please ignore Yezi. She doesn't know enough."

"You're right, Miss Wang. Chinese food's tasty, especially in my daughter's home," Agnes quickly added. Pointing to the teapot on the table, she asked demurely, "Would you like a cup of tea? Please, join us at the table."

"No, thank you." Miss Wang was curt. Glancing at her watch, she asked, "Can you be back at the guesthouse by 9:30 a.m.? I will pick you up and take you to a meeting."

"A meeting? Why?" Perplexed, Agnes turned toward her daughter and then looked at Miss Wang for an explanation.

"The Party's Secretary would like to express his greetings on behalf of the university. Teacher Wei should attend, too."

"Me?" Meihua's astonished eyes shifted from her mother to Miss Wang.

"Yes, that's why I am here." Before anybody could ask another question, Miss Wang said to Meihua, "Be ready. I'll be back at 9:30 a.m."

"You don't have to bother, Miss Wang. We can walk to the administration building," replied Meihua.

"No. I've already arranged a car." Miss Wang's voice was firm. "I'm supposed to meet you at the guesthouse, okay?"

"All right then, we shall see you there." Meihua nodded, trailing behind Miss Wang. "Let me get the door for you."

During Agnes's visit, Lon was permitted a week off from the mine. Yezi joined her parents and grandmother in most of their tours around the city—each accompanied by Miss Wang. They visited the Dragon Gate, the Golden Temple Park, the Black Dragon Pool and the Stone Forest—more places than she had ever visited in her entire life.

In the Stone Forest, towering, dark brown boulders formed a breathtaking sight, the sky a pale blue expanse above them. Wisps of clouds drifted and changed into various shapes. The breeze brought the pleasant scent of camellia from nearby bushes. Miss Wang pointed out specific stones and told them legends about each one. Her tight voice echoed sharply around the stones. Yezi's family followed her to a boulder shaped like a person which had been named, "Figure of Ashima." Miss Wang explained to Yezi's grandmother that "Ashima was the most beautiful girl of the Sani people." Yezi listened attentively even though she already knew the story. "Ashima and her brother Ahei had lived happily in their tribe until one day a wicked magician carried her off to his castle—"

Tugging her mother's hand, Yezi whispered, "Ahei was her lover—"

"Who told you that?" asked Meihua.

"Popo Yao said Ashima was kidnapped by the chief's son, but that her lover rescued her. He won over the chief's son with his beautiful songs and his magic arrows." She asked, "Why is Miss Wang telling a different story?"

Pausing for a second, her mother said, "Her story comes from a different source, but the ending's the same." She did not want Yezi to question Miss Wang's version of the tale out loud.

Entranced by the boulder, Yezi thought about how Ashima had died in the flood caused by the villain who had deliberately broken the dam, and how, in death, she was transformed into a stone. A cloud cast its shade over the figure. She could almost hear the water crashing and see the tears trickle down Ashima's face. Several skylarks darted around the top of the boulder. Their chirping brought her back to the reality of this lovely spring day, and the magic of sightseeing with her grandmother who had come from so far away.

The family spent a lot of time with Agnes, but it was hard to talk privately, because Miss Wang was always with them.

Meihua looked forward to their trip to Chengdu so that she could be alone with her mother, without the presence of Miss Wang hovering about and studying their every move. Despite the fact that Yezi continued to stay with her grandmother at night, she did not know English well enough for them to talk about anything at length.

One evening, seated together at the guesthouse, Agnes wrapped her arm around Yezi's shoulder, a gesture of affection and contentment. Yezi clasped her grandmother's hand. "I once dreamed of an old lady on the moon smiling at me. Now I know it was you."

Agnes smiled. "Honey, but what are your dreams for the future?"

"Going to university." Leaning on Agnes's arms, Yezi closed her eyes and added wistfully, "I really don't want to live in a camp."

Agnes's face suddenly darkened. She was filled with mixed feelings, and troubling thoughts. "Maybe you would like to come to the United States and live with me?"

"Maybe, someday. When I grow up, I will come to visit you in your country."

Agnes gently rocked her granddaughter in her arms. There didn't seem to be anything more to say.

Agnes and Meihua left for Chengdu, and Lon returned to work. Yezi resumed her daily routine at school. She had missed a whole week of school, and she needed to catch up with her class. She borrowed all the notes that Jian had taken in different classes. She didn't want to miss completing any of the necessary assignments as failing a course might lead to her rejection from junior high school.

One evening, while Yezi and Jian were finishing their homework together, Jian was particularly fidgety and distracted. Before leaving, Jian blurted out, "When are you going to the States?"

"What? What do you mean? Who told you I was going anywhere?" gasped Yezi.

"Some of the kids in our class said your grandmother came to take you away," Jian said, her questioning eyes on Yezi's face.

"That's not true," sighed Yezi. "Why do people gossip about me?" She fanned her book in the air as if to blow the gossip away.

"The teacher said American people are good. But that society is harmful because capitalism keeps most Americans in poverty," said Jian. "I'm more than confused."

"So am I. Wait a second." Walking over to the dresser, Yezi pulled open the top drawer and pulled out a dress. "This is from my grandmother. What do you think?"

"Wow, I like the square neckline and the lace." Jian narrowed her eyes and reached her hand out to touch the fabric. It looked like a dress she had seen in movies. "It's so nice! I like the floral pattern and the short, puffy sleeves. Put it on, let me take a look."

Yezi quickly slipped into the dress and spun around. "What do you think?"

"It's terrific," Jian said, clapping her hands. "Why don't you wear it to school tomorrow?"

"People would say it's too bourgeois." Yezi frowned. "They might nickname me Dress Wei, the same way my mother got her nickname."

"I like it so much. I wouldn't be afraid of wearing it if it were mine." Jian pursed her mouth. "Maybe I am just too bourgeois."

Yezi slipped out of her dress and then encouraged her friend to try it on. Then she examined Jian in the dress and beamed. "You look gorgeous!"

"Is your grandmother a capitalist?" Jian asked in an awkward tone, her hands sliding uncertainly over the crisp folds of the dress.

"No, she's a retired nurse." Yezi felt proud of having a non-capitalist grandmother.

"You mean she doesn't exploit people, but she can afford a trip to come here?" Jian asked with surprise. "I don't think my family can even pay for a train trip to Beijing," Jian added, unable to hide the pity she felt for her own circumstances.

"I don't think she's exploited anyone," said Yezi, even though she was not entirely certain what that meant. "Instead, she's been exploited by capitalists," she announced firmly.

"Why do you think that?" Jian was astonished.

"If capitalists exploit people, they must exploit working people," Yezi replied, trying to explain her logic. "My grandmother must have been exploited because she worked, just like we do."

"So, she isn't bourgeois, but has an eye for a nice dress!" Jian was not convinced.

"Hey, it's not only the bourgeoisie that like to dress up. Girls like us also appreciate pretty dresses," Yezi said in what she thought was a convincing tone of voice. Then she shook her head, adding, "But I don't think I'll wear it to school."

"I wish, someday, we could wear what we like. And not be afraid of gossip," Jian said, her voice conciliatory.

"I wish someday we could feel free to do what we want!" Yezi smiled broadly at her friend.

"Girls, bedtime," Yao called out as she came into the room. Plopping down on her own bed, Yao loosened her long, gray braid and sighed, "I don't know why you use those big words: 'capitalist,' 'bourgeoisie,' and so on. Life is life; talking is no use." She stretched her arms, opened her mouth wide and yawned.

"Good night," Jian said and then left for home.

When Meihua and her mother visited Chengdu, Agnes showed Meihua the formal West China Mission compound. They also visited Huaxi Medical University in which Meihua's father had studied. Without being watched by Miss Wang, Meihua and Agnes had a chance to share their memories of those past years. Agnes told Meihua how much she wished they had been able to find her father, Mei. Meihua told her she'd never given up hope.

After Agnes's visit, Yezi's family quickly fell back into their familiar routine. When Yezi returned to school, however, several classmates stared pointedly at her, and one of them chanted, "Yankee grandmother! High pointy-nose invader! Beaten by great Koreans!"

Before Yezi could respond, her teacher approached the chanting child and asked, "Who told you that?"

"I heard it from his sister," the child said, pointing to another boy in the seat behind him.

"Stop talking nonsense. Both of you. That's history. Yezi's grandmother is a very nice American," the teacher said, and she sent the children outside to play.

The incident bothered Yezi a lot. *Why did the American invade Korea?* She did not understand and did not get the answers she needed in her class. When she got home, Yezi told her mother what the children had said and asked her to explain what had happened between the Americans and Koreans. Meihua sucked in a deep breath. "There was a war between America and Korea in the early 1950s. But your grandmother didn't go to Korea, and she wasn't an invader."

"But why did the American soldiers go to Korea?" Yezi longed to know more.

"In order to answer your question, I must first read many history books. If you're really interested to know why it happened, you also need to read lots of books and do your research," Meihua explained. It was hard for Meihua to discuss political issues with her daughter. And it was dangerous to do so. She rose to her feet and pulled Yezi to her side. "Look at you! Soon you will be taller than I am. And when you grow up, you'll know a lot more than I do."

"Mama, can I study history at university?"

"Yes, of course, but maybe you'd better focus on science instead."

"Why?"

"Science is useful and practical." Meihua gazed into the distance. She turned toward Yezi, and asked, "What do you think about your eldest brother?"

"I'm proud of him."

"Why?"

"He's a hero. He fought for the revolution." Puzzled by the question, Yezi asked, "What do you think?"

"He was an idealist."

"What does 'idealist' mean?"

"An idealist is someone who cherishes high or noble principles. The most important thing for them is to fight for what they believe in." Meihua stifled her tears, "He shouldn't have died so young."

"Don't cry, Mama. It's no use. I, too, wish he could come back." Yezi embraced her mother, holding her protectively.

Meihua was reminded then of a conversation she'd had with her mother during their trip to Chengdu. Agnes had suggested Meihua consider getting medical help in Boston for her persistent headaches. She looked at Yezi and asked, "If I go to the States, would you like to come with me?"

"Do you mean we can afford to take a trip?"

"Tell me if you're willing to go with me."

"Yes, I am. But what about Popo Yao, Sang, and Baba?"

"I don't know the answer to that yet. I'm just considering a suggestion your grandmother made." Meihua stroked her daughter's back. "Please don't say anything to anyone else about this."

"What was Grandma's suggestion?"

"I'll tell you later. I need to discuss it with your father first."

20.
LOGAN INTERNATIONAL AIRPORT

YEZI TURNED THIRTEEN IN 1979. The year began with the recently launched reform movement called "The Realization of Four Modernizations." It was intended to strengthen the fields of agriculture, industry, national defense, science and technology, and to open China up to the outside world, and make it a great economic power. According to Hu Yaobang, the new General Secretary of the Central Party, branded rightists and people persecuted during the Cultural Revolution would have their cases reviewed and get rehabilitated. As a result, people who were in prison camps would be freed and allowed to return to their former work units. University students across the country initiated a free-speech movement with the hope that freedom and democracy would soon be practiced in China.

Yezi had more tests at school than ever before. After midterm exams, Jian and she were ranked top students. If they kept their grades up, they would both be assured a promising future: admission to a key high school and then, presumably, acceptance to a first-class university.

Completely immersing herself in studies, Yezi worked hard until her final exams. Finally, just as she was able to relax in front of the television, her mother returned home and with a big smile on her face, gestured for Yezi to come into her room. "Look at this." She took out a brown, wallet-sized booklet from the desk drawer.

Yezi read the words on the cover. "A passport!" she said with surprise. "Whose?"

"Yours."

"Mine? But where is yours?"

"It's a long story."

"They didn't permit you to have one." Yezi lowered her voice, "What about the medical help you need?"

"I can get medical help here." Meihua looked deeply into her daughter's eyes, and gently added, "Grandma is expecting you. You will be able to go to school there. It's a wonderful opportunity."

"Do you think I can catch up with students there?" Yezi hesitated, and then said, "I don't know English that well."

"You will learn quickly."

That night, Yezi sat on a stool next to Yao who, under the light, mended her apron. "I have a secret." Yezi pulled on Yao's arm and told her about the passport.

"Whoa! I have a needle in my hand." Yao stopped sewing. "You should go," she said, though she wished Yezi would stay and and had to fight back tears. To Yao, life seemed better in the United States. Yezi's grandmother could afford to come to China, when the people of China never travelled those distances. "I'll come and visit you there someday," she added encouragingly.

"Really?" Yezi linked Yao's arm. "Do you have enough money for a ticket?"

"I can save some."

"Maybe you should learn some English from my mother," Yezi teased.

"When I was a kid, I didn't even go to school to learn Chinese. How can I put English into this rusty head?" Yao rapped her knuckles on her head, her smile wide and toothy.

"Even though you didn't have the chance to go to school, you are really smart," said Yezi, stroking Yao's arm. "Don't worry. When you come to see me, I'll be your interpreter."

Yao nodded and continued mending her apron. Her eyes blurred; the stitches were hard to see.

"Promise me you'll come to see me." Yezi snuggled next to Yao.

"I promise," her husky voice softened.

In late July, Meihua told Yezi she had ordered a plane ticket for her. Like silk threads newly spun, feelings of enthusiasm and anxiety enveloped her like a cocoon. She felt as if she were a silkworm biting its way out. She longed to learn about her mother's birth country; but at the same time, she wondered and worried about what would become of her in that foreign place.

Yao wiped her eyes with a corner of her apron. "Poor little one, how will you bear the food there? Americans only eat tasteless milk and bread."

Yezi said, "Don't worry about me," Yezi said. "I will like milk and bread as much as I enjoy your food. And when I come back, I will eat lots of your good home-cooking."

Yao took Yezi to buy some fabric because she wanted to make her some clothes. Even though Yezi had not left yet, Yao already sensed the emptiness around her when they walked through the people-packed street.

After purchasing the fabric and returning home, Yao asked for a large sheet of white paper from Meihua. She placed the dress Agnes had given Yezi on the paper and traced around its edges, carefully measuring the puffed sleeves and ruffled hem. She sewed busily every day for the next week and managed to complete two dresses. She asked Yezi to try them on.

Fingering the garments made with fine stitches, Yezi gazed at Yao's sweaty face, her wrinkles like tiny, uneven cracks on dry land. It was the first time Yezi realized Yao looked old—even older than her grandmother, though Yao was only sixty-two. A sad feeling welled up inside her, but Yezi resolved to look cheerful. The dresses were almost identical to the one Agnes had given her. One was pale pink with white polka dots, the other a deep navy blue. "I'll wear the pink one when I get on the plane." She did not want to endure the gossip or taunts of bourgeois lifestyle, she knew would rise around her in a flurry should she wear either dress to school.

Yezi carefully wrapped the yellow floral dress that her grandmother had given her in a piece of newspaper. She decided to offer it as a keepsake to Jian who liked it so much.

In mid-August, after a twenty-hour flight from Shanghai, Yezi landed at Logan International Airport in Boston.

As she watched crowds rush into and out of a grand hall, and heard the chatter of English all around her, she knew she was in America—the country she felt close to in her dreams, but now, in its immediate presence, distant and strange.

An interpreter helped her during her interview with an immigration officer. As Yezi went to pick up her luggage, an announcement rose, "Mrs. Agnes McMillan, please come to Gate Eight."

Yezi pushed a cart with her luggage toward the exit gate. She was relieved when she spotted her grandmother, then surprised that she was wearing a bright red dress. Agnes rushed toward Yezi and immediately pulled her into her arms. "How was your flight? I am so happy you are here!"

Yezi nodded, feeling warm and happy. *I'm not alone. I have Grandma!* She touched her grandmother's burgundy silk scarf and buried her face in her grandmother's neck, catching the subtle aroma of lilacs. "I almost didn't recognize you, Grandma."

"Because of my dress?" Agnes chuckled, seeming to know what Yezi thought. "We old women like to wear colourful clothes, so we can feel young again."

Raising her head to look around, Yezi noticed that quite a few of the older people milling around were wearing colourful clothes. *Things are different here,* Yezi thought. Most of the older people in China only wore dark or gray clothes. She could scarcely imagine Yao in a brightly-coloured dress.

Agnes led Yezi to her car and helped Yezi put her luggage in the trunk. Wondering how her grandmother got the key from the driver, Yezi followed her to the passenger's side. Agnes opened the door. "Hop in, sweetie."

She hesitated. "Where are you going to sit?"

"You'll see." Agnes closed the car, walked past the front end and slid into the driver's seat. Yezi gasped as Agnes started the car. She could not help but exclaim, "Oh my, you're the driver!" Yezi's eyes widened. She had never thought her grandmother could drive a car!

As the car turned onto the freeway and zipped along, co-lourful ads, street signs, telephone poles and tall trees rushed by them. The cars around her formed glittery lines stretching to the end of the freeway. They exited the freeway and made their way through the city streets. Agnes finally turned into the driveway of a two-storey house and parked the car in front of the garage.

"Here we are," Agnes said, turning to Yezi, whose face had suddenly become white. "Are you all right?"

"I ... feel ... sick." Yezi opened the door and stumbled out of the car.

"Take deep breaths. I think you must be carsick," Agnes said, slowly taking Yezi by hand. "Come and sit here. You'll feel better in a minute." She led Yezi to a patio chair on the veranda.

Yezi plopped down, breathing deeply, her eyes absorbing the huge spruce tree in the centre of the front yard, surrounded by delicate pink and white mayflowers. Elegant rows of irises and daffodils lined the driveway. At sunset, everything looked shiny; the scent of honeysuckle drifted along with the breeze. "Such a nice garden," Yezi murmured.

"Would you like a drink? I have apple cider, fruit punch and grapefruit juice."

Yezi did not know what to choose. "I'll have whatever you are having."

"Okay." Agnes entered the house and returned with two glasses of grapefruit juice.

Yezi took one and slowly sipped from her glass.

"How do you like it?" asked Agnes.

"It is a little bitter."

"Grapefruit is good for blood pressure. That is why I drink it. Next time we will have the cider, it's sweeter."

Suddenly a black squirrel jumped from a branch low in the spruce tree and landed on the railing. Hand shaking, Yezi tilted her glass, spilling the juice. She screeched, "Did the squirrel get away from a zoo?"

"Oh, no. It lives here, in my trees. Here, squirrels are everywhere."

"I have only seen squirrels in picture books." Yezi watched the squirrel pat its head with its paws, her eyes gleaming with delight. "It's washing its face!"

"Do you like animals? I'll take you to the Franklin Park Zoo later."

Yezi nodded. "Is the zoo large?"

"Oh yes. There are about two hundred different species there. The zoo's more than sixty years old," explained Agnes. "We will definitely go. But now, let's have supper. And then you need to rest from your long flight."

"Okay," said Yezi, following her grandmother into the house.

Agnes motioned for her to sit at the table in the kitchen while she opened the refrigerator and took out a package. "I have Chinese won tons for you."

"Did you make them?" Yezi was surprised again.

"No, I bought them in Chinatown," Agnes spoke slowly, removing the lid of a round porcelain cookie jar and placing it in front of Yezi. "And look, here are some Chinese treats."

"Oh," Yezi said, peering inside. "Fried broad beans. China

... town?" She repeated the word in two parts, trying to understand it. "Yes, they have all kinds of Chinese food."

Yezi held the jar and pointed at the won tons. "Please do not buy these just for me. I like bread and milk. I'll eat your food."

"Well, let's eat this for now. Tomorrow you'll have American food." Laughing, she added, "And by the way, we eat more things than just bread and milk!"

After supper, Agnes showed Yezi around the house and finally to her bedroom. A giant fluffy teddy bear was perched on the bed, inviting her into her new room with an exaggerated smile. Yezi sprang forward and cuddled the bear in her arms. Exhausted, she lay down and promptly fell asleep.

The following morning, Yezi woke as the first sunlight peeked through the window curtains. At first she was puzzled. *Where's Popo Yao and her bed?* A framed painting of horses grazing in meadow on the wall across from her bed reminded her that she was in her grandmother's home. Quickly she got dressed, and then pulled the curtains open. An unfamiliar view appeared outside. Just beyond her grandmother's garden, on a spacious lawn, rows of headstones sat next to one another. *Is it a graveyard?* She rubbed her eyes with the back of her hand. *Why aren't there any mounds?* She remembered once seeing a number of round tombs in Kunming's suburbs, on a stretch of land that appeared to be abandoned; there were no people or houses around for miles. Indeed, the area was surrounded by wild trees and noisy crows. The memory faded and was replaced by a vision of the grave of her brother Dahai. A mound with a wooden marker stood in the wind, on which the words, "Rest in Peace" were carved. Her anxiety melted away. She opened the window. Sunshine poured in, along with the scent of sweet clovers. A new day in her new home had just begun.

Yezi was busy every day, learning the language and experiencing a different life. But eventually, homesickness crept into Yezi's heart. One morning, she decided to write letters to everyone back in China.

August 31, 1979

Dear Mama and Baba,

I've been here for two weeks. Grandma's letter must've reached you before mine. Grandma drives! She's very healthy and takes a long walk almost every day. She's busy even though she's retired. She volunteers a lot at the church and at a volunteer centre.

Grandma has hired a tutor, a university student, to help me with my English. The tutor takes me to parks and shopping centres. She teaches me how to play children's games, how to greet people, and how to ask for directions.

Yesterday, Grandma took me to a public school in the neighbourhood. We met with the principal and handed in my school report. In September, which is next week, I'll join the seventh grade.

Is there any news about Baba's job? When will he transfer back to Kunming?

Is Sang still very busy at the university? I hope he can come to America someday. Will you tell him that I miss him?

I'll write a letter to Popo Yao, please read it to her.

Your loving daughter, Yezi.

Yezi wrote a second letter.

Dear Popo Yao,

How're you doing? I'm missing you a lot. Grandma likes the dresses you made for me.

There's Chinese food in Chinatown, but I'm learning to eat American food. Besides milk and bread, there're pizza, pancakes, hamburgers, and Kentucky fried chicken. I'm sure you would like Kentucky fried chicken and French fries.

Forever yours, Yezi.

She also wrote to Jian telling her about the places she had visited and what she had seen in Boston. She ended the letter like this: "You asked me to find out if the moon is rounder in the United States. Jian, I'm not sure about the moon's shape, but it seems brighter here. By the way, have you been accepted to a top notch junior high school?"

She finished the three letters before lunchtime. In the kitchen, Agnes mixed canned tuna with mayonnaise. Yezi watched her grandmother making sandwiches. *It's easy. Soon I'll make them by myself*, she thought.

After lunch, Yezi drew a rectangle on a piece of paper and showed it to her grandmother. "Can I get this thing to put my letters in?"

Agnes chuckled and gave her several envelopes and also an address label sheet that she pulled out of one of the kitchen drawers. "These are envelopes and these labels have our address."

Yezi happily addressed each of the letters, and carefully placed the address labels on the corners of the envelopes.

"Let's go to a postal office to mail your letters," Agnes said, grabbing her purse as she waited for Yezi to seal the envelopes. Hand in hand, they sauntered out the front door.

21.
KUNG FU MAN

YEZI'S NEW LIFE WAS LIKE a kaleidoscope tube. Each time she looked into it, it would display a different complex pattern in various colours and shapes.

School began on September 2, the day after Labour Day. Escorted by her grandmother, Yezi walked the two blocks to a three-storey brick building covered with straggly ivy. At the entrance, Yezi asked her grandmother to return home. "I am okay, Grandma. I can go in by myself." She said she preferred to find the classroom on her own.

Agnes smiled and nodded. "Good girl. Enjoy your first day!"

Yezi climbed the stairs to the second floor and located her classroom. Students were already sitting at desks, chatting. A girl mouthed hello while a boy eyed Yezi skeptically. "Are you one of the boat people? Welcome to class."

Why does he think I came by boat? Surprised by his words, Yezi thought: *It would've taken me a couple of months to get here by boat.* "I came by airplane," she answered, wondering whether they would now refer to her as one of the "plane people."

The girl who had greeted her, tapped the back of the chair next to her. "Come, sit here. Was it more dangerous coming by plane?"

Sitting down, Yezi asked, "Why would it be dangerous?"

"People might shoot it down," replied the boy, hooking his

finger as if he were about to pull a trigger. "But how did you find an airplane? Most people escaped by boat."

"Why would people shoot at the plane?" asked Yezi, her puzzled eyes searching the boy's face for an answer.

Another boy had been listening. He suddenly piped up, "Aren't you from Vietnam?"

"No, why?" Yezi stared at him.

"Don't get me wrong." Shaking his head at Yezi, he chuckled at the assumptions his classmates had made. "You guys messed up. She isn't one of the boat people. She isn't even Vietnamese. That's why she got here by plane." He turned to Yezi and asked, "Where are you from, anyway?"

Before Yezi could reply, the bell rang, and more students entered the room. A blonde woman, wearing a pale green dress, walked to a wide desk in front of the blackboard.

"That's Ms. Shaw, our English teacher," the girl told Yezi.

"Welcome back to school!" The teacher scanned the class, a happy smile on her face. "I hope everybody had a good summer." Noticing the new girl, she walked over to Yezi, asked her name, and then introduced her to the class.

"If any of you are interested in China, ask Yezi." Ms. Shaw eyed the class. "Meanwhile give her a hand whenever she needs help, will you?"

What does 'give her a hand' mean? Yezi struggled to understand the logic of the teacher's words.

The teacher strolled back to the front desk. "For our first English lesson, I'd like you to write a story about your summer. First discuss it with someone next to you. Then write it on your own."

Yezi expected the teacher to explain the assignment in more detail, or read the class something from a textbook, but she did not. Instead, the students around her began talking with each other. "I love your name," said the girl sitting next to Yezi. She sported a long ponytail, and her hair was the colour of honey. "What does your name mean?"

"Leaf," Yezi said.

"Nice. It reminds me of summer. I had lots of fun this past summer."

Uncertain what she should say about her summer, Yezi responded anxiously, "What kind of story does Ms. Shaw want?" She was eager to know the teacher's expectations.

"Write whatever you like." The pony-tailed girl winked at her. "Do you have a boy friend?"

Startled, Yezi flushed. She shook her head, embarrassed.

"I'm going to write about my trip to Cape Cod with my folks." The girl opened her binder. Pencil in hand, she doodled on the corner of a page. "Did you go anywhere with your folks in the summer?"

"No, oh, yes. I came to Boston." She remembered looking out at the clouds through her window on the airplane. She imagined herself a swallow gliding effortlessly through the air. It would never again be like the time she dreamed she was a baby swallow being chased and not knowing where to go. This time, she was a free swallow, flying in a boundless sky.

"Okay, that's your story. I'm going to start writing mine." The girl began scribbling.

Yezi stared at a blank page in her own binder, as if her mind's eye were searching for an expansive scene in the emptiness. Ms. Shaw stopped in front of her desk, rescuing her from the void. "Follow me," she said, motioning Yezi to a chair next to the teacher's table. "Tell me anything about your summer in China." Ms. Shaw spoke slowly, smiling widely to encourage her. "Don't worry about writing."

As Yezi relaxed, memories flooded her mind: the plane ride from Shangai; arriving at Logan International Airport; her first hamburger. Yezi had trouble finding the right words to express herself clearly, but Ms. Shaw listened to her with interest.

Ms. Shaw told Yezi her task in the next period was to listen as others read their stories. Then she could write about one of the stories she had enjoyed the most when at home.

During the second period, Yezi had her binder open, ready to take notes. The first reader told about her experience playing in a swimming pool. The second one had a camping story. The third talked about a family trip to the seaside. One by one, twenty-five other students shared their stories. Yezi had a hard time following them, but she caught some episodes and discovered a buoyant tone in most of her classmates' stories. Listening, she thought that maybe some day she too would be able to tell stories like these.

For her homework, Yezi wrote about one girl's dog, even though she herself was afraid of dogs. Yezi could visualize the desperate, missing pet wandering for two days. Like a lost child wanting to get back to his or her mother, the dog strove to find his way home. At the end, Yezi mentioned that she did not understand why the girl had let the dog sleep on her bed, since bugs on the dog could have infected her.

Like a salmon smolt on its long journey to the ocean, Yezi dove into her new waters, and worked hard to catch up to her fellow students. In her spare time, she read books from her grandmother's shelves. Sometimes, with her grandmother, she went to the local library where she enjoyed immersing herself in a sea of magazines and books. Meanwhile, Agnes pored over various encyclopaedias, equipping herself with enough knowledge to answer Yezi's many questions.

A month later, Yezi received a thick envelope from her parents, which had letters also from Yao and Jian. Her father's case had been reviewed along with other branded "rightists" across the country; as a result of his rehabilitation, he would be allowed to return to Kunming at the beginning of the year. Her parents mentioned their appreciation for the Central Party's new policy that would help them reconstruct their life. Puzzled by their attitudes, Yezi thought they should feel angry about how they had been mistreated and incarcerated as anti-revolutionaries. She wondered who should be blamed for all those wronged cases. Yezi was glad to know her mother was taking some Chinese traditional medicine for her headaches, and that it had reduced some of the pain. Yao's letter, written by Jian, simply mentioned that she was content to hear about Yezi's new adventures, and hoped she still remembered the Chinese language. Jian wrote briefly about her hectic life at junior high school, where everybody went crazy with their studies and competed to earn higher grades.

One day, in music class, a male teacher, Mr. Tice, played the piano while the students sang "All in the Golden Afternoon" from the movie, *Alice in Wonderland*. The movie had delighted Yezi when she watched it with her grandmother. And now she sang along: "*Little bread and butterflies kiss the tulips / And the sun is like a toy balloon....*"

Suddenly, Kevin, a skinny boy sitting next to her cried out, "Ouch!" Yezi tilted her head and noticed a taller and seemingly fearless boy named Aaron, stabbing Kevin in the back with a pen. She stared at the annoying Aaron, who smirked back at her.

The class, unaware of the attack in their midst, continued to sing: "*There are dizzy daffodils on the hillside / Strings of violets are all in tune....*"

Aaron flung his pen at Kevin, who jumped up from his seat. With his hands on his head, Kevin ran toward the front of the room. Yezi turned and glared at the attacker, her tone firm, "Stop it!" Aaron did not say anything but grabbed another pen and this time threw it at her. Yezi ducked, then picked up an eraser from her own case and tossed it in his face. She had fought with Tao. This boy did not frighten her much. A girl shrieked as Aaron jerked out of his seat and fell to the floor.

The singing halted, and the entire class fell silent. Mr. Tice walked over to Yezi. His eyes flashed behind his glasses. "What's going on here?"

"Aaron bullied me!" skinny Kevin responded from a corner of the classroom.

"Aaron started it first," reported a girl.

Another girl said, "Yezi hit Aaron with something."

The teacher turned to Yezi. "What do you have to say for yourself?"

"I didn't—" Gaping at the teacher's thin moustache and shoulder-length hair, Yezi hesitated and wondered if she should express her true feelings; her grandmother had said that telling the truth was important. Finally she mumbled, "I can't be quite sure if you're a man or woman."

Muffled giggles spread through the class.

Mr. Tice glanced at his watch. "Aaron, Yezi and Kevin, go to the principal's office right now." He returned to the piano and spread out his arms. "Let's carry on."

Since that incident, Yezi had become quite popular for daring to face up to Aaron, the class bully. Several students befriended her and some invited her to join in their games, checkers at lunch, dodge ball on the playground, and Dungeons & Dragons on the weekend.

Helen, a student from another class, approached Yezi during the afternoon break. Her spiky, red hair looked like porcupine's quills. Helen begged Yezi for help with Chinese numbers. In exchange, she would help Yezi learn American songs and what was trendy. They began spending more and more time together and often strolled around the playground together.

One day, Yezi could not help but ask, "Can you tell me what your hair style is?"

"Punk. Do you like it?" Helen took Yezi's hand, "You can touch it."

Yezi pinched a stiff strand. "How does it stand up like that? It must be hard to do."

"It's easy. You use hair gel to hold it."

"What does 'punk' mean?"

"New music and fashion. I like new things."

"Aren't you afraid of what people will say or think about you?"

"Why should I? This is a free country. You can do what you want as long as you don't break the law." Helen asked Yezi, "Hey, do you still remember that song I taught you?"

"The one by the Free Rocks?" asked Yezi. "Yes! Listen!" She began chanting, "*I've got a mind of my own / I'm listening to no one...*"

Helen joined in, "*I wanna laugh out loud / Oh, yeah. I'm not afraid of Mao.*"

"I was afraid of Mao!" Yezi giggled. She asked Helen how the Free Rocks knew about Mao. Helen said punk musicians knew everything.

One Friday, at lunchtime, Helen pulled Yezi aside. "Do you have any plans for after school?"

"No. Why?"

"Let's go to Chinatown!" Helen exclaimed. "Let's find a Kung Fu man."

"What's a Kung Fu man?? And why do you need to find one?"

"Have you heard of Bruce Lee?"

"No." Yezi shook her head. "What about him?"

"He's a great Kung Fu man. I want to learn Kung Fu and jump on walls, just like he does. You need to see one of his movies." Helen leaped up and down, her spiked up hair glinting in the sun.

"Once I saw people break bricks with their hands." Yezi mimicked Helen, her skirt swinging back and forth as she too leapt up and down. "Okay, let's go find a Kung Fu man, but I must phone my grandmother first." Yezi had ten dollars tucked into her pocket that her grandmother had given for emergencies. She thought it would be more than enough for this unexpected after school trip.

When classes ended, they got on the bus that headed downtown, and then boarded the subway. They sat close together, knapsacks on their laps, staring at the crowds that got on and

off. Half an hour later, they were in Chinatown. Helen told
Yezi that Boston Common, the park, was near Chinatown.
Her parents used to take her to play there. She would point it
out to Yezi. From the subway station, Helen led Yezi through
the bustling Tremont Street and turned left into Oak Street. A
Chinese archway rose above them. People strolled under it; a
number of children played around it.

Helen pointed to the top of the archway. "Can you read
those words?"

"Sure," Yezi gazed at the characters. "*Li, Yi, Lian* and
Chi."

"What do they mean?"

Clasping her hands together and wrinkling her brow, Yezi tried
to translate their meaning. She was about to answer Helen's
question when an elderly Chinese man beside them came to
her rescue. "They mean courtesy, good manners, justice and
uprightness."

"Thank you," Helen said. As she walked to the back of the
archway, she gazed up at the characters on the other side.
"What about those words?"

The old man answered, "Serve the world as your duty."

"It sounds like something President George Washington once
said," replied Helen.

"It's a saying of Sun Yat-sen!" The elderly man stroked his
chin, his face lighting up. "He was the president of the Re-
public of China."

Both of the girls giggled and thanked him for his help. Then,
Yezi noticed a person sitting cross-legged at the foot of the
archway. A tin can with some change inside it lay in front of
the man, whose eyes wandered aimlessly around the street. *A
beggar?* Eyes widening, Yezi was surprised to find that poor
people also lived in the United States.

Helen fished two quarters out of her pocket and dropped
them into the can. The clink drew the homeless person's eyes
back from their roaming. "Thank you, Miss."

Yezi squatted beside the man. "Where is your home?"

"I don't have one any more." The man shook his head, his scraggly brown beard hiding the shy smile behind it.

"Why not?" She gazed at him with concern. To her, everybody had a home, even it was a tiny cluttered shelter that housed many family members.

"I lost it," the man said, looking away.

Yezi placed a dollar in the can. "Will you get it back someday?"

"Don't know." The homeless man tapped on the can with his fingers. "God bless you."

Yezi was touched by his words. Those words had always made her feel better. *I was lucky to have Popo Yao when my folks were sent away from us.* Yezi stood up and ran to catch up with Helen. Turning left onto Hudson Street, they peered into all the shop windows they passed, but did not spot anyone resembling a Kung Fu man. Many people streamed in and out of the stores, shopping bags dangling from their hands, looked like they might be Chinese. Yezi strained to hear what they were saying, but she could not understand most of them. They were not speaking in the Kunming dialect or Mandarin. Yezi and Helen strolled along several other streets in Chinatown, but still did not discover a single sign related to Kung Fu. Instead, the different aromas wafting from the restaurants and the inviting pictures of mouth-watering dishes advertised in their windows made them suddenly realize how hungry there were. They decided to get something to eat and entered a cozy diner. Yezi ordered rice noodles in chicken soup. Helen asked for fried rice with beef.

Satisfied after their meal, they entered a nearby jewellery store. Jade-coloured stones, amber-like bracelets, luminous earrings and glassy necklaces glistened under the store's harsh, interior light. Helen could not believe her eyes when she saw the prices. "They're so cheap," she told Yezi, who had no clue about jewellery or its prices. Fingering the smooth surfaces of the elegant items, Yezi eyed their glimmering colours and delicate shapes, but did not know what to buy. Finally, Helen purchased a silvery bracelet and green necklace for $1.98. Under Helen's suggestion, Yezi selected a stone with the picture of a horse, her zodiac sign, and a glass paperweight for her grandmother, for which she also paid $1.98.

The two girls continued to amble down the sidewalks under the light of lampposts. At a store window they paused to watch some colourful tropical fish swimming lazily in a big tank. Yezi noticed a man reflected in the glass; she had seen the same man somewhere before. She suddenly felt uneasy. She tugged at a corner of Helen's blouse. "I think that guy in the black T-shirt is following us."

"How do you know?"

"I remember now. I saw him when we went into the jewellery store. He came into the store after us. Now he's hanging around at the corner." Yao's anxious warnings about being kidnapping came to Yezi's mind.

"Let's find a crowded restaurant and lose him there," Helen said, taking Yezi's hand in hers.

They rushed across the road and merged into a crowd in front of Penang, a Chinese-Malaysian chophouse on Washington Street. When Yezi turned her head, her eyes sweeping the street, she spotted the same man crossing the road. "He's still after us," her voice quavered. In a panic, she dragged Helen into the dining hall, and they headed upstairs.

On the second floor, they reached a spacious room crowded with diners around the tables. Their loud conversations bounced off the walls as light blended with the hazy steam of hot dishes. A waitress guided them to a corner table for two and handed them menus. Yezi took a deep breath as she scanned the menu; most of the dishes cost more than $2 each. She did not have much left from her emergency money. Turning to the dessert page, she pointed to the Egg Tart. "This one, please." Helen ordered a cup of iced tea. The waitress stared at them with a twisted mouth. "That's all?" They bobbed their heads and looked knowingly at one another.

Though momentarily at ease, they still faced the problem of how to return home safely since they did not have enough money to take a taxi. Helen decided that the only thing to do was to ask her parents for help and went to a phone booth to call them.

Helen returned to the table where their orders sat and leaned toward Yezi. "My dad's coming to pick us up." It was hard to hear because of the buzzing conversations around them.

Yezi raised her voice. "What should we do if the guy comes in here?"

"We'll call the police." Helen's firm voice helped Yezi relax, but she still craned her neck every few moments to check the entrance of the restaurant, in case their stalker attempted to sneak in. It was 9:00 p.m. when Helen's father arrived at the restaurant to take them home. Yezi was not accustomed to being out this late. It was now dark out. At the door, Yezi peered anxiously up and down the street to see if the man might still be loitering around. The breeze had turned chilly, and the street had emptied. There were only a few pedestrians hurrying away. Yezi was not curious about Chinatown any more.

Yezi was relieved when she finally got home. Her grandmother was waiting for her in the living room. Book in hand, Agnes sat in an armchair, reading under the table lamp. Swallowing hard, Yezi felt guilty. "Grandma!"

Agnes laid the book on the end table. "You're back finally." Then she lifted the telephone and dialled a number. "Nancy, she's back. Thanks for waiting." It panged Yezi to see the worry in her grandmother's eyes.

"Sorry to keep you up so late." Yezi took the paperweight out of her pocket as she ran toward Agnes, her heart pounding. "This is for you."

Agnes reached up, took the glass ball and admired the shiny fish and water weeds at its the centre. "I got your message,

Yezi, but I really didn't expect you to stay out so late." There was a slight tremor in Agnes's hands, her voice soft but firm. "If you hadn't shown up by ten, my friends and I would have gone to Chinatown to search for you."

Agnes talked to her about several cases of missing children and teenagers she had read about in the newspaper, and stressed how important it was that she be careful, and that Agnes always know where she was, and who she was with. "Once you realized that it had gotten late," Agnes said, "you should have phoned me to let me know where you were and when you'd be home."

The shadowy image of the man in the black T-shirt that had followed them flashed through Yezi's mind and made her shiver. Yezi told her grandmother about her afternoon and evening, but skipped the episode of being followed to avoid worrying her grandmother any further. The adventure in Chinatown was over. Yezi promised her grandmother that she would always phone to let her know where she was and if she was going to be late.

22.
A SKELETON FOR CHRISTMAS

TWO WEEKS BEFORE CHRISTMAS, AGNES opened a box of decorations that she had brought down from the attic. Yezi helped her pick a spruce tree from the local market, which they brought home and set up in the living room. Together, they opened the box of decorations and pulled out all the ornaments that Agnes had collected over the years.

Picking out a tiny human figure from a box, Yezi exclaimed, "Oh, I like this one best!"

"That drummer was your mother's favourite, too," Agnes said, as she turned toward Yezi. "Did she tell you about it?"

"Never. Mama never said anything about Christmas." Yezi's fingertips ran over the miniature ornament. "But once I read a story called '*A Little Match Girl.*'"

"Was it in English?"

"No. I borrowed a Chinese version from Jian. I didn't know I had a Grandma then. Now I'm with you for Christmas!" She smiled gleefully as she wrapped herself around her grandmother's arm.

"Wait a second." Agnes hurried back to her room and returned with another box. Removing the cover, she carefully sorted out several postcards and displayed them on the table. "Tell me which one you like the best."

Yezi carefully examined all the postcards. They were all of paintings in different galleries. She singled out one that had an image of a man, his own hands squeezing the sides of his face:

"Scream" by Edvard Munch. "This one for sure," she said, holding the card up to the light so that she could examine it in more detail. Yezi wondered why she enjoyed that painting in particular. *The man's gawking eyes and gaping mouth are funny. Maybe I like the dark running river. Maybe I like the floating red-orange clouds.*

"You *are* your mother's daughter!" Agnes chuckled. "You didn't even spend enough time with her to—" She paused suddenly, her eyes misting over.

"Did Mama like that picture, too?"

"Yes, honey, she did. You are like two peas in a pod." She turned back toward the tree, and the box of ornaments, to hide the tears threatening to spill.

As she placed another ornament on the tree, she added, "By the way, your Aunt Dora and her family will also be here with us on Christmas."

"That's awesome," Yezi said, proud of the new words in English she had learned from her friends over the past months. Dora was Meihua's half-sister. Her mother had only mentioned her once, but Agnes had shown Yezi photographs of Dora with her husband and two children after she'd arrived in Boston. "How long does it take them to get here from Maine?"

"Six or seven hours."

Yezi was thoughtful for a moment. Thinking about meeting her mother's sister led her to think about her grandfather, Mei, her mother's birth father.

"Grandma, can you tell me about my grandfather?"

"Which one?"

"My mother's father. In China. The one who disappeared. The one my mother hasn't been able to find."

Gazing into the distance, Agnes answered slowly, "When you grow a little bit older, I'll let you read my journals. I wrote in them while I was in China. That was more than fifty years ago."

"Your diary's older than Mama!" Yezi exclaimed.

Agnes muttered with a softened voice, "Yes, it's my very old secret."

On the last day before the Christmas break, Yezi and Helen sauntered around the neighbourhood to admire the festive decorations. Yezi loved the twinkling, multicoloured lights on all the trees, the displays of reindeer pulling Santa's sleighs; the red, pink and cream-coloured poinsettias that dotted porches; and the nativity scene: baby Jesus nestled in a crib, his mother, Mary, kneeling by him, her gaze lovingly fixed on her child. Yezi had never seen anything like this. The colourful lights and decorations were like splashes of colour painted on the glittering white snow that blanketed the streets and the gardens in her neighbourhood. Yezi could hear music drifting through the lit houses on her grandmother's street. Of all the Christmas carols she had learned, Yezi cherished "The Twelve Days of Christmas" the most. Joining Helen, she would hum along, *"Twelve lords a-leaping, eleven ladies dancing, ten pipers piping..."* until she had to pause for breath.

Finally they wished each other happy holidays and headed home.

Aunt Dora and her family arrived on Christmas Eve. Dora hugged Agnes, and then Yezi. "You really look like Flora. Does your mom's Chinese name mean 'Mayflora?'"

"Her name has a double meaning," Yezi explained. "Mei in Chinese can mean 'beautiful' or 'America.' 'Hua' sounds like the word for 'flower' and is also the word for 'China.' So Mama's name means either 'beautiful flower' or 'America and China.'"

Aunt Dora was amazed. "My God. Chinese is such a complicated language. What does 'Yezi' mean?"

"Leaf," Yezi said.

"The daughter is a leaf. The mom is a flower." Aunt Dora laughed.

Uncle Marvin shook hands with Yezi. "I know two words:

ni hao, which I think means 'how do you do'? Is that right?"
He edged a child of nine forward and introduced him to Yezi.
"This is our son, Ralph."

Yezi led Ralph to the couch and brought several picture
books over to show him. "Where's your sister?"

"She went to visit her boyfriend's family," answered Ralph,
staring at Yezi. "She's older than me, so my parents let her
go." He looked puzzled. "You don't look Chinese."

"Why?"

"You don't have slanted eyes," the boy raised his voice.

Yezi chuckled. "I've only seen slanted-eyed Chinese people
in ancient stories." Disappointed, Ralph made a face.

Everybody went to midnight mass that evening. A fresh layer
of snow covered the church steps when they left the service.

On Christmas day, the family spent the morning opening
the gifts under the Christmas tree. Yezi opened more presents
than ever before in her life. Her hands were busy untying
shiny ribbons and tearing off colourful wrapping paper. Yezi
received a sweater with a deer pattern, a tan suede skirt, a
pink scarf with matching gloves, tapes of popular music, and
several books. One box wrapped in glimmering green paper
came from Ralph, but he asked her not to open it until later.
Everybody thanked Yezi for her gifts. She was delighted that
they liked her gifts. She had ordered something for each of
them from one of her favourite mail-order catalogues. For a
moment, she wondered what her parents were doing. It saddened her that Christmas was not celebrated in China. *It's
their Tuesday evening now. My parents should be at home.
Sang may be in class at his university. What is Popo Yao doing? Dozing in front of the TV?* Yezi sighed. She would have
liked to share this day with them.

Yezi enjoyed the roast turkey with cranberry sauce, and the
mashed potatoes and gravy they feasted on for Christmas dinner. The steamed turnips, roasted sweet potatoes and blanched
beans were not as inviting but once she tasted them, she thought

they were perfect.

When the adults settled to watch television that evening, it came time for Yezi to open Ralph's gift. She removed the shiny green wrapping paper and uncovered a rectangular box that featured a hand-painted a skull on the lid. Ralph grinned at her.

Eager to know what was in the box, Yezi quickly lifted the lid. Inside was something shaped like a human figure. *Is it a doll?* Peeling away the white tissue paper, Yezi caught sight of the skull of a mini skeleton; it had two deep, dark holes for eyes and shiny white teeth in its large mouth. Shocked, she dropped the skeleton on the coffee table.

Ralph laughed and picked it up. He waved it in front of her face, making the skeleton perform a funny dance. "It's my favourite,"he said as he passed it to Yezi. "Hold it. You'll get to like it. I've heard the Chinese have lots of ghost stories."

Ashamed of showing her fear, Yezi smiled. Gingerly cradling the skeleton in one of her arms, she asked politely, "How do you know the Chinese have ghost stories?"

"I've read some." Tilting his head, Ralph smirked. "Can you tell me one?"

"Do American kids like skeletons?" Yezi asked. When she pinched the skeleton's ribs, she could tell it was made of plastic.

"I don't know. But I like them." Ralph lowered his voice, "Guess what I want most." Before Yezi could respond, he said, "I want my dad's skull!"

"What?" Yezi gasped, not sure whether she had heard him correctly. "How?"

"I'll keep it after he dies. That's it."

"Why?" She stared at his face to see whether he was joking.

Ralph laughed hysterically. "What do you like best?" he asked.

Yezi shook her head. "I'm not sure." She thanked Ralph for

his surprising gift and asked him to tell her one of the Chinese ghost stories that he had read. Ralph's story was about twelve-year-old Bocai, who worked as a maid for Furen, and his wife, Pangpo. She had to scrub the floor, clean the tables, chairs and dishes, and do the family's laundry every day, but the couple never gave her enough food to eat. So, Bocai got sick and died. After she died, Furen and Pangpo started hearing a little girl crying in their bedroom each midnight, but they had found no one. Night after night, the girl's cries kept them awake. Finally, Pangpo figured out it was Bocai's ghost, so she placed a plate full of fruit at the door of their bedroom every day. After that the couple finally got some peace and quiet.

In exchange, Yezi told him about Yuanmou Man and how she dug for his bones on her visit to Popo Yao's village. Thinking about Popo Yao made her throat tighten. She suddenly realized how much she missed her, and how she longed to sit next to her and eat some of her noodles.

Ralph was intrigued by Yuanmou Man and asked her many questions about them. "I'll go there digging with you if you still want to do it," Ralph said.

Aunt Dora and her family returned home the following day. They invited Agnes and Yezi to visit them. Dora wanted Yezi to meet Ralph's sister, Brenda. Agnes promised that they would visit sometime soon.

Every year, Agnes celebrated New Year's Eve at the community centre. On the last day of 1979, she spent hours cooking her version of Boston's famous clam chowder. In the late after-noon, she and Yezi took the large pot of soup to the potluck that was being held at the centre. When they entered the hall, they were greeted by a large banner hanging over the stage that read, "Happy New Year!" A band was playing onstage, filling the hall with joyful music. Yezi's feet began moving with the rhythm of the music as her eyes lingered on the rain-bow coloured streamers that criss-crossed the ceiling, and the bunches of red and green balloons that bobbed lazily from the chairs and tables that filled the room. They approached a row of tables set with prepared dishes. Agnes laid her pot of clam chowder among them. An elderly woman dressed in red came over to greet them and asked, "Is this your granddaughter, Agnes? From China?"

Agnes nodded and turned to Yezi, "This is my old friend, Nancy. She's also your mother's godmother."

Yezi shyly greeted the woman, wondering if she had been close to her mother.

Nancy said, "It's nice that you are here with your grand-mother. Enjoy the party."

The room was full of people eating, and drinking, talking and singing, while children of all ages laughed and played around them. Yezi tried every single dish on the buffet until she was stuffed. Agnes and her friends sat around their tables and laughed and talked about almost everything. Yezi decided she needed to stretch her legs, so she ambled toward the band that played in front of the stage.

A girl who looked to be about the same age as Yezi joined her. "Hi, I'm Kay. I heard you are from China."

"Yes," Yezi replied. "My name's Yezi."

"Do you live with that old lady?" Kay pointed to Yezi's grandmother.

"Yes, why?"

"Did she buy— I mean did she pay for you?"

"I don't understand what you mean."

Kay tried to find the right words. "Well, about eight years ago, each student at my school was asked to donate whatever money we could, so we could save starving kids in China."

"Did you save any?"

"Yeah, I paid five bucks for a kid. Next time, I'll show you a photo of my girl. She should be about our age now."

"That woman didn't buy my photo. She's my grandmother," Yezi said.

Embarrassed, Kay asked, "Where are your parents?"

"In China."

"You must miss them." With a look of chagrin on her face, Kay took Yezi's hand and said, "Come and join us."

Yezi smiled, and they scurried over to a group of young teenagers who were blowing paper whistles. Their cheers mingled with the laughter and high-pitched sounds of the younger children.

Kay placed a red, cone-shaped paper hat on Yezi's head while another girl with a painted face grabbed a handful of glittery strips of foil and draped them over Yezi's shoulders and hair.

Soon it was time for the countdown. The entire crowd chanted in unison, "Ten! Nine! Eight—" At the last stroke of midnight, Yezi and the other children hugged one another and then blew their paper whistles riotously. Yezi's eyes searched for her grandmother in the crowd. She spotted her across the room, and waved to her with a smile on her face that went from ear to ear. At that moment almost everyone in the room started singing:

> For auld lang syne, my dear
> For auld lang syne,
> We'll take a cup o kindness yet,
> For auld lang syne.

Yezi closed her eyes and listened carefully to the words. The warm atmosphere and enthusiastic and friendly crowd in the colourful hall was forming a memorable complex in her kaleidoscope. And she was a part of it.

23.
UMBRELLA-SHAPED ELM

YEZI LIKED LIVING IN BOSTON. She enjoyed the fact that there were less restrictions and more leisure time in America than in China. Yezi had finally caught up with her classmates and was comfortable at school. Now, at the age of fourteen, she loved going to parties with her friends and dressing up in nice clothes and wearing shiny jewellery. She was no longer the girl who had decided not to wear a pretty dress because she was afraid of gossip. Shopping had also become her favourite activity.

She had also recently discovered that in America you could also shop from home. One afternoon, she flipped through a bunch of mail order catalogues that were regularly delivered to her grandmother's house and decided to pamper herself from head to toe. She chose items from the catalogues that she could afford with the allowance her grandmother gave her. All she had to do was fill out the order form and write out a cheque from the account her grandmother had recently opened for her. Several weeks later, a package of bobby pins and multicoloured hair bands arrived, followed by another parcel of white cotton socks trimmed with pink lace.

When the third parcel arrived, she was particularly excited. She whisked it into her bedroom, closed the door, and grabbed a pair of scissors to cut away the packaging. Inside were bottles and jars of Silky Vitamin E Face Cream, Goat Milk Hand Lotion, Lavender Cream for dry feet, and lipsticks and nail

212 ZOË S. ROY

polishes in a variety of colours. Jars of anti-aging face cream and wrinkle-reducing eye cream were also enclosed. These were for her grandmother, so she placed them on the shelf. Then she opened the other tubes and jars one by one, sniffing them and trying them on her skin. Yezi imagined how amazed her friends would be when she showed up at the next party smelling like tea roses and wearing red nail polish and lipstick. She forgot all about the time until she heard her grandmother call her downstairs for supper.

She brought the anti-aging and wrinkle-reducing creams with her into the kitchen. "Grandma, I think you'll like these."

At the dining table, her grandmother looked at the labels and smiled. "Thank you, Yezi. These are lovely. Hopefully they will make me look much younger."

"You think so? You are so beautiful anyway!"

"Well, all I wish for now is to watch you grow up," Agnes said.

"I am growing up, Grandma." Yezi smiled and began eating. "I can manage things by myself. I know how to order stuff."

"Did you order them by mail?" Agnes pointed to the cream jars.

"Yes. I got lots of stuff for myself, too." Yezi looked up at Agnes's concerned eyes. "Are you worried about something?"

Agnes turned her gaze to Yezi. "It's nothing, Yezi. I am happy to see you adapting to American life." She sipped from her bowl of chicken soup and added, "It's already November. I just hope that your parents have been able to get their visas by now."

Even though Agnes knew that foreign policy had been improving in China since the United States and China formally established embassies with each other in 1979, she was afraid that Meihua and Lon would not be permitted to visit the United States.

"Don't worry. We will soon hear from them." Yezi glanced

at the clock on the wall. "Hey, it's six o'clock. Time for Bugs Bunny." She carried her plate into the living room and turned on the television. Her grandmother did not mind if she ate her dinner in front of the TV. She sank into the couch and smiled at the cartoon characters that flickered across the screen.

Three months later, on a brisk, cold February evening in 1981, Yezi's parents, Meihua and Lon, arrived at Boston's Logan Airport.

As she exited from the gate, Meihua immediately spotted her mother, sister and daughter in the distance, their heads craning to look for her. "Do you see my sister, Dora, next to my mother?" Meihua said excitedly to Lon, gesturing in their direction. "She has reddish hair. When I left home, she was only thirteen years old."

"Well, I can see Yezi, even though she's dressed so strangely. I almost didn't recognize her!" Lon chuckled. He, too, was excited.

Taking two steps in one, Meihua threw herself into her mother's open arms. She whispered, "I'm home!" and buried her face into her mother's shoulder. She felt as if she were a tired hummingbird that had just flown back to its nest.

"Welcome home," Agnes murmured, "I've missed you so much. I am so happy you are finally here." Her face was brimming with tears of happiness. Her daughter had come home at last.

Meihua then turned to embrace Dora, murmuring over and over, "My baby sister, my baby sis...." Meihua laughed as old memories of the two of them running in the backyard, splashing in the bath, and playing games in their room flooded her mind.

Dora stood back, placing her hands on Meihua's shoulders. She was gazing at her so intently, as if to drink her in. "I'm not a child anymore, you know, big sister. I am so happy to see you too."

Lon hugged his daughter, Yezi, who fingered the cuffs of his gray coat. "This looks so different from the style that is popular here."

Her father teased back, "Your hair looks like straggly grass. What happened to it?"

"It's a new style." Wagging her head, she stroked her sleeves. "I'm wearing all the latest fashions. Do you like my gypsy blouse?"

Lon eyed her light blue cotton blouse, which was gathered at the neckline and hem. Little bells hung from the ends of the string at the collar and a geometric pattern was embroidered around the neckline and on the sleeves. He also noticed the makeup on her face and pink polish on her nails. He did not comment, but a look of subtle disapproval appeared on his face. Meihua had noticed the change in Yezi's appearance, too. When she hugged her daughter, "You're taller now," was all she said.

Before entering the car, Meihua scooped snow off the surface of the vehicle, and clenched it gently in her fist. For the past thirty-three years, she had missed the snow she had grown up with. She was elated to hold it in her hand, and tossed it mischievously in the direction of her husband, who laughed with her. Getting into the car, she sat beside Lon who held her cold hand in his, his heart swelling to see his wife so happy. The snow melting in her palm gave Meihua a feeling of freshness, a lightness of heart; the warmth of her husband's hand coursed through her body. She pulled her daughter close and breathed in the sweet scent of her hair.

Meihua recognized the street and visualized the red brick house long before the car turned into the driveway. Looking at the huge spruce tree surrounded by the snow-covered garden, Meihua remembered the times she and Dora would chase butterflies on warm and sunny afternoons. She could see the rows of irises and daffodils that would spring up along the driveway in the sweet month of May. She could even smell the honeysuckle, which permeated in the air in the spring. Home. Sweet home.

Once in the house, Meihua helped her mother set the table for supper while Yezi helped her father carry their luggage into the spare bedroom on the second floor. During supper, Yezi bombarded her parents with questions about Sang, and Popo Yao, and Jian. She was excited to hear all their news. Meihua and Lon laughed as they tried to keep up with Yezi's constant chatter, doing their best to share the events of the past year and a half.

After supper, the adults sat in the living room, talking and catching up on each other's lives. Yezi had gone upstairs to change into a long, red skirt and a purple paisley blouse. She appeared in the doorway of the living room, and said, "Sorry but I've got to go to a friend's party. I'll see you later!" She pulled on her tall black boots at the door, grabbed her winter jacket, and left.

Noticing Lon's scowling face, Agnes handed him a cup of tea. "This is her weekend routine. She'll be back before bed-time."

Meihua, in the rocking chair, comforted Lon. "Children her age enjoy going to parties, being with their friends."

"My daughter is just the same," Dora said. She sat next to Meihua and started asking questions about Deng Xiaoping's reform movement and the wind of change in China. Excited about the questions, Meihua talked about China's reform including the effort to boost foreign trade and Deng's Special Economic Zone along China's southern coastline to attract foreign companies. Dora suggested she give a talk on China at her school if the couple had time to visit Oceanville where she and her family lived. Meanwhile Meihua wanted to know more about how Dora had decided to become a teacher in the small town of Oceanville in Maine, and also about her husband and children. They had so many years to catch up on, it seemed the words couldn't come out fast enough.

Listening to Meihua and Dora talk as though they had never been apart at all, Agnes's mind travelled back over half a century to the time when her daughter was born in this very house. Agnes had named her Mayflora, partly because of the ship, the Mayflower, which symbolized her heritage, and partly because Mei had fathered her baby.

"Do you remember that story you told me about the baby hummingbirds when you picked strawberries in the summer of 1943?" Dora asked, looking into Meihua's eyes. Her eyes still shone with the same passion that Dora remembered seeing in them even as a child.

"Do you mean the birds that ate the strawberries?" Confused, Meihua searched through her memories.

"No, I mean the nest of baby hummingbirds you found at the strawberry farm. Remember? I was about six when you told me about them, and how you fed them to keep them alive."

"Yes, I do remember, now." Meihua said, nodding. "I saw those hummingbirds almost every day when I was picking tea leaves on the military farm." Meihua shook her head, with a look of worry furrowing her brow. She remembered that the Party's Secretary had asked her not to tell the others about her experiences in the labour camp.

"How do you know that?" Puzzled, Meihua looked at Dora. "I have never mentioned that to anybody."

Her words caught Lon's attention. Gesturing for Dora not to pursue the topic, he turned to Meihua and said encouragingly, "Why don't you tell Dora about your new paintings?"

"Yes," Meihua's eyes gleamed. "I have painted quite a few new canvases based on my old memories. In fact, I have one that I would like to give to you." Meihua ran upstairs to find her luggage and returned with a small painting of a teenaged Dora running after her older sister toward a ship at a wharf.

Dora and Agnes admired the painting, and Meihua content-edly told them about the other paintings she had finished since her discharge from the prison camp five years earlier. She had another canvas in her hand, that she was about to show them, that took her back over three decades.

She remembered the first time she went to China. She was standing on Peace Avenue in Chongqing City and looking up at a number affixed to the front door of a hardware store. Mayflora, only twenty-one-year-old, had just arrived from America. She had located the address of her father's parents. Behind an open counter, a middle-aged man in a high-collared, ankle-length black robe nodded to her. "Can I help you with anything? Do you need any kitchenware or household cleaning products?"

Looking at him, Mayflora wondered whether her grandfather, a schoolteacher, had opened the store and whether this was a clerk who worked for him.

Something is strange. She shook her head. "Could you please tell me if the Mei family lives here?" The palm of her hand was damp as she nervously pinched the corner of her blouse. "I've been trying to find a relative and I believe they used to live here."

"No, oh no," the man asked, shaking his head. "The entire street was destroyed during the Japanese bombing in the summer of '41. Most of the residents around here died. I built my store on the rubble six years ago. I guess the family didn't survive." He pointed to an old elm tree at the street corner. "Look. That tree out there still bears the scars of that bombing."

"Thank you," Mayflora said, turning to examine the tree. The sight of the mutilated tree startled her, and she shuddered, suddenly feeling very cold. Part of the trunk looked like smoke-stained stone, smooth and dark. The tree was cracked in two; most of the branches sprouted from its unburned side. It resembled an open umbrella, half of which had been slashed off. The elm was still alive but maimed. Did her father and his family survive the bomb? That was the moment, she real-

ized that her dream of finding her father would be difficult
to fulfill.

The disfigured elm tree had haunted Meihua for years until she
finally decided to paint it. "My favourite painting is this one.
I call it, 'History.'" She turned to Agnes and said, "I thought
you might like it." A young boy sat under the umbrella-shaped
elm, a book in hand. On his book's cover was a tree in full
bloom.

"I do like it," Agnes said. "What inspired you to paint
it?"

Meihua told her. The three decades she had lived in China
now slipped away. Once again Meihua was sitting in the
rocking chair in the living room of her old home. She could
hardly believe she was back in the same place where she had
begun, yet the image of her father remained elusive. She felt
a headache coming on. Her head started spinning, followed
by throbbing and searing pain, then numbness. "Lon, where
are the other paintings?" she asked, her voice barely rising
above a whisper.

"Are you okay?" Lon noticed her face had gone white. The
dampness visible on her forehead was a telltale sign of the
onset of one of her headaches. "I'll get the other paintings
later, Meihua. I think you need to rest."

Dora and Agnes also noticed Meihua's distress. "Mayflora,
Lon is right. You need to rest after such a long flight. We can
look at all your paintings tomorrow." Together, they led Meihua
upstairs, Agnes behind them, consumed with worry.

After the weekend, Dora returned home. She planned to come
back with her family the following weekend. Meihua wanted
to take Lon to the Childs Gallery, which she had missed so
much. She could not wait any longer. She had so many plans
and there were so many things she wanted to see and do during their short one-month visit.

On Monday morning, after getting off the transit at Copley station, Meihua and Lon trudged down the snow covered Boylston Street toward Newbury. The shovelled sidewalk looked like a dark gray scarf splayed over a white blanket. Linking her arm with Lon's, Meihua breathed the frosty air. "You'll get used to walking in the snow. I have missed it."

Lon exhaled; the warm breath from his mouth merged with the chilly air. He smiled back. "I'm enjoying it."

They entered the gallery. The paintings that graced the walls, seemed to welcome them, Meihua thought. She felt as if she were slipping into a fairytale. Her heart pounded fast, so she slowed her pace and breathed deeply. They strolled from hall to hall, lingering over the paintings they liked best

Meihua was struck by a watercolour, "Rhine Castle" by Gertrude Beals Bourne. The painting took her back to the the deck of that steamship so many years ago. She was leaning against the rail, entranced by the hills rearing along the shores of the Yangtze River.

"Are you all right?" Lon whispered beside her, his hand on her arm.

"Did you—" Meihua hesitated. "Oh, I love seeing all these paintings. Look at that house. Does it remind you of anything?" She pointed at the building in the painting.

Lon's eyes lit up. He turned to Meihua and said, "It reminds me of the houses on the mountainside along the Yangtze River."

"Yes. That's what I was thinking. Did we first meet on the ship to Chongqing or in a mountain house?"

"On the ship." Looking at Meihua's misty eyes, he realized she really could not remember where they had met.

"Do you need to sit down?" Lon asked, his mind drifting back to those days in 1948. Lon had been on the same ship as Meihua. He was travelling to his first job in Chongqing after having graduated as an English major from the National Central University in Nanjing. Lon had been standing beside her, also leaning against the rail, admiring the same hills.

"It seems I am reliving the day I met you." She held his hand. "If you're not tired, do you mind if we stay longer?"

"Sure, as long as you like. I'm enjoying this as much as you." Lon stepped toward, gently pulling her closer to him. They paused in front of an oil painting titled "Portrait of an American Clipper Ship." Lon carefully examined the picture; his eyes narrowed, then widened. "It's by Lai Fong!"

Meihua gazed at the fully-blown white sails, her mouth curving into a smile. "Did you recognize his work, or did you read his name on the placard next to the canvas?"

"You've mentioned Lai Fong and his paintings of ships several times. The scene has been stamped indelibly into my head. I think these images, this very painting, must have inspired you on your quest to find your birth father."

"Look at the ship, the blue sky and translucent clouds. You can fantasize about many things." Meihua's eyes wandered over the picture of the vessel painted about a hundred years earlier by the Chinese artist. Lon was right; the painting had been an inspiration.

She remembered the first time she had this painting by Lai Fong. It was in her Grade Nine art class. She hadn't been able to take her eyes off the canvas. She had pictured her mother on the ship, sailing to China. The ship's white sails fluttering above the dark blue sea had taken young Mayflora's imagination across the Pacific. The artist's Chinese name 'Lai Fong' reminded her of her father, Mei, whom she had never met. It was at that moment that she had resolved to learn the language and cross the ocean by ship to find him.

With time, her girlhood dream had become reality. She studied Chinese with a tutor her parents had hired for her in 1942. It was a difficult time. Her stepfather, Jensen, had left his engineering job to enlist in the army. Her mother had worked hard at a number of different part-time jobs to supplement the family income.

"I'm amazed to see this painting again after so long,"

Meihua sighed. "Everything seems to be happening as if in a dream."

Rubbing his eyes, Lon mumbled, "I recognized his ship at first sight."

They continued exploring the gallery, ending their visit with sculptures by Donald De Lue and the work of Bernard Brussel-Smith, who had been Meihua's professor at the Pennsylvania Academy of the Fine Arts.

Meihua wished they could stay at the gallery forever.

24.
THE RED LINE

BY THE TIME THEY LEFT the gallery and walked into the alley, the snow, glittering in the sun, had thickened. As they tread on the crisp snow to Green Briar on Washington Street, Meihua's nostalgia melted away. Her heart softened.

A waiter at Green Briar led them past several occupied tables to one in the corner. Meihua and Lon sat on cushioned wooden chairs while the Irish song, "Londonderry Air," coming from an old music box, flowed over the bar counter. The dining hall had timber beams and terra-cotta walls, trimmed with hand-painted green leaves of sweetbriars. Under the orange beams of the overhead lights, everything shone a rich coral. Lon scanned the pub, wondering why it was called "Green Briar."

Meihua explained, "The shamrock is the symbol of Irish culture. Green is a favourite colour. On St. Patrick's Day, the Irish decorate everything green; they even dress in green clothes! Youngsters wear green skirts, green trousers or green shirts or hats, and have green clovers painted on their faces."

She tapped two of her fingers on the tabletop along with the rhythm of the music. "My stepfather was Irish. We used to come here at least once a year. My parents would drink Irish ale." She sipped her beer. "Dora and I always ordered New England clam chowder. After dinner, everyone would get up for some Irish step dancing."

The waiter placed two bowls of clam chowder in front of them; then, he added a boat-shaped, wooden basket of freshly baked buns. Meihua sniffed at the bowl. "It's so good to smell fresh bread again."

Lon spooned some chowder into his mouth. "This is really tasty. What makes it white?"

"Milk." Meihua felt proud of her hometown. "This is a well-known Boston dish. People say that you know nothing about Boston if you haven't tasted its clam chowder."

"Are you serious?" asked Lon, looking at her bright, smiling face. "I'll have another bowl to prove that I really do know Boston now."

Meihua stroked the dark wall with her fingers while she reminisced about her childhood, remembering that the delightful music they danced to was like a bubbling creek running down a hill. "Dora was five at that time. She wanted to dance with the adults after she danced with me. Mom would bend forward so she could hold her hands while they danced. Dad would actually lift her high above his head. Dora would dance with her feet in the air. Her kicks almost hit Dad's chest!"

"I can imagine that happy time, especially when I'm sitting here with you, eating this delicious soup." Lon understood why, after four decades, Meihua was able to find her way to the restaurant without asking for directions. It was an important place for her. But it troubled him that her memory of the past seemed much better than her ability to recall recent events. He was worried about her ongoing headaches, and he wanted her to see a doctor about them, but Meihua kept insisting the headaches were caused by menopause. She seemed so happy right now that he could not bring himself to talk to her about this again, even though Agnes this morning had mentioned the name of a doctor she knew that would be willing to see her.

Another song was playing. Meihua hummed along with it and asked for another glass of Bass Ale. She told Lon that the song was her mother's favourite. Not familiar with the variety of beer available, Lon chose something called Blue Moon because he liked the name. Meihua dreamily sipped the ale from the glass, seemingly lost in thought, while Lon watched her, suddenly anxious. The song gradually came to the end.

> *When true hearts lie wither'd*
> *And fond ones are flow'n*
> *Oh! who would inhabit*
> *This bleak world alone?*

"This song seems so sad," Lon said. "What's it about?"

"It's 'The Last Rose of Summer'," answered Meihua, "by the Irish poet, Thomas Moore."

"I once read a poem called 'A Red, Red Rose' by Robert Burns. He is a Scottish poet," Lon said. "It's a sweet poem, and not so sad as this song."

"Let's toast." Meihua raised her glass.

A line of Burns' poem popped into Lon's head. *O my luve is like a red, red rose.* He touched the glass with his mug and recited the lyrics. "*O my luve is like a melody / that's sweetly play'd in tune.*"

Meihua swallowed her last sip. She gazed at Lon, but he was a blur. Suddenly, it was as if there were two of him sitting in front of her. Her blurred vision was making her nauseous, so she leaned into the table, grasping at the edge with one hand.

Lon noticed that her other hand was trembling when she stretched it toward him. He clasped it between his and asked, "Are you all right? Is there anywhere else you want to go?"

"Home. Let's go home," Meihua whispered, as if some invisible substance had entered her body, and changed her mood.

Taking her coat from the rack, Lon helped her into it carefully, as if he were afraid it it might hurt her. Then he quickly donned his own coat.

They walked back to the bus shelter just in time to catch a bus that was going in their direction. Sitting by the window, Meihua peered out at the darkened streets. Snowflakes landed against the glass, turning into crystal petals. She laid her fingers against the window as if to touch them. They melted and trickled down the glass. Cars and buses passed through the snow-blanketed city like pencils drawing sketches on paper sheets. Pedestrians moved on the sidewalks becoming spots of colour dotted here and there to complete the sketches. Her eyes felt hot, as though tears were about to spill. *Life is like a painting.*

When they reached the subway, Meihua ran down the stairs. She did not hear Lon's call, "We're not in a hurry!" She gripped the rail to help herself descend quickly. In her mind she was struggling to catch that train that would bring her home. She did not want to miss the train she had missed so many times in her dreams. Turning to Lon, in a throaty voice, she said, "Hurry."

Lon quickened his steps to catch up with her. Linking his arm through hers, he said breathlessly, "Slow down. I'm with you now."

Meihua drew a deep breath and relaxed. She had stopped running. The heavy sensation that had taken over her body gradually dissipated. A train pulled into the station. Following the other passengers, Meihua and Lon boarded. Noticing her sweaty, pale face, a young man offered her his seat.

Barely able to utter a few words, Meihua struggled to tell Lon, "Let's transfer to the Red Line at Park Street ... The Red Line ... Park Street!"

Lon nodded, placing his hand reassuringly on her shoulder. "Don't worry. I know where to transfer to the Red."

Meihua closed her eyes and envisioned a canvas she had painted recently. She called it "Nirvana." The painting was of a phoenix that whooshed past a giant flaming ball. The burnt tail feathers of the phoenix drifted away in the wind. New plumage on the phoenix's wings glinted in the fading sunlight. A strikingly red sun went down in the corner, its rays streaming across the darkening sky.

The train stopped, and Lon said, "We'll get off here and

transfer to the Red Line." Lon took her hand and tried to pull her to her feet.

Meihua opened her eyes, but only a crimson light registered in her vision. Rising from the seat, she blindly followed Lon off the train. People around them walked and talked, but Meihua could not see them. She was only aware of the smell their perfume and cologne. She could not see Lon, either. Red enveloped her; everything else lost its form. She mouthed "the Red," though she could not hear herself.

"What's wrong?" She heard Lon cry out, but she could not respond. Her head throbbed. A burning sensation enveloped her. Everything seemed to disappear, including herself.

Two pizzas arrived at 3333 Rindge Avenue at suppertime. Yezi carried the large boxes into the kitchen and laid them on the counter. She helped herself to a slice of pepperoni pizza and called out. "Grandma, I can't wait for Mama and Baba. I am so hungry!" She took her plate of pizza into the living room and plopped back on the couch to continue watching television.

Sitting at the kitchen table, Agnes untied a bundle of paper and flyers. As she scanned the *Boston Globe*, her stomach growled. She glanced at the mahogany clock on the wall. *Why aren't they back yet? Maybe I should eat now, too.* Agnes forked a slice of cheesy mushroom pizza onto a plate.

The phone rang just after Agnes had finished the last bite. She picked up the receiver and heard Lon's husky voice. "Where are you?" she asked. Her face went pale.

Half an hour later, Agnes and Yezi arrived at Emerson Hospital. In the waiting room beside the emergency room, Lon sat on a bench, hunched over with his head buried in his hands.

"Baba!" Yezi ran to him and grabbed his arm. Lon raised his head, his eyes dim. It was the first time Yezi had seen such desperation and hollowness on her father's face. She looked at her grandmother whose wrinkles had deepened. Worry and grief had washed over them both. Their faces were streaked with tears. Yezi's heart felt as though it would explode.

Several hours later, a doctor came to inform them that Meihua had regained consciousness but needed surgery immediately. Before her surgery, lying in bed, Meihua asked Yezi to come closer. Then she held Yezi's hand and said, "Remember no matter what happens I'm always with you," Yezi's heart skipped a beat, but she nodded and tried to smile.

After the operation, Yezi sat motionless by her mother's bed. An oxygen mask covered Meihua's nose. Intravenous injections remained connected to her arms. The expression on her face was peaceful. Her eyes were closed as if she had fallen into a deep sleep. Yezi held one of her mother's hands. From the other side of the bed, her father held Meihua's other hand. The room was warm, but Yezi's heart felt cold. *Mama, wake up. Mama, please don't die. We need you.* She was consumed by guilt. *I should've spent more time with you, Mama, after you arrived. We should have done things together.* When she turned her head, her father's eyes met hers with an anguished look.

Yezi felt her mother's hand move. She stood and looked down at her face, holding her breath. Meihua opened her eyes slowly. When she saw Yezi, she smiled. Meihua was diagnosed with Glioblastoma multiforme, the most malignant form of brain cancer. Years of malnutrition in jail had contributed to her already frail physical state. Surgery, a last resort, could not save her from the cancer's vicious attack. Three days later, she died.

For many days, Yezi moved puppet-like from one room to another. She was convinced her mother might not have died, had she stayed home the night they arrived. She was filled with remorse, and wished she had gone out with them and shown them around Boston.

Aunt Dora arrived with her family to mourn the sudden loss

of her sister. Agnes and Dora tearfully comforted each other.

Yezi's bosom friend, Helen, came with condolence messages from other classmates.

Lon was inconsolable. He sat motionless, as if a part of him gone with his wife. He couldn't get the words of "The Last Rose of Summer" out of his mind. "*Oh! who would inhabit / this bleak world alone?*" The lyrics seemed to have been written only for him.

After the wake, Lon kept repeating over and over, "She's home." He told Agnes that Meihua had liked to recite a line by an unknown Boston poet. "'Go back to Boston, friend. Heaven isn't good enough for you.'" Lon looked down at his hands, tears in his eyes, and said, "Maybe this is where she wanted her soul to rest."

Both Agnes and Dora offered to sponsor Lon to stay in the U.S., but he declined. To Yezi, America was a country of freedom and opportunity. People could do what they want. *Baba can learn to speak English more fluently. Getting a job won't be difficult.* She could not understand why her father would want to go back to China.

"Baba, are you afraid of staying here? Why do you have to go back?"

"I have many things to do back home." Lon searched for the right words, hoping to make Yezi understand. "I've been given back my teaching job. And I'm in the middle of a project that I need to finish. Besides, Yao's old and needs to be taken care of. I cannot leave her alone. And there's Sang."

Yezi frowned and then smiled. "Let's bring them both here, Baba. We can all be together again."

"We will need a place to stay. How will we pay for it?" Lon had a wry smile. "If I had to start over here, I couldn't even afford to find a place for all of us." Yezi was silent, her expression mournful. Lon blinked his eyes. "Something more important is—"

"What?" Yezi grabbed his sleeve.

"This is our secret." Lon lowered his voice. "I want to see if I can find your grandfather." Imagining the possibility of locating his late wife's birth father gave Lon a renewed sense of purpose.

"How?" Yezi held her breath.

"Do you remember Ling, your mama's colleague? She told your mama about a woman in her parents' neighbourhood, originally from Chongqing. Her maiden name was Mei."

"What's the point?"

"Your grandfather was from Chongqing. His family name is Mei."

"Where are Ling's parents?"

"In Mianyang. Ling's back there for the holidays. She'll find out if that woman has any connection to your grandfather's family."

Yezi willed herself to appear optimistic. "But is it possible? Grandpa's parents must be too old to be alive."

"Maybe not. But he may have had sisters, or brothers. Anything is possible." Lon's voice softened. "This was your mother's wish. I would like to do this for her."

Yezi's eyes moistened. "I'm also going to carry out one of her wishes: to go to university."

"Good girl!" Lon wrapped his arm around Yezi's shoulder. "I have been afraid you'd only lose yourself in this rich and free country. That you would only be interested in accumulating material things, which are so easily acquired here. I hope you will learn that objects are meaningless. Your life must have meaning. When your life has meaning, you will need very little, because you will already have what fulfills you. Sometimes I feel I have no right to say anything to you, or to try and teach you anything. As your father, I haven't taken enough responsibility for you. I was never around you enough."

"I'm sorry if I've disappointed you." Yezi pulled her father's hand to her face.

Lon softly dabbed her tears and stroked her hair. "You have

not disappointed me. A better education is what your mama and I have always hoped for you." He went upstairs and returned with a small envelope in his hand. "Look at this photo."

Yezi lifted the rectangular envelope and drew out a black and white snapshot. The yellowed photograph featured a young couple standing under a tree with picturesque mountains in the background. "My Grandpa?" Yezi fingered the photograph. "Did he have a Chinese wife?"

Lon shook his head. "That's your grandmother, the same one that lives right here in this house."

Yezi examined the woman who wore a long-sleeved, dark Chinese blouse. Her baggy pants ended at her ankles, and her feet were in a pair of cloth shoes. Yes, she was a young Agnes. Her eyes seemed to shine with vigour, Yezi thought. "Oh, they look like the people in ancient times."

"This is the only photo of your grandparents together. Your mother told me that each of your grandparents had a copy. Your mama had it reprinted before she left Boston for China." Lon sighed, thinking about Meihua's reason for going to China so many years ago. "I hope they can meet again someday."

Yezi placed the photograph back into the envelope and returned it to her father. *Will the miracle ever happen?*

Finally Lon boarded an airplane back to China, where he would carry on with his life. Engraved deeply in the bottom of his heart was the word, Nirvana, the title of the painting that Meihua had taken several months to complete. The physical form of his wife had passed, but her spirit was free, and it would accompany him on his remaining life journey.

At the airport, Yezi and her grandmother watched the plane take off. Yezi held her grandmother's hand all the way home.

25.
WHITE PAGODA STREET

A MONTH LATER, A LETTER FROM Yezi's father arrived informing her that while Ling had returned to Kunming, she had no new information about Mei. Lon's letter also enclosed a photograph of Yao. She was wearing the bright blue blouse Yezi had sent to her through her father. Yao's smiling face brought back many fond memories. Yezi framed it and placed the photograph on her dresser, next to the one of her parents and brother.

Two months later, Yezi turned fifteen and received Agnes's old diaries, as the birthday gift Agnes had promised.

In her bedroom, Yezi quickly unwrapped the package, eager to learn about her grandmother's history. The two books were covered with faded, pink brocade. They looked like mysterious chests inviting her to look inside for treasure. Carefully, she fingered the fabric on the cover, and then sniffed the pages that smelled faintly of mothballs. Each cover had the word "Diary" engraved on it. She opened the first book and began to read. It was dated Halifax, May 1923.

Agnes Willard of Wolfville, Nova Scotia was the youngest of four children from a doctor's family. After graduating from the Nurses' Training School affiliated with the Victoria General Hospital in Halifax, she studied at Pine Hill College preparing for a Christian mission overseas.In February of 1924, during a Christian fellowship meeting, her pastor informed her that her application for a missionary position in Japan had been rejected.

Agnes filled out another application for the West China Mission in Sichuan. Along with a reference letter from her pastor, she mailed the form to the Methodist Church in Toronto. In August, Agnes took holidays and visited her parents in Wolfville. Her parents held a family party, inviting friends and neighbours to a potluck picnic. Her siblings joined the party, as did her maiden aunt from Boston. Several tables, set in a row in her parents' backyard that looked over the Bay of Fundy, were filled with plates of broiled cod fillets, salted haddock, cold poached salmon, smoked herring, potato salad, coleslaw, and home-made bread. Among the dishes was a Caesar salad made by Agnes's aunt who had followed a recipe, recently created by Caesar Cardini, a restaurateur in California. Agnes's mother had invited a children's choir to perform at the party. All the guests joined the choir in singing "Summer Suns Are Glowing," a hymn by William Walsham How.

"*Summer suns are glowing over land and sea / Happy light is flowing, bountiful and free / Everything rejoices in the mellow rays...*" As Agnes sang the last line, "*Earth's tenthousand voices swell the psalm of praise*," she tried to imagine her future, and lost herself in thoughts of missions in far away and exotic places. One of the young men at the party was an ardent and persistent admirer. Joining her in line to fill their plates from the buffet, he said, "Agnes, you've been rejected twice by the foreign mission. Maybe that's God's will."

"I appreciate your concern, Bill, but I'm going to try again." Agnes carried her plate, laden with food, to a picnic table. He followed and sat down next to her. After a few minutes of silent eating, Agnes turned to him and said, "You're very kind, but you don't really understand me."

"Why won't you give me a chance?" Bill's face lit up.

Agnes was at a loss for words when spotted one of the young

women at the picnic staring pointedly at Bill. She stood up and beckoned for her to join them. She turned to Bill and said, "Eva's been looking for you. I think she would really like to talk to you."

Then, excusing herself, she walked over to her aunt, Joanne. "Are you enjoying the smoked fish? Mother and I smoked them a couple of days ago."

"Oh, really? It really is very good; it reminds me of my childhood." Joanne nodded, looking back at Bill. "He seems to like you."

"He's a nice man, but I'm hoping to leave for an overseas mission very soon. I cannot get involved with anyone right now."

"You could come to Boston and stay with me. You could easily get a job there," her aunt said with a smile. "Boston is a great city for a young, ambitious woman."

They finished their plates and then strolled to the shore. A cool breeze from the bay brought with it the smell of fish and salt. Agnes drew a deep breath. "I really want to go overseas. I believe people there need me and I want to do this work."

Water crashed against the shore. Aunt Joanne had to speak loudly to be heard. "But you might have to wait until next year for another opportunity. And even then, you don't know if you'll get a position."

"Thank you, Aunt Joanne. But I can get a part-time job in September. And I'll do some volunteer work at the hospital in Halifax while I wait for my next chance to apply."

They reached some crumbling sandcastles that had been built earlier by the children at the picnic. Agnes picked up a few pebbles and threw one at the bay's surface. It slipped into the water. She tossed another one, which flew into the air and then disappeared. She kept skimming stones. At last, the fifth pebble skipped twice before sinking into the water. Satisfied with her efforts, she eyed the waves thoughtfully.

Joanne linked her arm with Agnes's. "Your father insisted

on coming back to Wolfville after he got his medical degree from the New York Medical College, even though he could have more easily practiced in the States."

"Now, I understand why he's never interfered with what I want to do." Agnes laughed.

"Like father, like daughter," Joanne said. "All right, do what you want. But come with me to see your grandparents in Port Royal tomorrow."

"Certainly. I haven't seen them for a couple of years."

After her holiday, and back in Halifax, Agnes worked part-time as a nurse and volunteered at her neighbourhood church. On an August day in 1925, a year later, she received a telegram from the newly formed United Church in Toronto. They offered her an unexpected position in the West China Mission, due to the sudden sick leave of a missionary. They asked her to leave within ten days for Vancouver. From there she would go to Shanghai by ship.

Exhilarated, Agnes immediately confirmed her acceptance. But it was the end of October before she could finally board the Empress of Australia in Vancouver. Growing anti-western resentment in China had delayed all new missionary positions. When she arrived in Chengdu, the capital of Sichuan Province, it was already the end of November 1925. Agnes was housed in the West Mission Compound on White Pagoda Street where she would get lessons in the Chinese language for three months before beginning her missionary work.

Several days later, Agnes met with the Chinese tutor assigned to her in the compound meeting room. Mei looked to be in his early twenties. He wore a padded black robe and a short gray Chinese blazer with two rows of buttons reaching a tight, standing collar. He was tall and well-built. Handsome. Amazingly, he spoke fluent English. "Is this your first time speaking to a Chinese person?"

Agnes nodded. "Not only that, I thought I would be taller than you, but..."

"You also thought I'd be malnourished, right?" Mei said, his mouth curving into a smile.

Feeling her face flush, Agnes stammered, "This is something I have heard about before. I am sorry about that."

"No need to apologize. China's a weak country. My people need lots of help to escape famine and poverty."

Agnes learned that Mei, from a teacher's family, had been converted to Christianity at a missionary middle school. As a senior student, he had majored in medicine at the West China Union University, sponsored by missionaries from Canada, the United States and other western countries. Agnes met him several hours a day to practice Chinese. When he was not teaching her Chinese, Mei showed her around. She bought a long white Chinese blouse and a loose black skirt that Chinese girl students commonly wore. She found it more comfortable walking with Mei when she dressed like a Chinese girl student.

Four months later, in March of 1926, Agnes began to work as a nurse in a missionary hospital. One Monday, as she stepped out of the hospital building after work, she was surprised to find Mei leaning against the stairwell banister. "Let's celebrate your day!" he said, waving his hand at her.

"My day?" Agnes tried to think what he meant and then suddenly remembered. "March the eighth? International Women's Day?"

"Right. Don't you celebrate this day in Canada?"

"Not really. But I remember its founder, Clara Zetkin."

"Good! Because of her urging and help, Lenin established International Women's Day."

"Lenin? The Russian communist?"

Just then, a rickshaw abruptly halted in front of the gate. A man jumped down. "I need a doctor? Please help me!" he shouted, racing into the yard.

"What's happening?" Mei asked the man.

"My wife is in labour! Please come!"

"Is she in the wagon?" Agnes ran over to the rickshaw.

"No, no. She's at home. She can't move." The man wiped the sweat on his forehead with a handkerchief and looked at Agnes. "Can you help me?"

"Let me get something first." Agnes ran back into the building. The doctor on duty could not leave the hospital, so she was the only one who could help him. She returned with an emergency kit.

The man led her to the rickshaw. "Take her back to my house. Remember? It's 24 Black Horse Lane," he said to the rickshaw-puller. Mei helped Agnes clamber onto the seat.

"I'll follow you," Mei said. Maybe I can be of some help."

The rickshaw-puller began to run. Mei and the man raced after the rickshaw, dust rising from its wheels. Several pedestrians scurried out of the way while other passers-by cheered the rickshaw-puller on. Fifteen minutes later, the rickshaw pulled into a courtyard.

"You a doctor?" asked a boy who had waiting for them. He pointed to a door on their right. The door suddenly opened and a middle-aged woman hobbled out to grab Agnes's arm. "Please save the baby."

Agnes followed her into the room, noticing her tiny, bound feet, which caused her slow, shuffling steps. Mei and the husband were stopped at the door after they had rushed into the yard. The woman's panting and moaning filtered through the window accompanied by Agnes's reassuring voice, "Hold her legs, please."

The middle-aged woman inside asked in a husky, panicky tone, "What did you say?"

Mei shouted outside the window, "Lady, please listen to me." He interpreted Agnes's words from the outside.

"Take deep and slow breaths." "Shift your weight from one leg to the other." Blow through your mouth." Mei continued. "Push the baby out, gently."

The world seemed dead until a baby's cry broke the tension in the air. Finally Mei and the father were permitted to enter the room. Agnes fell into a chair, too tense to move. It was her first time delivering a baby. The foot-bound woman insisted they drink some tea before leaving. The husband thanked them profusely. After they left, he waved goodbye from the double doors of the yard gate. Emergency case in hand, Mei walked with Agnes back to the hospital.

It was too late for them to go to the performance of the female students at the university as Mei had planned. Instead, Agnes suggested going to a teahouse she had heard about, even though Mei mentioned that most of the patrons were male. To satisfy her curiosity, Mei led the way along a pebble-paved alley toward the Laoguang Teahouse. Agnes pulled her black scarf over her head to hide her blonde hair. Inside, middle-aged and elderly men lounged together at tables. A few women were sitting beside their husbands. Tobacco smoke spread through the room lit by a few burning oil lamps hanging precariously on the walls. Occasional coughs rose from the crowd.

Mei and Agnes found a small, square table made of bamboo near a window. A breeze blew in, diluting the smoke. Patrons sipped tea and ate snacks. Like most of the people in the teahouse, Mei ordered two cups of tea and a plate of deep fried fava beans and another of deep fried soybeans.

Agnes craned her head toward the stage. An elderly man with a long, white goatee was seated in front of a table in the centre of the stage. He spoke loudly, and bobbed his head. He was wearing a small, round, traditional Chinese cap that shook as his head bobbed, its sleek surface shining in the flickering light. Agnes asked under her breath, "What's that old man doing?"

"He is, as the folks here say, talking books. It's a kind of oral tradition for illiterate people, so they can also appreciate the classics." Mei passed a cup to Agnes. "This is Emei tea. It's rated the best in West China."

Sipping the tea and nibbling the beans, Agnes strove to understand what the elderly man was saying. He banged the table with a thick palm-sized bamboo sheet whenever the story reached a turning point or the protagonist had something important to do or say. Then the hall echoed with applause and cheers. At the next table, several men joined in the clapping. Their long, single braids drooped down their backs. Meanwhile they smacked their lips on long smoking pipes. Agnes understood some of the war stories of heroes from *The Legend of Three Kingdoms*. Later, though the clapping of the audience made it difficult for her to hear, she was able to make out the words "boxers," "righteous" and "harmonious fists" came from the mouth of the book talker. When she heard the phrase "foreign devils," she realized the story was about the Boxer Rebellion that had taken place more than two decades earlier.

"We should leave now," Mei whispered, noticing that one or two listeners sitting nearby were staring at them.

"Okay." Agnes stood up and began to follow him out. As they passed through the door, a heavy voice called behind them. "Get out of here. You fake foreign devils!"

Mei was relieved that they had mistaken Agnes for a Chinese girl student. In the eyes of ordinary people, college students were poisoned by foreign ideas. If the patrons had realized that Agnes was actually a westerner, some of them would have gotten even angrier; Boxer fighters had been opposing foreign imperialism and Christianity for decades and were responsible for widespread anti-western sentiment. Mei took Agnes's arm and said, "I hope you aren't upset by the stories in the teahouse. I regret taking you there."

"Don't regret it. I am glad we went there." Agnes stopped walking. "Now I've learned what ordinary people think."

"Some people welcome missionaries. Some don't. They are hostile to anyone who's been converted to Christianity or who gets new ideas from outside." Mei looked at the almost empty street. "I'll walk you back to the compound."

Walking with her arm through Mei's, Agnes felt safe. "I'm wondering when we can go to Mount Emei. I'm really eager to see it." She had read about the Buddha's Glory on the summit.

"I'll take you when my semester ends," Mei replied.

When they reached the compound yard, Agnes said, "Today is the most eventful International Women's Day I've ever had."

May 28, in the early morning, Agnes and Mei paid for a horse-drawn wagon ride to Mount Emei, which would take them almost an entire day to reach. Agnes wore a long-sleeved, blue blouse made of hand-woven cloth and light baggy pants bound at her ankles. Over the blouse she had on a white Chinese-style vest. She sported a pair of cloth shoes with rubber soles—the best walking shoes she could find. She rolled her long blond hair into a bun at the back of her head and covered it with a silky blue scarf. This way, people around her would barely notice that she was not Chinese. Mei, like most local peasants, was dressed in a short white robe and baggy pants with their cuffs bound at his ankles. A black waistband cinched his robe shut. He also had a bamboo hamper on his back, its two straps on his shoulders. Inside were provisions for the trip. The talked the entire way, never running out of things to tell each other.

The wagon deposited them at the foot of Mount Emei the following morning. Immediately they started to climb along the path winding up the mountain. A number of tourists had hired carriers—two men to carry them on sedan chairs. Each carrier held two poles, attached to a chair, resting on both shoulders.

Half way up, when Agnes and Mei decided to rest for a moment under a pine tree, Mei pulled a bunch of bananas from his hamper and passed them to Agnes. "Help yourself."

Before Agnes's hand could reach for the fruit, a monkey unexpectedly dropped from a branch in the tree. Mei, startled, dropped the fruit and the monkey, seizing his opportunity, snatched it. Startled, Agnes screamed as more monkeys arrived and hopped excitedly around them.

"I should've told you about the monkeys," Mei laughed. "They're everywhere on the mountain, but they won't hurt you. Watch that one."

Looking to where Mei pointed, Agnes spotted the monkey with the banana perched on a rock several steps away. A baby monkey clung to her stomach as the mother peeled the fruit, tore off bite-sized pieces, and began to feed it. "It's so cute," Agnes chuckled.

"They're nice to you if you give them food. If you hurt them, they'll fight back." Mei took a handful of longan nuts from the hamper and gave them to Agnes. "Here. Try feeding them with these."

As Agnes tossed the nuts to the monkeys, they jumped to catch them. One or two in hand, each monkey hunkered down, their long nails cutting expertly into the shells, popping the nuts into their mouths as the shells dropped away.

Agnes and Mei laughed and ate their snacks, tossing the monkeys their scraps when they finished.

The diary ended there. Yezi closed the book, wondering how long it had would take them to reach the summit. She glanced at her radio clock on the end table. *It's 11:00 p.m. I have school tomorrow.* She decided to read the second book the following day after school. Yezi had heard about the legend of the Buddha's Glory on Mount Emei from Yao. *Did Grandma and Mei see the Buddha's Glory?* She couldn't wait to continue reading.

26.
BUDDHA'S GLORY

YEZI DID NOT GO TO the mall with her friends after school the next day, but went straight home. Plopping herself onto her bed, she leaned against the headboard and opened the second diary. It was a beautiful day in May, 1926, and her grandmother was climbing the path to Mount Emei.

After Agnes and Mei had walked for several hours, the sun inched toward the edge of the mountain range. The sun spilled through branches and limbs, glinting on the weed-covered path.

"What's that?" Agnes saw something shivering in the grass several steps away from them.

"Don't move. Let me take a look." Mei stepped forward. "It's a woman," he said with surprise. "She's lying down."

Agnes waded through the jumble of grass and bushes. A middle-aged woman was lying on her back, staring into space. Her eyes were hidden by long strands of hair that fell over her haggard face.

"Do you need any help?" asked Agnes.

"I need something to eat," the woman groaned, her dull eyes looking up at Agnes wearily.

"Just a minute." Mei pulled the hamper off his back. He pulled out two buns and several bananas and quickly passed them to her.

Sitting up, the woman hastily grabbed the food, stuffing it

bit by bit into her mouth. Then she wiped her mouth with her sleeve, a grateful smile on her dirty face. "Thank you. Kind people are everywhere. Buddha bless you."

"Are you a Buddhist pilgrim?" asked Mei.

The woman nodded as she spoke. "I'm from Hunan Province. I want to see the Buddha's Glory on the Golden Summit." As she talked, her face brightened. "It took me half a year to get here."

Agnes asked, "What made you do this?"

"Two wishes. I wish that my daughter would have a son." The woman pursed her mouth, a sigh escaping her nose. Her husky voice rose again. "I am a widow. I had to raise my daughter alone. Now my daughter's married. Her husband and in-laws dislike her because she has two daughters but no sons. I wish for her a son. My second wish is to be a man in my next life." The woman uttered a deep moan when she finished her story.

"What do you do for a living?" Agnes asked.

"I do everything I can. I clean houses and do laundry. I make straw shoes. I sell used stuff that I scavenge from the garbage."

"You work hard. You deserve a better life," Agnes said, smiling warmly at the woman.

"Thank you for saying that." The woman looked relieved, though her eyes were still guarded. "Buddha's taking care of me. People have given me food along my way coming here. Now, I have also met you kind people on this sacred mount."

Agnes had noticed the numerous patches on her faded dress and flimsy jacket. Agnes took a silver yuan from her purse and placed it in the woman's hand. "Take this, please."

The woman gasped when she saw the coin. "This is half-a-month's pay. I haven't done anything for you—"

"I wish you and your daughter a better life," Agnes said, her eyes full of compassion.

Pulling more buns and bananas from the hamper, Mei

passed them to the woman. "Have you heard of the Saviour, Jesus?"

"Yes, but I'm not sure if I believe in him."

"Why?"

"He's from foreign devils. They set fires in China, and kill people."

"The foreign army did those things, but foreign missionaries are here to help us Chinese."

"Maybe. This lady looks like a foreign devil, but she's very generous." The old woman pressed her palms together in front of her chest, praying, "You merciful folks, may Buddha bless you. If Jesus is nice, he should please bless this lady."

Agnes and Mei resumed their uphill journey to the summit.

At sunset, they approached the Golden Summit plateau where the Huazang Temple Monastery was located. The temple, surrounded by marble balustrades, stood among towering pine trees that seemed to form a canopy, protecting the sanctuary. The layer of yellow glaze on the tiles on the roof had faded and weeds were sprouting from the edges of broken tiles, but the pillars, doors and window frames, made of burnished copper, sparkled in the sunset. As their eyes scanned the plateau, the last red cloud fell behind the summit; the crows' sad cries spread through the woods.

"*Green mountains still remain / Crimson rays come from the sunset*." The couplet from *The Legend of the Three Kingdoms,* which Agnes had learned from Mei, leapt to her mind.

Visitors were scattered all around the temple. Some sat under trees; others walked in and out of the double doors that led to the temple interior. Several sedan chair carriers napped on their seats while young monks in black robes carried pails of drinking water to newcomers.

Agnes and Mei ate buns for supper. They paid forty copper coins to stay in the Bronze Hall of the temple for the night, where each pilgrim was provided with a pallet, a quilt, and a pillow.

Mei chose a pallet that had been placed in a corner against the wall for Agnes, and the one next to it for himself.

"How are your feet?" asked Mei. "You must have some blisters."

"I think so." Agnes removed her shoes and socks and felt the blisters that had formed on her heels during their climb. Mei went to find an oil lamp and placed it in front of Agnes's feet. Then he pulled a sewing needle from his wallet. "Let me burst the blisters, so they won't get worse tomorrow." Burning the needle's point in the lamp flame for half a minute, he pierced the blisters one by one.

"Now, let me do yours." Agnes cleaned the serum with a piece of paper.

"I don't have any new blisters. The old ones have already turned into calluses."

Just then, a monk entered the chamber and added soy oil to the lamps in the niches before bedtime. Mei returned the lamp to its place.

Agnes lay fully clothed under the quilt, as did Mei, after setting his bamboo hamper in the place between their straw-filled mattresses. Mountain winds whistled through the rustling trees, and wood crackled in the bonfire lit by those who could not afford a bed inside. In a low, fervent voice, a man intoned a Sichuan folk song called "Kangding Love Song": "*A cloud floats over running horses on the mountain / A beautiful girl of the Li family comes from Kangding Town....*" The melody lulled them both to sleep.

Agnes woke early. The people sleeping inside the temple had begun to stir; their quiet voices and muffled movements had encouraged the late sleepers to rise. Agnes turned her head to look at Mei. He was sitting with his back against the wall. "What's going on?" Agnes asked.

"The pilgrims don't want to miss Buddha's Glory. A monk has reported a shower under the golden summit. That means there is a very good chance to see a halo."

"Let's go!" Excited, Agnes quickly slipped on her shoes, knowing that not many mountain visitors had the good fortune to see the great rainbow that might form over the mountain's peak. In the ancient Chinese legend, the rainbow formed a halo over Buddha's head and that is why it was called Buddha's Glory.

They followed the crowd out of the temple and headed toward the eastern cliffs. Clouds flowed past them and the fog, like an ample rug, blanketed the mount. Agnes felt as if they were on a ship sailing on a turbulent sea.

The wind blew through their clothing. She shivered. Mei took off his short robe and wrapped it around her shoulders. Suddenly, the sun emerged from behind the clouds and glowed through the mist. Exhilarated, the flocks of people cheered. Some even cried out when they saw the fog dissipate and the green mountains become visible in the sunshine. A rainbow gradually appeared over the massive cliffs as whispering prayers rose around Agnes and Mei. The chanting of the pilgrims echoed and wafted around them.

A person, wrapped in a piece of gray fleece from head to foot, shuffled toward the cliff and stopped only a few steps in front of Agnes and Mei. The rainbow glowed in the sun while the gray apparition bent over, its covering loose and touching the ground. Before Agnes realized what was happening, the figure threw itself toward the chromatic halo, a desperate leap for nirvana. Mei rushed forward and clutched at the gray robe, pulling the figure back from the cliff. He fell back when the person collapsed on him; several stones crashed down the bluff. The hollow echoes of the falling rocks sounded like the cries of someone in distress. Two men ran toward Mei to help, lifting the person who had fallen on top of him, and laying her gently on the ground. It was an elderly woman.

Agnes bent and placed her arm under Mei's head, gently lifting it. "You saved a woman!" She looked at him. "Are you hurt?" she asked.

"I'm okay. How is she?" Mei sat up.

"She's safe." Agnes checked his arm. "But your elbow is bleeding."

Mei raised his arm. "Just a scratch. I can move it without any problem. Let's make sure this poor woman is okay."

He stood and they turned their attention to the woman on the ground. A man pressed his thumb between her lips and nose. Mei noticed Agnes's bafflement and explained, "Pressing that acupuncture point can quickly bring her back from unconsciousness."

Agnes and Mei were stunned to realize that the woman was the pilgrim they had spoken to a day earlier. Underneath the gray fleece, she was clad in clean clothes, and her gray hair was streaming down the length of her back.

Agnes touched the pilgrim's wrist and then her forehead. The woman opened her eyes. "I'm still alive?" She sounded disappointed.

Someone pushed Mei toward her. "This is your saviour," he said.

The pilgrim sobbed when she saw Mei and Agnes. "I wanted to follow Buddha's Glory into my next life. You should've let me go."

In a soft voice, Agnes said, "If you live well, you can help your daughter."

Hearing about her daughter, the pilgrim stopped weeping. When Agnes helped her sit, the woman stared at her bare feet. "I've lost my shoes!"

An elderly head monk in a black robe strode toward them, his head bent, his hands clasped in front of his chest. "Buddha's light is brilliant. A life is rescued." He bent over the pilgrim. "You are blessed."

The woman stood up and bowed low to him. He raised his head toward a group of praying monks and called out, "Monk Zhi, come to help." Then he turned toward the woman, "One of my students will carry you down to the temple. You can rest there. We will also find you another pair of shoes."

The woman thanked Mei before a young monk hoisted her onto his back. And then the monk carried the old woman and tramped down toward the monastery.

Waving goodbye to others, Agnes and Mei decided it was time for them to go back.

It was the end of the tiring hiking and late in the afternoon. They boarded another horse-drawn wagon to make their way back to Chengdu. Exhausted, they dozed off, along with the other passengers, to the rhythm and motion of the rolling wooden wheels.

Agnes dreamed that she and her father were in a boat jigging for fish in the Bay of Fundy. They had caught a boatload of cod and mackerel. She kept moving her jigger jerkily up and down while her father yelled, "Stop it! We have way too many fish." The fish filled the boat and flapped on the floor, causing the vessel to capsize. She was falling and hit something before she could utter a word.

"Agnes! Agnes!" She heard her name and opened her eyes. Bright stars in the dark sky above sparkled. "Are you okay?" Mei was holding her shoulders.

"What happened?" she asked as her hands touched the wet grass and soil.

"The horses slipped, and the wagon fell into the ditch."

"Where are the others?"

"I'm here, behind your husband," said the wagon owner, who sat against a stone, stretching his head toward her. "We're lucky. Nobody got killed. One of my horses broke its leg though. And my wagon's been damaged so I won't be able to carry you any further until it's repaired."

"How far is it from here to Chengdu?" asked Agnes.

"Maybe twenty kilometres," answered the wagon owner, "but I'm not going anywhere. You will have to find your own way home.

Mei asked, "What are you going to do with your horse and wagon?"

"I'll nap until daylight. Then I will find some help from the nearby village. People around here know me."

"Which direction is Chengdu?"

The wagon owner craned his head and examined the stars in the sky. "That way!" He pointed off to the right.

Agnes stood and said to Mei, "I can walk. Let's go on foot."

"Are you sure?" Mei could not locate his hamper, so he told the wagon owner, "If you find my basket, it's yours."

"Thanks. I might also find some of the lost chickens and ducks that fell of the wagon too, if their owners don't catch them first." The wagon owner chuckled.

Agnes and Mei clambered up to the road and lumbered toward the West Gate of the city. The fields were peaceful; only the barking of a solitary dog rose in the darkness. On that dark night, Agnes did not have fear. As she stopped to stare into Mei's gentle face, she realized she was in love.

Back in Chengdu, Agnes and Mei became inseparable. They dreamt that they could break the cultural taboos that haunted them, and that in the future could be together and have a family.

A few days later, after she distributed medicine to her patients, Agnes went to the staff room for lunch. It was Monday, June 7, 1926—a day Agnes would never forget As she pulled a chair up to the table, ready to have her lunch, she was surprised to see Mei rush into the room, his face sweaty, fear in his eyes. Before she could question him, he said in a frantic voice, "Don't go anywhere by yourself from now on."

"Why?" Agnes looked puzzled.

Mei hissed. "Mrs. Sibley was killed this morning."

"Killed?" Agnes's heart throbbed. "How?"

"When she was walking along a street near White Pagoda

this morning," Mei wiped his face with a handkerchief. "A swordsman from behind cut off her head—"

"What? My God!" Shocked at the news, she asked in a trembling voice, "It's not true, is it? It can't be."

Mei held onto her shoulders. "I didn't believe it at first. But then I rushed to the alley and saw the police milling around the pool of blood that marked the spot."

Agnes shivered as she listened to Mei. Several times at the compound, she had met Mrs. Sibley, a Canadian missionary who had been in Chengdu for the past nineteen years. "Who was the swordsman?"

"People say he was a member of the Red Lantern Society, a kind of traditional secret society that hates foreigners," answered Mei. "From now on, I'll walk you between the hospital and home."

Why on earth does such hatred exist? Agnes felt a sense of despair come over her.

In the evening a meeting for the compound residents was held, during which the murder of Mrs. Edith Sibley was confirmed and discussed. Every missionary was advised to avoid travelling the streets alone at any time of the day or night.

On the following days, Mei appeared more often in the compound since he accompanied Agnes back there every day after their lessons, and after her work day was over at the hospital. When Agnes's supervisor asked about Mei, Agnes had to admit that their relationship was intimate. Her supervisor reported her to the West China Mission committee. Missionaries were not allowed to become involved with the local people. A few weeks later, Agnes was informed that she had been ordered to return to Canada.

Agnes was devastated. She didn't know what to do. The increasing anti-western sentiment was pushing missionaries away from the country. Meanwhile regulations forbade her from staying on the mission. Mei could not bring himself to ask her to stay. He knew she would only suffer. And he was afraid for her life. She did not have any choice, but to obey the orders of her mission.

Heartbroken, she said farewell to Mei on July 2, 1926, and left for Shanghai to board the ship that would take her back to Vancouver. From there, she would make her way back to Wolfville. Endless waters separated her from her heart's love, and China was now a remote corner of the earth. She clung to the ship's rail until she could no longer discern the receding Chinese coastline. That evening Agnes wrote in her journal.

July 31, 1926
At this quiet moment, I can hear the sea roaring outside the ship. The passenger across from my bed is sleeping soundly. I'm still wondering whether there's a corner in this world where love isn't restrained by rules, but is only immersed in sweetness... I miss him so much.

In her bedroom, Yezi's eyes lingered on the page. Holding Agnes's diary in her hands, she imagined her grandmother's sitting in the darkness of the ship, hot tears streaming down her face.

27.
AN ENDLESS OCEAN APART

AFTER SUPPER THE FOLLOWING DAY, Yezi rushed back to her bedroom and immersed herself once again in her grandmother's diaries. She travelled back with her grandmother to Wolfville, Nova Scotia, August 25, 1926.

The bus finally pulled over in town this afternoon. Agnes was both physically and emotionally exhausted. Everything looked the same, but she knew she had changed a lot these past months. A young girl at the station recognized her. "You back from China? Let me help you." She took one of Agnes's travel bags and walked with her back to her parents' house.

Agnes's mother was hanging the laundry on the clothesline in the back yard. The bed sheets and towels fluttered in the air when the sea breezes slapped them. It was a beautiful, sunny day. Agnes's mother flicked a shirt with her fingers and cocked her head; she seemed to hear their approaching steps. She ran to the front and pulled Agnes tightly into her arms before Agnes could call out to her.

Agnes could feel the tears welling up in her eyes, but she didn't cry; her mother did, though. The sun shining on her wet face made her mother's cheeks glow. She let her mother hold her, then walk her slowly into the house. She was home.

Agnes's mother pampered her and Agnes gradually recuperated from the long, draining journey. China was a faraway place; everything that happened there seemed to have turned into a secret dream. But an unexpected reality suddenly hit her one morning: she felt seasick as she walked into the kitchen. Momentarily confused, she looked around the kitchen, recognizing the door and kitchen walls, but the rolling waves of the sea were still washing over her. Her father was sitting at the kitchen table and her mother had just served him fresh milk from a porcelain jug.

"Good morning," Agnes said, as she carefully sat down, but the smell of the milk made her feel even queasier.

"Do you want some breakfast?" her mother asked, placing a plate of toasted bread on the oak table.

Agnes took a deep breath. "No, thanks. I feel dizzy." She shook her head. "I think I'll go back to bed."

Her father's concerned eyes followed her as she left the room. "She seems to have lost her spirit in China." He rose and picked up his black briefcase. "I'm going to the clinic."

The next morning, Agnes felt the same. The nausea hit her in waves as she made her way gingerly to the kitchen. She was suddenly stunned by a thought: *Am I pregnant?* She sat down, her legs trembling slightly. She placed her hands on her belly, and stroked it, allowing herself to feel the wonder of the possibility that a new life might be growing inside her. She didn't know whether to feel great joy or deep sorrow. It distressed that she could not share the news with Mei, that they would not be able to raise their child together. She made her way back to her room, lay back on the bed and wept.

Her mother knocked on the door. "Agnes, there's some mail for you from China."

Agnes jumped out of bed, ran to the door and took the letter from her mother's hand. Recognizing Mei's handwriting made her heart flip. She could not hide the delight she felt.

Her mother noticed the change on Agnes's face. "Who is the letter from?"

"My tutor!" She tore open the envelope, which had been mailed from Wuhan City, Hubei Province.

August 7, 1926

Dear Agnes,

Since your departure, I've sometimes regretted that I didn't ask you to stay. I miss you so much, but maybe it's God's will that you had to leave. The situation here worsened after the June 7 incident, although the murderer was caught and executed. Since then, a number of violent riots have disrupted the city. Most of the missionaries are leaving the West China Mission, and my university is facing closure.

Even if I can graduate next year, I don't know whether I'll be able to practice medicine when a war seems inevitable. It seems the Northern Expedition will end the warlord era and establish a unique country. China is in evolution. People need a better life. I think joining the Expedition is my best chance at serving the cause of the social gospel.

I'll never forget those precious days we spent together. And now ranges of mountains and endless waters separate us. I wish we could see each other again.

I have resigned myself to the notion that I can't do anything about it. I will pray for you. And I will love you always.

Yours, Mei.

Agnes sighed and walked over to the window. The weeds at the shore waved in the breeze, the ocean ripples merging with the sky's large, gray clouds, making it difficult to distinguish the bay from sky. She wondered what she would do. It seemed fortuitous somehow to have received a letter from Mei just as she had discovered she was pregnant. But having a baby as a single woman, let alone a baby fathered by a Chinese man, would be considered unacceptable, and scandalous, in her Christian family and society. She would have to make some hard choices.

Several days later, Agnes helped her mother set the table, and the family sat down to boiled corn and a roast ham for supper.

Agnes told her parents that she had decided to move to Boston to find a job. "I won't stop you," her father said, sighing, "although I'd like you to stay." A descendant of a loyalist family, her father preferred to keep his family roots in Canada.

Agnes did not say anything more, but, on the same day, she sent a telegraph to her Aunt Joanne telling her she would be leaving for Boston the next week. She wrote a letter to Mei as well. She wanted him to know about the baby. Aware that Mei was on the expedition to Beijing, and not knowing where else to send the letter, Agnes decided to mail it to Mei's parents in Chongqing.

Agnes found a part-time job as a nurse at a busy clinic in Boston. In early May, 1927, she gave birth to a baby girl. She named her Mayflora.

That was the last page of the diaries, which took Yezi a few days to read through. On the very last page, Agnes had glued her copy of the photograph of the two of them at the summit of Mount Emei. Yezi let her fingers run gently over the photograph. They looked so happy. Reluctantly, she closed the book, but she still had questions: *Why didn't Grandma ever get a letter back from Mei? Did he ever receive her letter?* She remembered what her father had written to her in his last letter a week ago.

Lon had met with Ling after her return from Chengdu, but she had not discovered any further information about Mei. Ling had said that the woman called Mei and her husband had apparently gone to visit relatives in Hong Kong and that they planned to remain in Japan for several months.

Eager to get to the bottom of her questions, Yezi ran down to the living room. Agnes was easing back on the couch after a day of her volunteer work as the treasurer of the church. A stack of files rested on the table. "Grandma, are you okay?"

Agnes turned her head, "I'm fine, dear." She looked tired, but her face gleamed when she saw Yezi with the diaries in her hand. "How did you like them?"

Yezi wrapped her arm around her grandmother's neck and kissed her cheek. "I'd like reading them very much, Grandma. It's the greatest stuff I've ever read. I wish that you had continued writing in the journals."

"I didn't keep writing after your mother's birth. I don't know why. You can ask me anything you want to know." Agnes took the books and stroked the aged covers and engraved letters. "I hope you understand my experience."

"I think so," Yezi hesitated. "Why didn't you think of marrying Mei at that time?"

"I would have if I could've stayed in China or if he could've followed me here." Agnes simplified her explanation for Yezi. "But under the circumstances, I just didn't have time to work out a solution or make any decisions. Everything happened too suddenly."

"But why did the mission send you back to Canada?"

"At one time I was very angry with the mission for sending me back, but they had very firm rules. Relationships between people of different races were frowned upon at that time. And the mission was concerned that those kinds of relationships would interfere with the goals of their mission. I had to obey their rules, so I had no choice but to give up my position. It was a very painful thing for me to do. Without the benefit of being under their wing in China, the only thing option left to me was to return to China as a non-missionary. Then I would have been free to join Mei. But then I discovered I was pregnant and I couldn't take the rist of travelling pregnant and alone."

"Your parents, my great-grandparents, were not happy about your having the baby, weren't they?"

"That's true, but I can't blame them. A single mother, at that time, was considered a sin, and shameful, especially if she had a baby of mixed race." Agnes motioned for Yezi to join her on the couch. "Do you understand?"

"Yes. There are offensive words that refer to people of

mixed races." Yezi thought of a few she had heard. "Words like 'mongrel' and 'bastard'...."

Agnes scowled. "They're swear words."

"Was my mother abused with these words?"

"Not really. I don't think so." Agnes's mind returned to an incident that occurred in 1937.

Ten-year-old Mayflora was playing with two-year-old Dora on the living room carpet. "Sit still, my baby." She placed a small hand mirror into Dora's hand. "I am going to comb your hair." Dora took the mirror and looked into it. Flora ran a comb lightly through Dora's hair and then tied a bright blue ribbon around it. "Mom, why is Dora's hair red but mine isn't?"

Agnes's foot hung over the treadle of a sewing machine. The spinning wheel stopped turning as she thought how best to answer. She looked tenderly at Flora's and then said thoughtfully, "Dora looks like Daddy, but you look like me."

"Really?" Flora held Dora in her arms and cradled her little sister's head against her own. Dora giggled and then squirmed in Flora's arms. "My eyes are smaller than Dora's. One of my classmates calls me 'China Girl,' and calls Susan 'Africa Girl.' Do I look Chinese?"

Startled by the question, Agnes remained silent. She and her husband, Jensen, had discussed this before and resolved to keep information about Flora's birth father a secret for as long as possible so as to avoid any disturbance to Flora's life and happiness. Agnes got onto the floor and sat with her daughters, wrapping her arms around them. "Does Susan look African?"

Flora shook her head. "She has a nice suntan, that's all."

The door opened just then. It was Jensen returning home after work. "Hello everyone! I've got potatoes and steaks for dinner." He placed a paper bag on the kitchen table and walked over to where they were sitting.

"Daddy!" The two girls opened their arms; Jensen kneeled

to kiss them one by one.

"What's new?" he asked. "Who has a suntan?"

"Susan," Flora giggled. "I wish I had a suntan. Do I look Chinese?"

"Hmm," Jenson hesitated. "Yes, a little bit. Do you feel bad about that?" He sat on the floor beside her and watched her face.

"No. But I don't like it when the girl at school calls me that."

"Tell her you are American!" Jensen gave her a big hug. "In America, people are from many different cultures and races. This is our nation. Together, we're Americans."

"Okay, I will." Flora jumped up from the carpet. "Mom, I'm hungry. Are we going to have steaks? Hurray!"

"Hurray!" Dora's arms jerked in the air.

Yezi gently stroked Agnes's arm. "Are you okay?"

"Oh yes. Your mother didn't face any problem regarding her mixed racial background. Maybe because of the war, people dealing with many more stressful situations. Maybe because she didn't really know about her background. How about you? Any problems?"

"Not really. Helen became my friend because she wanted to learn numbers in Chinese. But sometimes I feel embarrassed when I have no clue about the music or games my friends are talking about."

"You can learn if you're interested. But you don't need to learn everything others know. Everybody is unique. You have your own personality and interests. \You have your own strengths."

"What are they?"

"You know two languages. You have cross-cultural experiences. Besides, you're bright and beautiful like your mother."

"Thank you. Sometimes I think you understand me better than my father."

"He's just worried about you. Having gone through many troubles in his own life, he's afraid you might lose your direction. He and your mother both hated that they didn't have the chance to be with you more when you were a little girl."

"Sometimes, I'm not sure if I'm Chinese or American." Yezi recalled the incident in the first grade, during which she had proclaimed "I'm Chinese!" She had changed a lot during these two years in Boston with her grandmother. *Who am I?* she wondered. "Did my mother have the same problem?"

"She didn't know about her birth father until she was fourteen. Then she became interested in everything Chinese, and she started to learn the language." Agnes told Yezi how Mayflora kept asking questions about her father after she saw the photograph of Agnes and Mei taken at Mount Emei. "Your mother read as many books as she could to find about China and she learned a lot."

Agnes told Yezi about one of Pearl Buck's novels, *East Wind: West Wind*. The protagonist, a Chinese woman named Kwei-lan, had been betrothed to a Chinese man before her birth. The man, who had been trained as a doctor in the States, objected to foot binding. Finally he fell in love with Kwei-lan when she asked him to unbind her feet. "Your mother played the part of Kwei-lan when her drama teacher organized a play adapted from the novel."

"Was she a good actress?"

"She certainly was," replied Agnes with pride. "The teacher asked me to be their consultant when she learned I'd been to China."

Yezi pictured her mother in a long black gown, her single, waist-length braid swinging lightly against her back. On stage, Mayflora looked up into the sky and proclaimed, "I've stood up as a new woman! Unbound, my feet no longer hurt. Thanks to God the Supreme, my soul has been liberated from the shackles of a thousand years." Mayflora's eyes would have flashed with joy, just as if she had turned into the Chinese woman she was imitating. Yezi imagined how much her mother must have enjoyed playing the main character in *East Wind: West Wind*.

"During the war, the life was stressful," Agnes continued. 'Your grandfather was in the army. I had a part-time job and then took care of your mother and aunt Dora. There was less food. Sugar, meat and canned food were rationed, but we managed," said Agnes.

Yezi said in an admiring tone, "I didn't know my mother could act."

"You know, your mother had many talents. She won second prize in an Irish step dancing contest. She made many friends. Susan was her best friend even after she revealed her Chinese background. And then, to your mother's surprise, Susan revealed that she had a black great-grandmother. They were friends for many, many years. One New Year's Eve, their resolution was to go to university."

"Did they go to university together?"

"They went to different universities. Your mother majored in Fine Arts. Susan studied American History."

"What does Susan do now?"

"Sadly, I lost touch with her after your mother left for China." An idea dawned on Agnes. "But you know what? I have some of your mother's old letters. I'll find them for you."

"Great! I want to learn more about her."

Agnes glanced at the clock on the wall. "It's after 10:30. You should go to bed. We'll find the letters tomorrow."

Yezi bounced from the chair. "Tomorrow is a big day."

"Why?"

"It's an engagement!" Noticing her grandmother's astonishment, Yezi made a face. "Anyhow, it's a secret."

"What secret?" Agnes eyed her.

"Don't worry. It's not mine," Yezi added as she hurried into the bathroom.

Agnes drew a breath and simply said, "Good night."

28.
THE LONG MARCH HOME

AT THE END OF LAST class on the following day, Yezi stuffed her books and pencil case into her knapsack. Angela, in a seat several aisles behind her, called to Yezi, waving her hand. "Helen is at the door."

Angela and Yezi hurried out the door and into the hallway where Helen was pacing. She looked shorter, as she no longer wore her hair spiked up, but now let it hang loosely over her shoulders under a purple headband. "Let's get cracking. My mom's waiting." She motioned to Yezi and Angela to follow, and rushed outside to a waiting car at the curb.

Helen's mother dropped the three girls off in front of Angela's home, a mansion on Ivy Street. Angela led Yezi and Helen through a tree-canopied garden and up the stone steps to the front door. She fished out a chain from around her neck; at the end of it, was a key. She pulled the chain off, and opened the door. "Come on in," she said, waving her arm with a flourish.

The living room was covered with a thick, soft, scarlet carpet. Two crystal chandeliers suspending from the ceiling twinkled in the sunlight coming through the windows. A grand chesterfield lay in the centre of the room, flanked by two armchairs like guards. Helen plopped in one of them, her head perched on one arm and her legs on the other. She called the position Mom's Cradle. Yezi enjoyed sitting in a corner of the chesterfield. Her hand brushed the black leather of the chair's arm next to her. It gave her the feeling that she had become a baby again, stroking Yao's arm before falling asleep.

"Help yourselves." Angela placed several cans of Pepsi and a bowl of potato chips on the coffee table in front of the chesterfield. "My parents won't be back before 9:00 p.m., so we can do whatever we feel like!"

"Remember? We're here to watch your sister's engagement." Yezi tapped her fingers the chair's arm again.

"Oops, I almost forget." Angela replaced her pop on the table. "Helen, can you find the remote control and turn on the VCR?"

Helen got up and walked over to a small wooden cabinet in a corner. Pulling out a drawer, she rummaged through videotapes.

Yezi glanced at the shiny dinnerware in the cabinet and the paintings on the wall. They were all abstract art, so she wasn't entirely sure what they intended to depict, but they were colourful and interesting. She couldn't help but wonder what her mother might have thought about them.

Angela inserted the tape in the VCR, and then, on the screen, grand hall appeared, where men in tuxedoes and women in beautiful dresses walked around, chatting with one another, holding drinks in their hands.

A teenaged girl in a short pink dress, its sleeves and hem trimmed with lace, ran into the hall. Her waist-length dark hair shone under the bright lights; two long, pink silky ribbons decorated with beads decorated her hair. "Mom! I'm sorry I'm late, but I've found my necklace." When she turned her head toward the camera, a pendant sparkled against her skin.

"It's you, Angela!" Yezi gasped at the pretty face on the screen.

Angela giggled. "I always forget things. Mom says it's because I always have my head in the clouds."

"Hey! Can you put your dress on?" Helen stared at Angela. She sipped from a Pepsi can. "I love it."

"Really?" Angela's eyes flashed with joy. "I like that party dress, too. But you know my Dad...."

"What about him?" asked Helen.

"He doesn't like me wearing something that short."

"Why?"

"He says I'll get arthritis when I get older. He wants me to wear skirts or dresses that cover my knees."

"He seems to have a good excuse," Yezi said. Helen and Angela burst out laughing.

"Look, Angela. Is that your sister?" Yezi grabbed her friend's arm while her eyes lingered on the screen. A young woman wearing a long white satin dress with a ruffled collar was being given a sparkling diamond ring. It had a yellow gold band and in the centre, around diamond, were four baguette sapphires. Her fiancé was dressed in a black tuxedo with a red bow under his collar, and his arm was draped casually around her shoulder.

"Yeah. It's a real diamond and costs a grand." Angela's gaze switched from the screen to Yezi. "Do you like the ring?"

"It costs so much!" Yezi exclaimed.

"Wow," Helen pointed to the screen. "What is that pendant made of?"

"My mom's? It's a gold cross with diamonds all around it. It's probably worth a couple of grand." Angela jumped off the couch. "Do you want to watch the party or look at my dress?"

Both Yezi and Helen answered, "Your dress, now!"

Angela climbed upstairs, and, in a few minutes, returned wearing the pink dress and her mother's necklace. "What do you think?"

Yezi clapped her hands. "So fresh! You look exactly like you did in the video."

"Ooooh, can I look at your necklace?" Helen touched the sparkling pendant with awe.

"Hey, how about this?" Angela spun around. "Come to my

bedroom. I have a bunch of dresses. You can try them on."

The three girls giggled and raced to Angela's bedroom. In five minutes, clothes of various colours and styles cluttered the bed. Yezi examined her reflection in the full-length mirror on the closet door: she wore a black dress with a square silver neckline and black spaghetti straps. Her dark brown hair, pulled back with a blue headband, reached her shoulders.

Helen said, "Yezi looks like a college student."

"I wore it only once. I don't think I will wear it again," said Angela.

"Why?" asked Yezi.

"It's so plain and old-fashioned," Angela said matter-of-factly. "If you like it, you can take it home with you."

"It's great. Thank you," Yezi said.

"You have so many fancy clothes and so much jewellery. I don't think I could ever afford to live like this," Helen said as she placed a pearl necklace back into the jewellery box on the dresser.

"Don't worry." Angela winked. "Your fiancé or husband will pay for it."

"I don't even know if I'll get engaged or married for that matter." Helen swirled around and watched Angela's pink-hemmed black skirt flutter around her ankles.

"Why?" Yezi and Angela exclaimed in unison.

"Haven't you ever heard of the women's movement? Women should be independent. I don't want to rely on a husband."

"You may run across a rich, cool guy who really loves you." Angela grinned.

"If you don't get married, what are you going to do?" Yezi gazed at Helen with curiosity.

"I have no idea." Helen closed her eyes and imagined a young man on his knees, a glistening ring in his hand. She opened eyes and chuckled. "I'll go to university first."

"Me, too." Yezi nodded.

"Really?" Angela asked. "Are you guys serious? I may go

to college. That's enough for me."

"My mom graduated from Harvard," said Helen.

"That's an important university." Angela seemed familiar with all kinds of costs. "The tuition is double that of other universities."

"I can save money. I'll look for a summer job." Helen said. "What about you, Yezi?"

"I can work in the summer, too." Yezi's eyes glowed. "If I get three dollars an hour and work forty hours a week, I can make almost one thousand dollars in a summer. That'll be tuition for half a term." Yezi was excited by the thought.

"Do you think you'll work through the whole summer?" asked Angela.

"Why not?" Helen clasped her hands. "Why don't you think about a summer job?"

"Maybe." Angela's eyebrows raised. She was disappointed to see her friends take an interest in something like going to university. It was not something she herself was interested in. As Yezi began to change out of the dress, Angela shook her head. "Yezi, you can keep the dress. Helen, are we going to have a party this weekend?"

"Maybe." Helen changed back into her white blouse and red-and-black plaid skirt.

"Thanks," Yezi said, folding the dress neatly and putting it on the table for her to take later.

"How about a slice of pizza before Helen's mom picks you girls up?" Angela led the way to the kitchen downstairs.

Yezi began scanning job ads in the classified sections of local papers in the library after school. Many of the jobs excited her, but she wasn't sure what to say if she called any of the potential employers. After her grandmother suggested she get more information at school, she located a workshop that helped students with job hunting.

Since then, she had busied herself with learning about writing a résumé and cover letter as well as developing interview skills. She thought she would be tired out before she even began working. It seemed to her that finding a job was more work than actually working.

One afternoon, she arrived home and picked up a letter in the mailbox. It was from her father. Excited, she tore the envelope open immediately and skimmed the page. *Grandpa?* When she saw the word, her heart pounded. Then she read the sentence again.

Lon wrote: "Your grandpa, Mei, is still alive! He is a retired doctor in Hong Kong. The lady Mei in Chongqing is his sister." Yezi's eyes widened at the news. *I have to tell Grandma!* She pushed opened the door and called out, but saw nobody and got no response. Yezi remembered that she was going to one of her meetings that afternoon, so she ran up to her room to read the letter again, this time more carefully. .

Plumping herself on the bed, she placed the letter next to her and smoothed out the creases. Besides that exciting news, Lon also mentioned that Sang had just started to work as an intern at Spring City General Hospital and would graduate in half a year. Yao was trying to learn from Lon how to read, as she wanted to read Yezi's letters instead of asking others to read for her.

Things were going well! Yezi was happy to hear that her family had moved on and were living their lives contentedly. But she was puzzled about Mei, and couldn't understand how he could have disappeared for over fifty years. *After all this time, could this really be him?* After reading her father's words over a third time, she jumped off the bed and paced the floor. Then she had an idea of what to do.

That evening, Yezi sat beside her grandmother on the couch. "Do you mind if I ask you some personal questions?"

Agnes closed the book in her hand and removed her reading-glasses. "I'm all ears, and willing to answer any of your questions."

"Do you love my grandfather?"

"What a question!" Agnes gasped. "Well, I certainly did at one time. And I do still care for him."

"Why haven't you looked for him all these years?"

"Well, I wrote him a couple of letters, but I never got a response. In fact, many years later, I learned that he had written to me, too. But my parents never told me, nor gave me his letters."

"Why? Because they disliked him?"

Agnes lost herself in remembering her father's funeral in 1947. It was during the funeral that her mother asked her to forgive them for disposing of several letters from China after Agnes had moved to Boston and they had become aware of her pregnancy.

"At that time, my parents couldn't accept me as a single mother or my child. So your mother never actually met them. The first time your mother met my mother, it was at my father's funeral." Agnes looked into Yezi's puzzled eyes and upset face. "Don't blame them. Everybody learns from their mistakes. When your mother made the decision to search for her birth father in China, her grandmother supported her financially."

"Do you think Grandpa got your letters?"

"Maybe not. Otherwise he would have known I lived in Boston. He wouldn't have sent mail to Wolfville."

"I remember Mama said she flew to Halifax, not Wolfville, for my great-grandfather's funeral."

"That's right. My parents had moved to Halifax before the war. So your mother met her grandmother in Halifax."

"If Grandpa is still alive, would you like to see him again?" Yezi looked up at Agnes, a smile lighting up her face.

"That's a good question. What would I tell him if I saw him again? He doesn't even know he had a daughter, your mother...." Agnes's heart pounded. "You know, your mother went to Chongqing. She discovered that Mei's parents' home had been bombed, and she wasn't able to find any trace of

Mei. During the war, anything could have happened to him. I doubt he's still alive." Agnes's hand joined Yezi's. "Don't let something like this get you down. Let's talk about your prospects for work this summer instead. What's up with your job hunting? "

"My workshop teacher has arranged a tour of the YMCA for tomorrow. I am going to drop off an application for a job as an Early Child Education assistant."

"Oh, that sounds great. I'll cross my fingers for you."

A few days later, on Sunday morning, after Agnes went to church, Yezi copied a phone number from her father's letter and made an overseas call.

"May I speak to Mei?" Yezi heard her own voice tremble.

A sturdy voice answered, "Speaking!"

"I'm Yezi." Suddenly questions flew out of her mouth. "Do you remember Agnes McMillan? You don't know me, but you are my grandfather. Why have you never searched for us?"

After a moment of awkward silence, the man replied hesitantly, "Well, Yezi, I didn't know your mother or you existed."

Yezi also hesitated before uttering the question she had been longing to ask. "Did you ever get my grandmother's letters?"

"Letters? No. I never got any letters. But I sent her some."

Yezi knew what had happened to those letters. "Your parents must have kept them away from you, just like my Grandma's parents kept your letters from her. But did you ever try to look for her?"

"Yes. Many years ago, I went to Wolfville to try and find her..."

Yezi finished his sentence. "But you didn't find anybody there?"

"I only found her parent's old house. Your grandmother's parents had already moved to Halifax. So, I went to Halifax."

"Did you meet them?" Yezi asked, excited.

"No. That was in 1955. All I found were their headstones in the cemetery. Someone who saw me there and knew them told me that your grandmother was married and had two children. Because I never received any letters from her, I thought she had probably forgotten me. I thought it best not to disturb her." The old man sucked in a deep breath. He seemed to know what Yezi's next question would be. "Your father told me that your mother tried to find me in China, in 1948, but I had already moved to Hong Kong and there I remained."

"I am glad we found you! Now, would you like to see my Grandma again?"

"Yes, of course. But I don't know if your grandmother will want to see me. I could fly to Boston if you think she would welcome a visit."

"Oh, yes! Yes! I'm sure she would like that very much," Yezi replied, ecstatic. "After you get a ticket, would you please let me know when to expect you?"

"I will try to come in the next couple of weeks. I can phone you from my hotel after I arrive in Boston. I will explain everything in person. So please don't tell her everything. Let's surprise her, okay?"

"Oh yes!"

After the phone call, Yezi wrote to her father about her phone call to Mei. She wished her father had a phone so she could talk to him right away, but telephone services were not readily available to most people in China.

Yezi had phoned Mei a second time, to find out if he had booked his ticket. Since then, she had been checking the calendar every day. July 2nd was not too far away. Yezi had lied to her grandmother and told her that her father was coming to Boston for a visit, and they would have to pick him up at the airport. The day finally arrived. Yezi hopped into the passenger seat as her grandmother started the car. They were going to the airport at last.

"Your father will notice you're taller now."

"He has wonderful news for you." Yezi hinted at the surprise, not wanting to shock her grandmother too much.

"Oh? Well, that's nice. But why didn't your father tell me he was coming?" Agnes was a little puzzled, suspecting that something was going on, but didn't have any idea what it could be. Yezi remained silent. "Well, we will see him very soon! By the way, do you remember Susan, your mother's close friend that I told you about?"

"Yes?"

"Well, talking to you about her motivated me and I managed to track her down. She lives in Pittsburgh now. She's is planning to come over on Sunday. She wants to meet you so much."

So many things are happening this weekend, Yezi thought, rubbing her eyes. It was all a little overwhelming.

They car came to a stop in the tunnel to the airport. "Why is the traffic slowing down?" Yezi asked.

A police car passed by, its siren blaring. "I hope it's just a fender-bender," said Agnes.

Yezi was chewing her fingers anxiously. "We'll be late."

"Don't worry. I don't see an ambulance." Agnes sat back. "Your father will wait for us."

"No, he won't. He doesn't even know we're coming to the airport," said Yezi, making a face. "I wanted to surprise him."

Half an hour later, they were at the arrivals. The plane from Hong Kong had landed. Yezi's eyes scanned the crowd, looking for an elderly man, while Agnes searched for Lon.

Almost simultaneously, Yezi and Agnes turned to a crowd of people walking in the direction of the cab stand. Yezi darted toward a tall, elderly, gray-haired man in a white shirt and black slacks standing by a pole.

"Your father is there!" Agnes shouted behind her.

Another man in a crisp white shirt was standing next to the gray-haired man. The both turned their heads.

Yezi gasped and called out, "Baba!" She had not expected him! She couldn't believe he was here, at the airport!

At that moment, Agnes walked toward them, a broad smile on her face. The gray-haired man next to Lon stepped forward, his arms outstretched. "Agnes?"

Agnes's gaze fell on the man's wrinkled face. His eyes, under glasses, resembled deep wells with ripples, as if a stone had just been dropped into them moments before. Agnes moved forward slowly, as if in a dream. She felt as though her mind and body had been transported in time, and she was back in 1925, the first time she had looked deeply into those dark eyes. "Mei! I can't believe it's you." Her hands joined his.

Agnes and Mei were still, their eyes fixed on each other. At last, Mei wrapped his arms around Agnes, and she smiled at him with a warmth that even Lon and Yezi, standing next to them, could feel.

"I have a photo to show you, Yezi." Mei took out a pocket-sized frame and passed it to her. It was the photograph of Mei and Agnes that had been taken fifty-five years ago, the same one her mother had copied and brought to China, the same one that Agnes had taped to the last page of her second journal.

Lon walked over to Yezi then and put his arm around her shoulder. He was smiling and crying at the same time. He had made her mother's wish come true. Yezi hugged him tightly. Then she wrapped her arms around her grandparents, holding them in a big bear hug. No words were necessary.

Yezi could see her mother's smiling face. She closed her eyes: *Mama, I know you can see your father now. You can rest in peace now. You are home, dear Mama. And I am at home, too.*

When they made it to Agnes's car, parked outside, Yezi looked up into the sky and saw a swallow gracefully joining a flock of birds that were soaring effortlessly, swooping and weaving in long ribbons, flying freely in the clear, blue sky.

ACKNOWLEDGEMENTS

I am deeply grateful to my editor at Inanna Publications, Luciana Ricciutelli, for her dedicated editing and brilliant suggestions that have made all the difference.

I would like to thank the Toronto Arts Council for its grant assistance to this writing project.

My thanks also go to my critique pals: Marlene Ritchie, Manda Djinn, Loretta Hemstead, Paul Ulrich and Katharine Williams, who read the manuscript in its earlier version and provided me with their honest and useful feedback.

I owe personal notes of thanks to Marie Laing, Penelope Stuart, Carol Mortensen and Dorothy Rawrek, who are always there for me.

Last, but certainly not least, I am thankful to my husband, Jean-Marc, and to my son, Shu, for their patience and forever support of my writing.

Born in China, Zoë S. Roy was an eyewitness to the Red Terror under Mao's regime. Her short fiction has appeared in *Canadian Stories* and *Thought Magazine*. She holds an M.ED. in Adult Education and an MA in Atlantic Canada Studies from the University of New Brunswick and Saint Mary's University. She lives and works in Toronto as an adult educator. Her first book, an acclaimed collection of short stories, *Butterfly Tears*, was published by Inanna Publications in 2009. This is her first novel.